TED TAYLER

STILL STANDING

BOOKS

TED TAYLER

STILL
STANDING

vinci
BOOKS

By Ted Tayler

The Freeman Files

Red Herring Season
Gathering Clouds
Still Standing

Vinci Books

vinci-books.com

Published by Vinci Books Ltd in 2025

1

A CIP catalogue record for this book is available from the British Library.
Paperback ISBN: 9781036705107

Chapter One

"DO you think you'll hear anything from Geoff Mercer today about when you'll get back to work, darling?" asked Suzie.

"That rather depends on who's pulling the strings," said Gus.

"Surely, Kenneth still has the final say? He doesn't hand over the reins until the end of March. The name of his replacement hasn't even officially been announced."

"Don't worry about me. I'll be okay," said Gus. "Just eat your breakfast, sweetheart, or you'll be late."

"I'll keep my eyes and ears open at London Road if you wish," said Suzie.

Gus could tell Suzie wasn't going to let it go.

"A quick chat with Vera might prove beneficial," he suggested. "Nothing much goes on between the four walls of HQ without her knowing."

"Do you think Vera knows you're off to Bourne Hill this morning?" asked Suzie.

"If she does, there will be roadblocks at either end of the lane," said Gus.

"Don't joke," said Suzie. "If someone was watching us at the weekend, we'll both be for the high jump."

Gus drained his coffee mug and collected their empty plates. If he was to be on the road to Salisbury within the hour, he had to get a move on. So Suzie went to the bedroom to finish getting ready for work while he loaded the dishwasher.

When Suzie reappeared in her uniform, with her hair pinned, Gus joined her in the hallway.

"Have a nice day," he said.

"Just be careful," said Suzie. "I'll see you at the usual time tonight. Love you."

Gus nodded, and they kissed.

"Do you want me to walk you to the car?" he asked.

"Will you make a habit of it?" asked Suzie.

"Probably not," said Gus.

Suzie kissed him on the cheek, scooped up her car keys from the hall table and closed the front door behind her as she left.

AS GUS GOT himself ready for the day ahead, he reflected on the hectic weekend they had just shared. Something he'd heard in one of his first conversations about the Rampart Road murders had refused to go away. It was ever thus. In his early days as a DC in Salisbury, his sergeant shook his head when Gus told him he had an inkling.

"Follow the tried and trusted method, young Freeman," he'd say. "It's there for a reason."

"I feel I'm right, sarge," Gus said, "even though I don't *know* that I am."

When Gus's intuition proved invaluable in solving a case, his sergeant put it down to beginner's luck. Nevertheless, they joked about it several years later when Gus had earned his three stripes.

"Either you're the luckiest copper that ever lived, young Freeman," said his sergeant at his retirement party, "or perhaps you'll turn out to be one of the best."

Gus hadn't realised the significance of his most recent niggle until last Wednesday morning when he visited Sally Woodman at her home in Wessex Road. After their conversation, everything fell into place. But because he was on gardening leave, Gus couldn't share his new knowledge with many people.

Suzie didn't get the full story until they'd driven across the border into Hampshire on Saturday afternoon, and Divya Yadav hadn't had any context to attach to the search requests Gus had asked her to carry out.

Bob Mears had called on Thursday to tell Gus the two detectives who had assumed full responsibility for the Crees and Howard case were following a false trail to South Wales. The news cheered Gus, as it meant they were out from under his feet. Finally, he could check he had the final pieces of the jigsaw without incurring the wrath of their boss, Phil Crocker. One more complaining phone call from Phil to London Road would be curtains.

Gus would have loved to have the rest of his team with him, but even before Geoff Mercer ordered him to stay home, his colleagues were scattered across the county. Amazing Grace and Blessing were ankle-deep in turnips near Bromham. Poor Lydia had to suffer long days at

Gablecross, listening to Raj Sengupta wittering on about the value of statistics.

At least Alex Hardy had been doing something worthwhile in Swindon last week, assisting the early-intervention teams. But Gus knew Alex was worthy of so much more, as was Neil Davis. So on Friday, when they all met up in the Waggon & Horses for a much-needed social night, they celebrated the arrival of Neil and Melody's bouncing baby daughter, Beatrice. Neil would be on paternity leave now, while the other team members were due to stay away from the Old Police Station office until the Christmas break.

As Gus had hoped, Divya had found the final missing pieces for his jigsaw, and the surfeit of good news meant he was drunk when the team left the pub. He'd spent Saturday morning recovering. By the time he and Suzie had returned to the bungalow in the early evening, they had discovered Tim Harding's address.

Suzie had first driven them to Winchester, where they paid a brief visit to the Post Office. Gus knew there was zero chance they would learn anything specific from staff due to the usual privacy restraints, but Suzie had a plan. Divya had done her best to enhance the image from Harding's driving licence, and Suzie used her charms on the young man behind the counter.

Resistance was futile. The young man agreed it *did* look like the guy who collected the post that arrived for him, although his hair was shorter. Gus asked whether they were expecting Mr Harding to call in anytime soon.

"I couldn't swear to when we last saw him, sir," said the youngster. "The whole point of setting up a poste restante is because you don't want people to know your permanent address, or you don't have one for a short period. So all I will say is that that man has been a regular visitor over the past eighteen months I've worked here."

"Would it be too much to ask whether he receives a lot of mail?" asked Suzie.

"How much would *you* receive if you subtracted the junk mail?" asked the young man.

"I take your point," said Suzie. "So, a handful of items on each occasion; is that fair?"

The young clerk nodded, then looked over his shoulder to see if anyone was listening.

"A few official-looking envelopes, a music magazine, and the occasional small package which needed a signature. That's about it."

Gus and Suzie thanked him and returned to the Golf.

"Divya confirmed Tim Harding has no social media activity," said Gus, "and we know he liked to be paid in cash wherever possible. I wonder whether he avoids the internet altogether?"

"Lucky chap, if he does," said Suzie. "Where to next?"

"Divya pointed me towards King's Worthy," said Gus. "Follow the High Street to Easton Lane, and that will take us to Winnall in ten minutes. But, first, we want the A34 out of Winnall, and then we look for caravans."

Divya's information was correct; there were several caravan sites to check. After cruising around two sites with no sign of a Vauxhall Combo van, Gus wondered whether they would be out of luck. However, he needn't have worried. As Suzie drove them slowly past yet another neat row of caravans on the third site, he spotted the van dead ahead.

"Okay, keep going at the same speed, Suzie," said Gus. "We're not stopping for a chat. They're all even numbers on this side, so Harding lives at number twenty-eight."

"Don't worry, I haven't looked directly at the caravan," said Suzie. "In case Harding is watching, I'll cover every inch of roadway to convince him we're prospective buyers rather than someone interested in him."

"When we get home, I'll spend half an hour putting the finishing touches to the case," said Gus. "Then we can enjoy the rest of the weekend."

After completing the circuit of the caravan site, Suzie eased the Golf into mid-afternoon traffic on the A34 and returned to Winchester. Gus kept an eye on the wing mirror for any sign they were being followed. He saw nothing to cause undue alarm, and sixty minutes after leaving Winchester, Suzie swung the Golf through the gateway at the bungalow. As she parked next to the Focus, her dash-board clock showed five-fifteen.

"Good timing," she said as they stepped into the hall-way. "Could you work in the kitchen until six o'clock? Meanwhile, I will put my feet up in the lounge and watch TV. I need my rest before another busy evening."

"Of course, darling," said Gus. "What time are we meeting Brett and Clemency?"

"Trust you not to be listening on Wednesday night," said Suzie. "We're picking them up at seven-thirty. Our table at the Fox & Hounds is booked for eight."

"In that case, I think it's high time I drove," said Gus. "You've done more than your fair share at the wheel today. Since I over-indulged last night, I'll be the designated driver. We need to take the Focus tonight, anyway."

"Brett will feel guilty," said Suzie.

"He's getting married in little over a fortnight. So he needs to take every opportunity for a pint while he can."

Suzie dropped her car keys on the hall table and disap-peared into the lounge. Gus fetched his file folder from the bedroom and made himself comfortable at the kitchen table. As the clock on the wall reached six, he was already reading through his final contributions.

The file should be sufficient for DI Stanton and DS Baker to bring the Rampart Road murders to a close after six years. But, of course, DCI Crocker wouldn't be happy, and his old pal, Bob Martin, would have a few words to say. He might suggest Gus wasn't handing Bourne Hill detectives a present, but instead, he was lighting the blue touchpaper and withdrawing before the firework exploded.

Gus returned the file to the bedside drawer and joined Suzie in the lounge. The TV sound was muted, and she was asleep, with her hands clasped on her bump. Gus let her rest and headed for the shower. As he dried himself, he heard a knock at the bathroom door.

"I've got the coffee on," said Suzie. "I must have nodded off."

Gus joined her in the kitchen five minutes later.

"Everything okay?" he asked.

"Tired, that's all," said Suzie. "Nothing to worry about. The little one was active while I was resting my eyes earlier."

"I didn't listen to Neil's every word about the birth on Friday night," said Gus. "March will be on us before we know it, and things will never be the same, no matter what Sylvia Robbins has up her sleeve."

"I didn't hear anything from Neil to frighten us," said Suzie. "Okay, Beatrice kept Melody hanging around for several days after her due date, but this one will arrive when ready. Every check-up I've had so far has shown there's nothing to worry about."

"I do hope so," said Gus.

Suzie knew Gus was concerned that with several guaranteed negatives in the first quarter of 2019, things might continue in the same vein regarding their child.

They drank their coffee in silence, and then Suzie went to get ready. They left the bungalow a few minutes after seven, and Gus drove them to the Rectory.

"The Reverend peeked through the curtains," said Suzie. "They know we're here."

"She's being sensible," said Gus. "No point standing outside on a night like this."

One minute later, Brett and Clemency hurried down the path and got into the back of the Focus.

"How are you both?" asked Suzie.

"Cold and hungry," said Clemency.

Gus drove to Nursteed Road and parked in the Fox & Hounds car park. With Christmas around the corner, plenty of people were already inside, and hopes of a quiet chat were out of the question.

Clem and Suzie went to find their table while Gus and Brett waited, in turn, to get served.

"Any news, Brett?" asked Gus.

"I wish there were something positive to tell you, Gus," he said. "Bert's causing Irene a few concerns. She told us this afternoon that he's called her Cora on more than one occasion."

"I never met his wife," said Gus. "Bert told me they'd been married for fifty years when she died in 2005."

"Irene reckons Bert's become more confused since that bout of flu," said Brett.

"I suppose sharing a house with someone different after you've been alone for thirteen years, could be enough reason for a slip of the tongue."

"Fair comment, Gus," said Brett. "But Irene said Bert has stopped leaving the house for his regular constitutional to the allotment and the Lamb. Instead, he spends hours just sitting in his chair."

"Not unusual for someone his age, Brett," said Gus.

"A couple of times this week, Irene said she spoke to him, and Bert didn't seem to hear. Irene thought he'd nodded off, but when she repeated the question, it was as if he didn't know where he was for a while before answering."

"Did Irene call a doctor?" asked Gus.

"Bert told her not to bother," said Brett. "You know what he's like with the medical profession."

"I do," said Gus. "He avoided visiting the Lamb for years when he knew the local GP would be in the bar, holding court over a gin and tonic."

"Bert's view is if he made regular visits to the surgery, that would be the finish of him. They'd start him on tablets for symptoms he'd managed himself for decades, and kick-start ailments he'd never suffered before."

"Bert believes in traditional methods of healing," said Gus. "Hard work and a regular dose of cider. What does Clemency think?"

"Clem's seen similar symptoms among her parishioners," sighed Brett. "It's generally a sign the brain is shutting down, one tiny bit at a time. They don't have a major stroke but a succession of episodes where they drift off in the manner Irene described. So we're even more convinced we made the right choice in bringing the date forward for the wedding. We can only hope we still have time, I'm afraid."

A member of the bar staff finally caught their eye, and they ordered their drinks. Brett didn't comment when Gus ordered a slimline tonic. When they edged through the crowded bar, Gus spotted Suzie and the Reverend deep in conversation.

"Sorry we took so long," said Brett. "This place is busy tonight, isn't it?"

"Did you girls get a chance to study the menus?" asked Gus.

"We've ordered," said Suzie. "Clem could see you two chatting at the other end of the bar, so we grabbed the opportunity when the landlord stood idle. With the Christmas menu in force since the first of the month, there's less choice than usual."

"Brett would have ordered steak if he'd been here," said Clemency. "So, I took an executive decision."

"So did I," said Suzie. "You're having what he's having."

"I can't argue with that," said Gus. "It's far too early for a Christmas dinner."

Although he enjoyed his succulent steak, plus all the trimmings, Gus was more concerned with Brett's news about Bert. Gus made a mental note to visit his old friend after he returned from Bourne Hill.

For the first time in ages, the girls didn't want a dessert, so while Brett chatted to Gus about the latest animals to come through his office door, Clemency brought Suzie up to speed with the wedding preparations. Finally, just before closing, they threaded their way through the crowds to the front door and into the car park.

Gus drove them back to Urchfont and dropped Brett and the Reverend at the Rectory.

"Will we see you on Wednesday?" asked Suzie.

"I'll call you if there's a problem," said Brett. "I promise."

Gus and Suzie had made the short trip to the bungalow and were in bed before eleven, which made a welcome change from the previous night. In the morning, Gus had made their breakfast, or rather brunch.

"I'm going to drop in to see Bert and Irene tomorrow morning after I've dropped the file into Bourne Hill," said Gus. "Perhaps, I can persuade the old buzzard to see a doctor."

"Good luck with that," said Suzie. "Have you seen the weather out there? It's decidedly cold, wet, and windy, so we'd be wise to stay indoors and keep warm."

Gus couldn't argue, so they listened to the wind buffeting the bungalow walls and the sleet rattling against the window panes for thirty minutes. Then, they took turns selecting a vinyl album.

"I wonder what genre of music our little one will prefer?" asked Suzie.

"Their education has already begun, perhaps?" said Gus. "Are you getting any feedback? Lots of kicks during Fleetwood Mac to suggest dancing, or no activity to indicate disinterest when your middle-of-the-road selection is playing."

"Experts say you should play classical music, or lullabies, to soothe them," said Suzie. "What our child just made of Sister Rosetta Tharp; I can't imagine."

Gus had leafed through his albums for an early Bob Dylan. Suzie agreed it was quieter and more soothing than his earlier choice, but they had argued whether it was a classic until bedtime.

GUS SMILED AT THE WEEKENDS' memories, grabbed his coat and scarf, and carried the folder to the car. The wind was still gusting, but the sleety rain had stopped during the night. He eyed the dark clouds scudding across the treetops and shivered—roll on the spring and warmer temperatures.

A watery sun was breaking through the clouds when he arrived in Salisbury. Gus parked in the visitors' car park at Bourne Hill and looked north. The blue-black sky suggested there was a storm brewing twenty-five miles away. Hard to tell from this distance, but Gus could almost hear Kassie Trotter moaning that the shortest day wasn't due until Friday week.

Gus walked into Reception with fingers crossed. He was in luck, Bob Martin on duty.

"I wasn't sure we'd see you again, Gus," he said. "That lanyard I issued you with won't get you very far, I'm afraid. You've been cancelled."

"I come bearing gifts, Bob," said Gus. "I don't doubt Phil Crocker was on the blower to you when he heard from Geoff Mercer. Bob Mears called me on Thursday evening, which shows not everyone here considers me persona non grata, despite my being on gardening leave. Have you seen Stanton and Baker this morning?"

"They're back from the valleys," said Bob. "A complete waste of time was how they described it. I couldn't fathom why they spent four days there, but Cardiff played Southampton on Saturday afternoon. I reckon they had a few beers in the city centre in the evening, and whoever was driving couldn't risk it until the afternoon."

"I'm guessing that was football," said Gus. "Look, could you see Dumb and Dummer get this folder, please? There are no long words, and it's self-explanatory."

"Have you done their job for them, despite being told not to?" asked Bob.

"I was ninety-nine percent of the way there before I received the instruction to stop, Bob," said Gus. "It seemed churlish not to complete the task. Tell them I'd be thrilled for them to take full credit. With luck, that will stop them from dropping me in it."

"I'll do my best, Gus," said Bob. "Don't worry. I won't breathe a word to Phil Crocker."

"Thanks, Bob. I'd better make tracks," said Gus. "Look after yourself."

"You too, Gus. Oh, before you disappear into the sunset, I heard good news at the weekend. Maxine Devereux has agreed to return to work full-time."

"Now that *is* something to put a spring in my step," said Gus. "Maxine and her husband live out at Winterslow, on the border with Hampshire. I visited her a few months back during the Kendal Guthrie enquiry and was introduced to her son, Oliver. He'll be seven months old now. I doubted whether we would ever see Maxine at Bourne Hill again; she seemed content. Why would anyone swap that life for the greasy pole?"

"Rumour has it Maxine is returning as a Detective Inspector," said Bob. "The salary increase might have persuaded her to tear herself away from little Oliver. However, her husband's situation probably impacted her decision more."

"His name was Gary, wasn't it?" said Gus. "I'm afraid I don't follow the sports pages as assiduously as Neil Davis, one of my sergeants. Has Maxine's husband lost his place in the team?"

"Gary suffered an injury a month into the new season, and although it wasn't career-ending, the club has younger players who can play in his position. So, no doubt, they'll be keen as mustard to cement their place in the first team while he's out of action. You know what young guns are like. Gary's forecasted to get back to full fitness by the end of the season, but, likely, he'll only be guaranteed second-team appearances next season. So, the Devereux family will feel the pinch."

"I don't suppose I'll get to see Maxine at work," laughed Gus. "Who do you think will be the lucky DS to work with her?"

"I don't know too many people from Dorchester HQ out at Winfrith," said Bob. "That's where I've heard she's heading."

"Our loss is Dorset's gain," sighed Gus. "Why is it every piece of good news has a 'but' attached lately?"

The phone on the desk in front of Bob rang, and he shrugged.

"No rest for the wicked, Gus," he said with a wry smile.

Gus left the building and returned to the Focus. His work here was done, and to heck with the consequences. As he drove across the Plain towards the tenebrous skies he'd observed earlier Gus hoped he could find a bright light somewhere in his day.

An hour later, with noon fast approaching, he drew up outside Bert Penman's home. He walked up the path to the front door, glancing at the front garden as he went. There was never much to brighten the mood in mid-December. Everyone's garden was dormant.

Gus remembered Bert and Irene had worked together in the autumn, tending the shrubs and deciduous trees. Whether they'd had the energy to tackle the orchard at the rear of the property was another matter. Gus made a mental note to ask Brett if he'd helped his grandfather keep things in order this year. His old friend wouldn't want his place to become as untidy and unloved as a few others in the village. Bert was a stickler for standards—fat chance of finding an old pram or discarded sofa in his garden.

Irene North answered the door when Gus rang the bell.

"Mr Freeman," she said. "What brings you here?"

"I feel guilty, Irene," said Gus. "My visit is long overdue. Suzie and I haven't seen the pair of you in the Lamb for weeks. Brett told us the flu jab had come with an unwelcome bonus."

"I should say," said Irene. "Come into the kitchen. It's too cold to stand on the doorstep."

As Gus followed Irene into the kitchen, he heard the radio in the next room.

"Coffee?" asked Irene.

"Black, without," said Gus. "Bring me up to date, Irene."

"I kept clear of coughs and colds for years, but the surgery kept badgering me about needing extra protection this winter. They had the cheek to say we were vulnerable. Bertie wanted to tell them where to stick their needle, but I finally talked him around. I thought it would be more beneficial for him, being that much older than me. I only went with him to make sure he didn't back out. Within a week, we were in bed: separate beds, Mr Freeman. So you can drop that raised eyebrow. That bout of flu knocked us both sideways, so it did."

"Brett told us," said Gus. "You seem more like your old self now, Irene."

"Cheeky," said Irene. "I've never been short of a word, Mr Freeman. My late husband, Frank, would have confirmed that. But as the years have flown by, talking is the only thing I can still do at the same pace as when I was a young woman. But, no, it's not me; Bertie is causing us the greater concern."

"Is he sat in his chair next door?" asked Gus.

"That's about all he does these days," said Irene. "He

might be awake if you'd like to go in. I'll bring your drink through in a tick. I made Bertie a cuppa not thirty minutes before you arrived, and we don't tend to have lunch until half-past one. He won't mind hanging on for a while."

Gus left Irene pottering in the kitchen and opened the front room door. Bert was staring out of the front window, perhaps listening to the voice of a female presenter. The time signal on the hour confirmed Bert was tuned to Wiltshire Radio and a topical conversation.

"Hello there, Bert," said Gus stepping into the room.

Bert turned his head slowly. Then, when he recognised his visitor, he scolded:

"You should be at work, Mr Freeman. Gus, I mean."

Gus took a chair from the table in the centre of the room and sat beside his old friend.

"I know you'll find this hard to believe, Bert," said Gus. "But I've been a naughty boy. My bosses have put me on gardening leave with no definite date for me to return."

"They must want their heads read," said Bert. "Turn off that radio, will you? Cora switched it on when she brought me a drink. I'd rather have her company than that silly woman prattling on about the economy."

Just then, Irene came in with Gus's black coffee. He got up to switch off the radio.

"Many thanks, Irene," said Gus.

"He does that a lot, Mr Freeman," whispered Irene. "I don't mind. We're good friends, that's all, but Bertie never used to get my name wrong before he had that blessed flu."

Irene returned to the kitchen. Gus didn't stop her. He could tell she didn't want Bert to see she was upset.

"Brett tells me you haven't been to the Lamb lately, Bert," said Gus. "Nor the allotment, although not much needs to be done this side of Christmas. I've spent less time there myself due to the cases we were looking into before I got my marching orders. Do you think you'll feel up to visiting the allotment soon? My time's my own for the foreseeable, so I can drive you whenever you say. If you spot something that needs urgent attention, I can deal with it, under your guidance, of course. Afterwards, we could drop in the pub for a pint."

"I haven't felt like walking to the Lamb. It's been cold and wet," said Bert. "I've got a couple of flagons of cider in the house if I want it, but apart from a whisky, or a brandy, to warm me, I haven't bothered."

"I could tell the two of you tidied the front garden before you were taken ill," said Gus. "Irene must be a comfort?"

"She does her best," said Bert, "but she's not my Cora. We didn't get around to the greenhouses and the trees at the back, though. Brett reckons I should phone for a tree surgeon to see to my orchard in future. What's the point of me if I haven't got something to keep me going? I never thought it would come to this. I'm tired, Mr Freeman, ready to go on."

"Do you remember when I moved here, Bert?" asked Gus. "I hardly knew one end of a rake from the other, and the Four Seasons were a bunch of lads from Newark, New Jersey. After Tess died, I spent days sitting outside my garden shed, asking why me. You coaxed me back from the precipice with a few words here and there. The hours we've spent together have been some of the best of my life."

"It was my pleasure, Mr Freeman," said Bert. "You weren't like the others, like Frank North. You listened. How long is it you've been in the village now?"

"A little over four years," said Gus.

"Then it's too soon to say you'll make a good gardener," said Bert, "but you're on the right track."

"I need you around to keep me on the right track, Bert," said Gus. "I'm not the only one. Brett and Clemency need your guidance too. Married life can be tricky, and you and Cora had fifty years together. You raised two children, and you can pass on the wisdom you learned from that experience if, and when, the time comes."

"Is Miss Ferris, Suzie, keeping well?" asked Bert.

"She's fine, Bert," said Gus. "You'll be able to raise a glass to our little bundle before spring has had a chance to settle in."

Bert chuckled and gazed out of the window.

"That would be good, Mr Freeman," he said.

"Call me when you're ready, Bert," said Gus. "You and Irene enjoy the rest of your day."

Chapter Two

GUS TOOK his empty cup back to Irene in the kitchen.

"He's not right, is he?" she said.

"Bert's eighty-six, Irene, and none of us can expect to be in perfect health at that age. So I've told him I can be available during the day to give him a lift anywhere he wants to go."

"Perhaps I can get Bertie interested in going out, Mr Freeman. He might snap out of his melancholy if we all do our bit without pressuring him. I overheard you telling Bertie you weren't working at present. Do you ever regret coming out of retirement?"

"Heavens, no," said Gus. "I've made new friends, kept my brain active solving a few mysteries, and I would never have met Suzie if I'd spent the rest of my days feeling sorry for myself."

"There's an upside to everything, isn't there? Well, thank you for calling, Mr Freeman," said Irene. "It means a lot. I'm sure it means a lot to Bertie, too. He thinks highly of you."

"The feeling's mutual, Irene," said Gus. "Even if I suddenly get a frantic call from the Chief Constable saying they can't cope without me, I won't be a stranger. I'll pop along the lane to see you both as often as possible. I promise."

Irene walked with Gus to the front door. When Gus sat in the car, he looked back. Irene was wiping a tear from her eye as she closed the door.

Gus drove slowly along the lane to the bungalow, swung the Focus through the gateway, and parked under the rambling roses. As he stepped into the hallway, he thought a bowl of soup was called for. Twenty-five minutes later, thanks to his store of fresh vegetables and his invaluable soup maker, he had a bowl full of goodness, plus a doorstep hunk of bread from the end of a wholemeal loaf. It wouldn't make everything right in the world, but it helped.

After tidying the kitchen and checking whether Suzie had left a list of chores he'd overlooked, Gus sat in the lounge. He noticed the vinyl albums they'd listened to had been put back in a rather haphazard fashion. Nine months ago, that would have annoyed him.

Times had changed, and anyway, with Suzie's eclectic taste added to the mix, there was little point in applying logic to how they were stored. So Gus made another mental note, not to mention that to her.

Gus was daydreaming when the phone rang in the hallway. He came back to the present with a start. Could it be the lady who once asked for Dorothy? Was she back again after so many months?

"The Freeman residence," said Gus.

"Behave yourself, Gus," said Vera. "Kenneth wants a word."

"Oops," said Gus. "I thought I had a day or two's grace, at least."

"I've no idea what that's supposed to mean," said Vera. "I'll put him through."

Gus held the phone away from his ear, just in case.

"Freeman, are you there?"

"Yes, sir," said Gus. "How may I help?"

"You can't," said the Chief Constable. "I just want you to listen. The PCC has been in touch concerning Ms Logan Barre."

Gus suddenly recalled a brief conversation he'd had with Lydia on Friday night.

What was it she'd said? Morris Beard had made a courtesy call to Raj Sengupta, informing him his colleague, Rosie Allison, would visit Lydia at Gablecross this week to chat.

Blimey, they were quick off the mark. Gus had already had a few drinks that night and perhaps unwisely told Lydia there was no problem listening to what Rosie had to say. Was that a schoolboy error?

"Freeman, are you still there?"

"Of course, sir," said Gus. "I was waiting for the punchline."

"Their initial conversation was concluded this morning," said Kenneth. "Ms Logan Barre is going to the Old Police Station office tomorrow morning to meet the other team members."

"Good idea, sir," said Gus. "It never pays to be too hasty, though. Was there anything else?"

"I doubt you'll be happy to hear this, but the official announcement regarding my replacement will be made on Friday. ACC Robbins will face the Wiltshire press corps for the first time on the steps outside this building."

"Best tell her to wrap up warm, sir," said Gus. "If the weather isn't frosty, the reception from the media will more than make up for it."

"You sound remarkably cheerful considering your present circumstances, Freeman," said the Chief Constable. "I can't help thinking you've pulled a fast one. Something I've yet to hear about."

"If there's nothing else, I must go, sir," said Gus. "I thought I heard the postman outside."

Gus rang off before Kenneth could grill him further, went to the lounge, and turned on the TV. After watching two antique dealers on a road trip in Wales for an hour, he realised he was dreading the next two weeks. He needed another case to solve.

Suzie arrived home at five-thirty to find Gus hard at work in the kitchen.

"Something smells delicious," she said. "I'm not complaining, but this *is* Monday."

"I was bored," said Gus.

" How was Bourne Hill?" asked Suzie.

"I only stayed long enough to deliver the case folder. Then Bob Martin told me Maxine Devereux was ending her maternity leave and moving to Dorset, which wasn't welcome news."

"That's a shame," said Suzie. "You hoped to persuade Kenneth that Maxine would be the perfect fit for the Crime Review Team."

"That was weeks ago," said Gus. "When I still hoped the team would stay together regardless of whether I was there."

"You've heard the announcement about ACC Robbins' appointment then?" said Suzie.

"Kenneth rang this afternoon," said Gus. "Not about

her Friday meet-and-greet with the press. I fear the PCC's team are already trying to poach Lydia. Kenneth told me Rosie Allison spoke to Lydia this morning, and tomorrow your friend Sarah will continue the PR campaign in our office."

"You knew Lydia was bound to move on at some point, Gus," said Suzie. "Kenneth warned you not to rely on her being in the office throughout the coming months. He wanted Geoff Mercer to send her to different departments to show Lydia what was available. Sooner or later, your rising star will decide which path she wants to follow. I'm going to shower and change. How long before dinner?"

"Fifteen minutes," said Gus.

After they'd eaten, they sat in the lounge with a coffee, and Gus told Suzie about his visit to Bert and Irene. She sympathised with Irene's lot and agreed they must drop in whenever they could over the coming weeks to offer what support they could.

"We need to be subtle," she said. "Not something you're good at, darling. Bert will dig his heels in and refuse to budge if he thinks we're interfering. Perhaps I can persuade the Reverend to involve Irene in the wedding preparations. That will keep Irene busy, and with odd reminders lying about the front room, Bert will realise he does have something to look forward to."

"That's a good idea," said Gus. "It could be beneficial for me, too. Can you put together a list of things you'd like done between now and Christmas? Anything to keep me from daytime television."

Suzie lay her head on Gus's shoulder.

"Poor you," she said.

Tuesday, 11 December 2018

IN CHIPPENHAM, Alex Hardy was wide awake at half-past seven. He'd heard Lydia moving around downstairs when he first stirred, some twenty minutes earlier. It was unlike her to have trouble sleeping, but he sensed she was bothered by something when she'd arrived home last night.

"A bad day with Raj?" he'd asked.

"No worse than any other," said Lydia. "I had an early meeting with the girl from the PCC's office I told you about on Friday. Our short session went okay, and after she left, Raj Sengupta lumbered me with a stack of filing. Just before I left Gablecross this evening, I had a phone call from Morris Beard inviting me into the office tomorrow morning. According to Rosie Allison's boss, I'd impressed her so much they wanted to introduce me to the rest of the team."

"That sounds good," said Alex. "Apart from 'inviting' you into your own office. It's as if they've forgotten we work there."

They had then watched a film before going to bed, but Alex knew Lydia's thoughts were elsewhere. So he rechecked his watch, got out of bed, and joined Lydia in the kitchen.

"Couldn't sleep?" he asked.

"I don't like having to make a decision without discussing things with Gus," said Lydia. "If only the team were in the office like we used to be."

"You might be jumping the gun," said Alex. "Did Rosie say there was even a vacancy on the PCC's team?"

"Not really," said Lydia.

"What did Gus say on Friday night?"

"He said there was no harm in listening to what they had to say," said Lydia.

"That's fair enough," said Alex. "If what they say doesn't feel right for you, thank them for their interest, and drive back to Gablecross. Geoff Mercer has promised to throw up other opportunities in the New Year. There's no rush. Now, I want something to eat before I leave for Swindon. What about you?"

Ten minutes later, Alex tucked into his poached egg on toast while Lydia nibbled on a crispbread covered with cream cheese. Then, finally, he left the house at eight-thirty to drive to Swindon for another riveting day of early-intervention sessions with local school kids.

Lydia left ten minutes later and hammered down the Lacock by-pass in her red Mini to reach the Old Police Station office by nine. She parked in a vacant parking bay adjacent to the lift doors. The cars beside her showed that the rest of the PCC's team was already upstairs. Lydia took a deep breath and called the lift.

Rosie Allison was waiting for her when the lift doors opened.

"Good morning, Lydia," she said. "Would you like a coffee?"

"My mug should be on the shelf next to the Gaggia," said Lydia.

"It's still there, don't worry," said Rosie. "I take it yours is the one with 'I'm Scottish, We Don't Keep Calm' written on it? Lead on. I'll get a drink for the others while we're at it."

Lydia returned from the restroom with her black, one sugar, while Rosie carried three white coffees on a tray. Rosie introduced Lydia to Morris Beard and Sarah Holland.

Lydia sat on a spare chair and soon faced three eager-looking faces. She felt like a goldfish.

"What was it you wanted to talk about?" she asked. "Rosie didn't give me any specifics yesterday."

"DS Mercer put your name forward," said Morris. "The PCC has a small team, and even adding one new member will be viewed in some quarters as excessive. So, if we were to have someone in mind, they would need to be the best candidate available."

"We want people passionate about public service," said Sarah. "Someone dynamic and experienced in delivering projects. We're looking for an individual who will support the Strategic Delivery Lead for Prevention and Youth to deliver improvements and drive forward the partnership's work within the portfolio area."

"That's me," said Morris.

"I thought it might be. It sounds like an interesting concept," said Lydia. "What would I be doing, though?"

"You would support several priority areas," said Rosie, "including youth diversion, youth justice, community safety, and crime prevention."

"Point-of-arrest youth diversion schemes are a way of addressing low-level criminal behaviour without putting young people through the formal criminal justice process," said Morris.

"I've heard of it," said Lydia. "Offenders can be dealt with through out-of-court disposals rather than the formal system that can result in a criminal conviction and other negative consequences."

"Quite," said Morris.

"If you were to join us, you would be part of the team which helps deliver the PCC's Police and Crime Plan," said Sarah. "We work with partners across our communities to deliver improvements for the public, including Wiltshire Police, Youth Justice Services, Local Authorities, health services and voluntary and community groups."

"That sounds like a lot of variety," said Lydia. "But that doesn't faze me. I have a passion for the idea of influencing and shaping services for young people. I believe I can use my initiative and demonstrate excellent problem-solving skills. I've always wanted to help make a difference in the community."

Morris Beard then explained how Wiltshire's Youth Offending Team worked with children and young people involved in offending behaviour.

"We do this by working with the young person, their parents or carers, the victims of crime, volunteers and the local community," he said. "The team comprises staff from various organisations, including the police, probation service, education, and children's social care, all working together to tackle youth crime in Wiltshire."

"Prevention is paramount," added Sarah. "Some young people may be at risk of getting into trouble but have not yet committed an offence. So the team supervises and supports them to prevent them from entering the criminal justice system. But, of course, some young people have already committed offences, and the team attempts to change their behaviour and stop them from re-offending."

"Through restorative justice, we work with victims of crime to ensure they are given a voice within the criminal justice system," said Morris.

"It sounds like you've got all the angles covered," said Lydia.

"It's a struggle we engage in twenty-four-seven," said Rosie.

"It's no picnic," said Morris, "but colleagues in other

parts of the country where the crime rate is three or even four times higher would love to work in Wiltshire. We're among the top ten safest counties in the country."

"This department is a fast-paced, dynamic environment, making a difference, Lydia," said Sarah Holland. "A transfer to us could be just what you're looking for."

"When would you need an answer?" asked Lydia. "I'd like to talk to my partner first. It's a big step."

"We understand," said Morris. "Look, take your time. There's no mad panic, Lydia."

"We're off to Scotland to stay with my mother for Christmas," said Lydia. "I'll let you know before we leave."

"Terrific," said Sarah.

Rosie and Lydia returned to the restroom. Lydia washed her mug and paused as she put it back on the shelf next to those belonging to the rest of the team.

"I suppose you'll call your boss too, won't you?" asked Rosie.

"Gus has been a great person to work with," said Lydia. "He's taught me so much these past nine months."

"You'll benefit from that knowledge moving forward," said Rosie. "Mr Freeman won't be around forever, and you have thirty years ahead of you to make your mark."

Rosie walked with Lydia to the lift.

"Bye, for now, Lydia," she said. "Hope to hear from you soon."

Lydia nodded, entered the lift, and descended to the ground floor. She sent Alex a text before driving to Gablecross.

'Calling in to see Gus on my way home tonight. I might be late x.'

MEANWHILE, in Urchfont, Gus was emptying kitchen cupboards. Last night, Suzie reckoned she couldn't remember that happening since she moved in. Gus had checked the TV schedules and decided a stocktake was a better option.

There was a method to Suzie's sudden desire for order. Before leaving for London Road this morning, she'd explained her logic to Gus over breakfast.

"Although the end of March seems a long way off when December's icy fingers have you in its grip, it's only a matter of weeks. Friday night, and the big shop, come around quicker with each passing birthday. As a result, there might be tins or packets of items well past their best-before date lurking in there. As for crockery and utensils stored in hard-to-reach corners, they're there for a reason. We need to make room for things used constantly when the baby arrives."

By the time he stopped for lunch, Gus had identified two food items well beyond the safety limit. So far, although every shelf was now pristine and neatly arranged, he hadn't created room for much more than a packet of rusks.

Later, he knelt before the ground floor cupboards, wondering whether he'd be able to get up again, and started on the crockery. Would they ever use that fancy dinner service again? He could remember how happy Tess had been to receive it as a wedding present. It was complete and had rarely been used. How many plates did two people need, anyway? They had acquired more functional plates, mugs, and bowls over the years, and since Suzie moved in, the dishwasher was on friendly terms with no more than two dozen pieces of crockery, cutlery, and cookware.

Gus heard the familiar ringtone on his mobile. He levered himself from the cold floor and went to the hallway to check who had sent him a message. Lydia wanted to know if dropping in at around six this evening was okay. He made an executive decision and sent back:

'Only if you bring pizza for three.'

Gus returned to the kitchen and emptied the ground floor cupboards and drawers. Sorry, Tess, he thought, but much of this must go. Then, at four o'clock, he was impressed with the results. They now had clean shelves, three completely empty, and the three C's washed, dried, and back within easy reach. Outside, the Focus was loaded with items destined for the recycling centre in the morning.

While he sat with a coffee in the lounge, waiting for Suzie to get home, Gus made a mental note to declutter the fridge and chest freezer. That was a task for tomorrow.

Suzie came through the front door at five-thirty and headed straight for the kitchen.

Gus waited.

It was too quiet. Gus finished his coffee and crossed the hallway to join Suzie.

"What have you done with the dinner service?" she asked.

"Tess and I rarely used it, and we never have," said Gus. "We can always get something more to your liking if there are more mouths to feed in the future."

"I didn't want you to get rid of all your memories, darling," said Suzie crossing the kitchen to hug him.

"All the stuff I'm taking to the recycling centre is in the car," said Gus. "I'll rescue the sauce boat if it helps. I can remember the rest of the set once I've seen that. What's my overall score?"

"Nine and a half out of ten," said Suzie. "We'll have plenty of room for the baby equipment now. I'd better get changed and start dinner. You've had a busy day."

"No need," said Gus. "Lydia's bringing pizza. She wanted a chat."

Suzie squeezed Gus and kissed him.

"That sounds like she needs your help with a decision she has to make," she said. "I'll get changed."

Gus heard Lydia's Mini in the driveway a few minutes after six and went to open the door. She looked all arms and legs, juggling with three pizza boxes, an oversized bag, and her car keys.

"Evening, guv," said Lydia. "Thanks for getting the door. I thought I'd have to use my nose to ring the bell. I brought three varieties of topping because you didn't give me a hint in your text message."

"Variety is the spice of life, Lydia," said Gus.

"Good to see you, Lydia," said Suzie, who had just emerged from the bedroom. "How was Gablecross?"

"I only spent half a day there today," said Lydia. "It wasn't as much fun as the week we worked together."

"Yes, that *was* fun. We got a result too, which was a bonus," laughed Suzie.

"Let's eat around the kitchen table," said Gus. "We can delve into whichever box takes our fancy."

"Can I get you a drink, Lydia?" asked Suzie.

"A coffee, please," she replied.

"Black, one sugar," said Gus as he plucked the pizza cutter from the drawer where he'd put it an hour ago.

It didn't take long to demolish the pizzas, and Gus knew Lydia hadn't dropped in for a social visit. He wasn't looking forward to what might come next, but there was nothing for it.

"How did the meeting with Morris Beard and his team go this morning?" he asked.

Lydia told them what had been said and that she'd

promised to give them an answer before Friday the twenty-first.

"I imagine you haven't discussed it yet with Alex," said Gus. "What he thinks is more important than what I think, surely?"

"When Mr Truelove wrote, telling me I'd been successful in getting a job with Wiltshire Police, I had no idea where I would end up working. While I went through my induction period, I was a long way from home, living in digs, and found it difficult to make new friends. As soon as I met you, Alex, and Neil in the office that first morning, I immediately felt at home."

"I hadn't realised," said Gus. "You always appeared so resilient, afraid of nothing."

"Nine months later, I feel guilty about considering a transfer, guv," said Lydia. "Alex and I owe you so much. We wouldn't have been allowed to work together if we'd been at London Road or Gablecross once our superiors learned we were a couple."

"I admit I did have to keep it under my hat," said Gus. "Geoff Mercer sussed what was going on, but because we were continuing to produce results, he somehow forgot to tell the boss."

"Something Morris Beard mentioned this morning made me think I could cause you even more trouble by accepting their offer, guv. He pointed out the PCC had to be very careful not to bring undue attention to the small team he has working for him."

"I take it you don't mean Morris Beard might ask you to wear longer skirts and control that mop of hair," said Suzie.

Gus saw what Lydia was driving at.

"The PCC's team has a high profile," said Gus. "A lot more people in the county will be made aware of who you are and who you work for. If your partner is sitting two desks away in the Old Police Station office, pressure will be brought to have him transferred."

"I liked the sound of everything they told me this morning, guv," said Lydia. "It will be tough to match the past nine months working with you in the Crime Review Team, but the Chief Constable told me a management position should be my target once I'd served my apprenticeship in crime investigation. I'd feel awful if my move dealt you a second blow."

"You must do what's best for you, Lydia," said Gus.

"I haven't told Alex about my concerns for his future yet," said Lydia.

"I'm sure Alex wouldn't want you to sacrifice this opportunity," said Lydia. "He's a good detective and will be okay whatever you decide."

"I'd better get home," said Lydia. "Alex will have guessed why I came here first. Whatever happens, I'm not rushing to a decision. Morris Beard was happy to let me think it over for another ten days."

Lydia gathered her things, said goodbye to Suzie, and Gus followed her outside.

"When will we get back to the office, guv?" she asked. "With everyone scattered to the four winds, it feels strange."

"I wish I could tell you, Lydia," said Gus. "I'm as much in the dark as you are. Everyone kept telling me it was temporary. Although, that was before I upset DCI Crocker at Bourne Hill. However, my gut tells me the Chief Constable has his hands tied. But I've known him for years, and if he has a chance for one more rebellious act before he retires, he'll grab it."

"Nothing can happen until the New Year," said Lydia.

"Perhaps I should wish you Happy Christmas now, in case we don't see one another. Goodnight, guv."

Gus watched her red Mini disappear through the gateway and listened as it sprinted along the lane—time to get indoors, away from the cold wind.

"I'm in the lounge with a coffee, darling," called Suzie.

"I fear that's one brick in the wall gone," sighed Gus when he sat beside her.

"Inevitable, and you know it," said Suzie.

Gus knew Suzie was right, but it wouldn't make the loss easier to bear.

Chapter Three

SUZIE WAS in the kitchen when Gus surfaced. After two days of cleaning and tidying, plus a couple of visits to the recycling centre, he was flagging.

"Come on, sleepyhead," said Suzie. "It's Friday, the end of another week."

"Every day's the same when you're on gardening leave," he moaned.

"It's allowed you to progress in other areas," said Suzie. "The kitchen is now unrecognisable. You found time for a haircut yesterday, and we had a productive session with Brett and Clemency on Wednesday night. Irene's helping with table decorations to be delivered to the Lamb on the wedding day."

"We couldn't persuade Bert to let me drive him to the Lamb yesterday, though," said Gus.

"There's always tomorrow," said Suzie.

"Not much to show for a week's work," said Gus.

The landline rang in the hallway.

"That's early," said Gus. "Which is *never* good."

"It doesn't *have* to be bad news," said Suzie.

Gus picked up the phone. He recognised the number.

"Morning, Geoff. What gets you out of bed so early?"

"I thought you would appreciate some good news," said Geoff. "I don't know how they managed it, but Bourne Hill has improved their clear-up rate. I heard a whisper late yesterday afternoon that an arrest had been made outside Winchester Post Office."

"So, they picked up Tim Harding, or Ash, as many music fans remember him," said Gus.

"Harding's been held in connection with the murders of John Crees, Mandy Howard, and Gillian Lye."

"We can only hope the CPS don't screw it up when it reaches court," said Gus.

"I believe Kenneth called you the other day?" asked Geoff. "Did he tell you Sylvia Robbins is visiting London Road later this morning?"

"He did," said Gus. "What time will she be unveiled? If you get my drift."

"Why?" asked Geoff. "Did you think about coming into town to hear what she has to say?"

"I don't have any pressing appointments on my calendar," said Gus.

"Just keep a low profile if you drop by," said Geoff. "I'm doing everything I can to get Kenneth to allow you to return to work. We've only got a few weeks left before our retirement to leave a lasting impression."

"You want me to help you go out in a blaze of glory," said Gus.

"I want you to help me sleep at night when I'm retired," said Geoff. "Something triggered a memory in the past ten days. I can't put my finger on where or when. We had a murder case in the county twenty years ago, where a woman's body was found on an embankment beside the M4."

"Was that on the long stretch between Junction 15 and 16?" asked Gus.

"That's the one. Stephanie Harford was the victim. Do you remember the case?" asked Geoff.

"I remember reading about it in the Salisbury Journal," said Gus. "We had enough to keep us busy at Bourne Hill, so I never got close enough to the case to hear the details. Police thought the daughter's boyfriend did it but couldn't get the evidence to charge him."

"Both detectives who worked that case have long since retired. DI Gordon Flowers was running the show, and DS Ricky Lenham was his second-in-command. They were old hands, who had worked together at Gablecross for ages, but they'd never dealt with anything like the Harford case."

"Is this one of the murder files Kenneth has had in his desk drawer since I returned to work?" asked Gus.

"No," said Geoff. "He knows nothing about it. I woke up in a cold sweat the other night thinking someone had said something that didn't fit. You should know what that's like."

"If Kenneth doesn't know about it," said Gus. "Then why couldn't I investigate it off the books? I'll drive into Devizes later this morning, listen to what the new Chief Constable says, and we'll meet up afterwards."

"Don't park at London Road," said Geoff. "We need to keep this under our hats. Instead, drive to Caen Hill locks. You pass the entrance every day when you drive to the office. Meet me there thirty minutes after Ms Robbins has charmed the media gang."

Geoff rang off, and Gus clapped his hands.

Suzie was standing by the front door, ready to leave for work.

"I told you it wasn't bad news," she said. "What's got you so excited?"

"Geoff Mercer extended an olive branch. We're meeting for a chat this afternoon."

"I wonder what he has up his sleeve?" asked Suzie. "Anyway, I must go. I'll see you tonight."

"Okay, darling," said Gus. "I'll get a list together for our big shop."

"This domesticated version of you won't last long if Geoff has found a way to get you back to work," said Suzie with a grin. "Ah well, it was good while it lasted."

She closed the front door behind her, and Gus heard the Golf make its usual dash for the gateway. He stood in the hallway, intrigued by the conversation he'd just had with his boss. Gus had never heard Geoff Mercer sound so nervous. Unless he was mistaken, the less Suzie knew about what he would investigate, the better.

Gus couldn't concentrate on the few items Suzie had cheekily added to the initial list of chores when he wasn't looking. There was nothing that couldn't wait a week or two. So, he searched online for press reports on the Harford case.

Stephanie Harford had gone missing on Sunday, the sixteenth of April, twenty years ago. Her parents last saw Stephanie on Saturday night. Doug and Mary Thompson had attended a forty-third birthday party organised by Stephanie's twenty-year-old daughter, Bethany. The party had been held at a restaurant in Swindon. The only other person in attendance was Adie Lawrence, Bethany's twenty-five-year-old boyfriend. Adrian Lawrence was a motor mechanic, while Bethany worked as a supermarket checkout operator. They had been seeing one another for fifteen months.

Doug and Mary Thompson had returned home by taxi at the end of the night, while Adie had driven to a house on Lime Kiln in Royal Wootton Bassett, where Stephanie lived with her daughter. Her marriage had ended a decade earlier, and the whereabouts of her ex-husband was unknown.

Her parents were both retired and lived on a new estate at Grange Park, the other side of the M4 motorway, on the western outskirts of Swindon.

Stephanie had worked at one of several farm shops, also on the other side of the M4, near Lydiard Millicent for six years. She made the four-mile journey on her bicycle six days a week, with a half-day on Wednesday. The shop was closed on Mondays.

Gus hunted through several press reports before he found what he was looking for.

Adie Lawrence worked at a garage in Chiseldon and lived with his parents in Wroughton. Gus made a note of names, addresses, and employers. Much would have changed in the decades since the murder, but a trip to the various locations was in order.

He successfully whiled away the hours before he needed to drive into Devizes. When he reached the supermarket car park he and Suzie would use later, he took advantage of the free parking. He hoped Sylvia Robbins hadn't written too long a speech. Gus walked to London Road, entered the car park at the far end fifteen minutes later, and found a quiet spot from where he could observe the steps in front of the main building without drawing attention to himself.

Invitations had been sent to the great and the good from

the town, plus the press corps. Both regional television companies had vans on site, and as the witching hour of midday approached, the front doors opened, and Stuart Midwinter appeared.

The PCC was followed by Kenneth Truelove in his best uniform. Every Assistant Chief Constable the county possessed left the building and filled the top step. Gus spotted ACC Sylvia Robbins in the centre.

Stuart Midwinter made an opening statement, thanking Kenneth for his unstinting support and reminding the media of the headline ambitions of his Police and Crime Plan. The time had come for new blood, he said, a Chief Constable who could take the county force forward over the next three to five years.

Gus wondered whether a bright spark from the press corps might ask why anyone would want to be a Chief Constable. Did they know too few candidates were throwing their caps into the ring these days? Was anyone at the Home Office asking why and doing something about it?

Two candidates were the national average for a Chief Constable post, and many ACCs had severe reservations about taking the role. Maybe that was why the faces in the back row looked so happy. They knew they could relax for a few years. Nobody would be asking them if they fancied the job.

When he'd been in Kenneth's office, Gus recalled the PCC referred to Sylvia Robbins as the best candidate. Maybe the other candidate was happy he hadn't got the nod. After all, there had been a substantial increase in turnover in recent years. The average tenure for chief constables was now three and a half years, and Wiltshire fared no better.

Policing was already under strain dealing with rising

crime. How could it cope with a more complex demand and an unprecedented terror threat with fewer officers unless it attracted the right people? Surely, we needed someone to lead from the front for a lengthy period. However, based on current evidence, the PCC was overly optimistic in hoping Sylvia Robbins would stick the pace for five years.

Gus knew Kenneth had found being Chief Constable hugely demanding, and given his responsibility; it was only fitting he'd been subject to significant scrutiny. The very best officers were needed to serve in such an important role.

In Gus's opinion, Kenneth was one of the best, and Wiltshire had been lucky to have him. Whether the diminutive, middle-aged woman waiting in the wings would match her predecessor's accomplishments remained to be seen.

Stuart Midwinter formally announced that ACC Sylvia Robbins from Durham would become the county's new Chief Constable on April the first, 2019. Polite applause from her colleagues on either side echoed around the car park as Ms Robbins joined the PCC by the microphone.

"I am grateful to the PCC for setting a clear, realistic, and ambitious Police and Crime Plan," she said. "This plan strongly aligns with my vision and priorities for the Force in the coming years. We will be tough on crime, keep people safe and put victims first. We have a shared ambition of making Wiltshire the safest county and remaining one of the finest police forces in the country. I will work relentlessly to assess the current capabilities of the Force to deliver the plan, identify and implement a road map to meeting it and ensure I develop the strategy, priorities, and infrastructure to deliver it. I will undertake a forensic examination of Force expenditure and identify where savings can be achieved and where we need to invest in transformation and new approaches."

As Sylvia Robbins paused to turn to the next page of her speech, Gus pondered the prospect of transformation and new approaches. So, the new approaches mentioned when considering his options four years ago had already been shown not to work.

"We must tackle developing crime threats and improve visible policing," continued Sylvia. "I have a programme to provide more officers tackling criminals who cause misery to parts of our communities, improved ways of being available to our public, ensuring a relentless pursuit of organised crime gangs involved in county lines drug supply. I recognise the importance of a continued need to ensure every penny we have is spent wisely. My team will be tasked to challenge costs to ensure we reinvest what we currently have in areas that deliver the very best for our communities."

Gus studied the heads of the press corps, the mayor, and several other dignitaries from Devizes. He didn't see Monty Jennings among them. Reporters weren't taking copious notes. They all carried smart phones that could record everything they required when they returned to a warm office. If this speech went on much longer, there was a danger of frostbitten toes.

"I've already identified several priority areas. Wiltshire Police will deliver the new rural crime strategy, expand our capability to tackle organised crime and protect business owners and those in isolated communities. I will invest in a new approach to targeting organised drug supply, increasing proactive policing, and working with forces across the UK to prevent offending in Wiltshire. I will continue to work with our partners to reduce crime, protect the vulnerable and relentlessly pursue offenders, bringing them to justice."

Gus continued to scan the small crowd looking for a

familiar face. Sylvia Robbins had stepped back to be replaced at the microphone by Stuart Midwinter.

"I'm delighted to welcome Sylvia Robbins to Wiltshire Police," said the PCC. "I look forward to working closely with her to ensure a safer Wiltshire for all who live and work here. I am confident Sylvia will drive the necessary change, and we are both clear that improving trust, confidence, standards and delivering a policing service the public wants, and deserves, is of paramount importance."

Gus spotted Geoff Mercer on the far side of the main building. His car was usually parked close to where Gus was standing. Geoff must have had the forethought to move it, so he could slip away unnoticed. That could only mean one thing.

The PCC and his party were already back inside the main building. Gus retraced his steps, left the car park, returned to London Road, and then walked to where he'd left the Focus. Finally, he drove away from Estcourt Street and headed towards Wadworth's brewery.

Gus turned right at the mini roundabout to join the A361 and was soon on Bath Road, crossing the Kennet & Avon canal as he drove past the Black Horse pub. Soon after, he turned into Mayenne Place. Access to the miracle of canal engineering was ahead within this small housing estate, but Gus was looking for somewhere to park other than where Geoff Mercer had chosen. He'd kept an eye on his rear-view mirror and was confident nobody had followed him.

He checked his watch and waited in the Focus for a few minutes. Then he walked onto the towpath beside the canal. He could see Geoff Mercer two hundred yards ahead. Two white swans were coming towards him from the centre of the large pool at the top of the rise.

"It's okay, lads," said Gus. "I don't need an escort."

Gus set off along the towpath.

"What did you make of the speech?" asked Geoff when they met.

"It ticked all the right boxes," said Gus. "Although, I was surprised not to hear her mention diversity or inclusivity. It's high on the list of priorities for most speakers these days. But, of course, the writing is on the wall for the Crime Review Team. We might be successful, but we're not using these new methods. We're merely perpetuating the myth dinosaurs aren't extinct."

Geoff smiled.

"Thankfully, Kenneth and I won't be around to hear the clamour for a fresh approach five years from now. Let's walk towards Foxhangers. Have you visited this place before, Gus?"

"I've heard about it from Neil," said Gus. "He's our resident canal expert."

"We're walking beside one of the country's longest continuous flight of locks. Twenty-nine locks with a rise of two hundred and thirty-seven feet over two miles. The sixteen locks that form the steepest part are scheduled ancient monuments. Two hundred years ago, seventy-sixty-ton barges were working this stretch of water, mostly carrying stone and coal. It might have taken over three days to get from Bath to Newbury, but it was faster and cheaper than by road."

"Until Isambard Kingdom Brunel and the railways came along," said Gus.

"That killed the cargo trade, and for the past sixty years, there's been a major rebuilding operation," said Geoff. "Thanks to that, Caen Hill gets ten million visitors each year. The Kennet & Avon canal supports many thriving businesses, from boat builders and repairers, marinas, miscellaneous makers, and artisans, to the many pubs and eateries that line its route."

"I can't see how these locks relate to the murder of Stephanie Harford," said Gus.

"They don't, but do you see many people around?" asked Geoff.

"There's nothing on the water now and only two couples on the towpath."

"Exactly," said Geoff. "It's quiet; we're not likely to be seen, nor will our conversation be overheard. We can see two hundred yards from where we're standing in both directions. Nobody can creep up on us unobserved. I brought you here because I understand why the original investigation struggled to make a case against Adie Lawrence."

"Did Flowers and Lenham realise Stephanie hadn't been killed by someone close to her?"

"You would need to ask them that question," said Geoff. "But, before I outline my thoughts, tell me what you've found online."

Gus told Geoff what he'd read about the case and what he intended to do next.

"You like to analyse locations, and distances, Gus," said Geoff. "I wish I could give you more, but I can't get hold of the case files from Gablecross."

"I already know the problems Gablecross have," said Gus. "Some recent cases are stored in the main building, while others have been sent to an industrial site. So, a twenty-year-old case might be hard to trace there. Its data might not still be intact and scattered around the facility."

"Which is perfect for someone who doesn't want the evidence re-examined," said Geoff.

"I could tell from your tone this morning that whatever

you heard spooked you. We could have held this meeting in your office. Do you suspect a serving police officer was responsible for the murder of Stephanie Harford?"

"It's not certain she was the only victim," said Geoff. "Are you sure you want to go ahead with this, Gus? It might be dangerous."

"You need to fill in the gaps in my knowledge," said Gus. "Is there somewhere we can do that where it's warmer?"

"We'll drive back to the Wharf café on Couch Lane," said Geoff. "I'll leave first. If I see anyone I recognise or who looks suspicious, I'll call, and you should drive straight home."

Fifteen minutes later, Gus joined Geoff inside the café. He'd parked twenty spaces from Geoff's car, and when Gus collected a black coffee from the bored-looking staff member on the counter, only three elderly couples were indoors enjoying an afternoon break.

"What happened after the birthday party?" asked Gus. "That was the last time her parents saw Stephanie."

"On Sunday morning, Stephanie told Bethany she was going to visit a friend's house after they finished work at the farm shop."

"The friend worked with Stephanie at Lydiard Millicent; I take it?"

"Alice Venton," said Geoff. "A widow in her early sixties who lived in the village."

"How many people live in the village?" asked Gus.

"Fifteen hundred," said Geoff. "A typical village on the outskirts of a large town like Swindon. The original church, school, pub, large country house in the centre, and the newer residential properties closer to Swindon. Alice Venton lived at Chestnut Springs, a new development of bungalows, where she had moved after the sudden death of her husband in 1996. Mrs Venton died around six years ago."

"So, when did the daughter realise something was amiss?" asked Gus.

"On Monday morning, Bethany realised her mother hadn't come home but assumed she'd slept at her friend's house. So Bethany left for work at the supermarket at the usual time and didn't call her grandparents until she returned to Lime Kiln in the evening."

"So, does that mean Bethany was the last person to see her mother alive?" asked Gus. "What about Alice Venton? Did Stephanie reach her home in Lydiard Millicent on Sunday?"

"Mrs Venton felt ill on Sunday morning, and called in sick," said Geoff.

"Who called Alice Venton?" asked Gus.

"Doug Thompson did," said Geoff. "He drove to see Bethany as soon as he received her worried call on Monday evening. Doug found an address book by the telephone in the hallway and contacted Alice Venton. Then he tried every other likely contact number without success. They phoned the police at nine forty-five and reported her missing."

"When was the body discovered?" asked Gus.

"That wasn't until October," said Geoff. "Work was being carried out alongside the motorway after a prolonged spell of rain. They needed to stabilise a steep wooded embankment which was slipping by a rate of about four inches a month. The body was found in a shallow grave behind a row of maple trees at the top of the embankment."

"What did the subsequent post-mortem reveal?" asked Gus.

"The hyoid bone was broken," said Geoff. "Stephanie Harford had been strangled."

"What do we know of the period between that phone call and the discovery of the body?"

"Stephanie's debit card was used to withdraw six hundred pounds on Monday morning. The killer had wrapped Stephanie in thick black polythene sheeting and thrown personal items such as her handbag and mobile phone beside the body. It wasn't known how much cash she had in her purse, but the killer had emptied it."

"How was the sheeting secured?" asked Gus.

"Zip-tied top and bottom," said Geoff. "The sheeting and ties showed no trace of DNA. The killer wore gloves, and the materials used were as common as muck. It was impossible to identify where they might have been purchased or when."

"What did the logs from her mobile phone tell DI Flowers and DS Lenham?" asked Gus.

"Stephanie made and received calls on Sunday," said Geoff. "She called her parents, thanking them for the surprise birthday party. Friends from the farm shop who weren't working on Sunday called with birthday greetings."

"Belated greetings?" asked Gus.

"No, her birthday was actually on Sunday. Bethany hadn't been able to book the restaurant that night, and anyway, she knew Doug and his wife were confirmed churchgoers. So they didn't hold with enjoying themselves on Sundays."

"Anything else from the phone?" asked Gus.

"There was nothing after seven o'clock on Sunday night, apart from missed calls from Doug Thompson."

"Was that it?" asked Gus.

"Doug Thompson had cancelled his daughter's debit

and credit cards on Tuesday morning. When the monthly statement arrived, he checked it before handing it to DI Flowers. On Sunday night, at eleven twenty-seven, Stephanie had booked a hotel room for the night."

"Where?" asked Gus.

"A budget hotel on Great Western Way," said Geoff. "Just three miles from the farm shop."

"Stephanie regularly cycled fifteen minutes from home in Royal Wootton Bassett to work and home again. So why on earth would she need to sleep elsewhere? Did she arrive for work on Sunday?"

"Yes," said Geoff. "Arrived on time, worked her full shift, and left just after six when the shop closed."

"Did anyone see her cycle away from the farm shop?" asked Gus.

"No," said Geoff. "Although, that was understandable. Back then, they had fewer people working on Sundays. Most of them drove to work or walked from their homes in the village. The manager told DS Lenham that Stephanie's bicycle was stored in a secure lockup at the rear of the premises. The others would only have been gone for a few minutes, but that was long enough for her to be the last to leave. Also, Stephanie would have cycled in the opposite direction to many of her colleagues."

"What was the weather like?" asked Gus.

"It was a mild and cloudy night. Nothing to suggest she would have struggled to get home," said Geoff.

"She could have had a puncture," said Gus. "Or her brakes were playing up. Even so, she had her mobile phone. She could have organised something. Why not call her daughter's boyfriend?"

"There was no record of any call to Lawrence in the phone logs that night," said Geoff.

"Where could she have gone between six and when she made the hotel booking?" asked Gus. "Why did she book the hotel room anyway?"

"That was never explained, and the room was never used," said Geoff. "Nobody turned up using Stephanie Harford's name or anyone else that night. They didn't see a Mr and Mrs Smith, which might have been behind the booking."

"Her marriage had ended ages before," said Gus. "Did the family or her work colleagues know of a new relationship?"

"There was no evidence to suggest there was anyone, male or female," said Geoff. "There were no male contacts on her phone Doug Thompson didn't recognise. Police eliminated the window cleaner, painter and decorator, electrician, and plumber who Stephanie called on to keep her property in good order."

"How soon after the discovery of the body was it established the remains were those of Stephanie Harford?" asked Gus.

"It took a week to identify her using medical and dental records. Stephanie didn't wear jewellery to work."

"What happened to her bicycle?" asked Gus.

"The farm shop manager confirmed Stephanie had retrieved her bicycle and locked the store room before she left the property. It was never seen again."

"So, she disappeared from her place of work and wasn't found for six months," said Gus. "Did the autopsy determine when she died?"

"Hard to tell with any accuracy," said Geoff.

"I wonder whether Eve Northwood can help," said Gus. "It was before her time as a locum police surgeon, but she'll be able to give me the benefit of her wisdom. Without access to the original files, that may have to suffice."

"You could always ask Eve to check who carried out the post-mortem, Gus," said Geoff. "The coroner's reports will be readily accessible to her. It has its dangers, of course."

"Eve could alert the killer if she suddenly looked into a historic case," said Gus.

"Quite," said Geoff. "We don't know how deep this goes."

Gus was starting to realise why his friend had sounded so nervous on the phone this morning. What were they dealing with here?

Chapter Four

GUS THOUGHT back over what Geoff had told him.

"The bank cards," said Gus. "Were they found with the body?"

"Yes," said Geoff. "The only activity on her cards after she left home on Sunday morning was that hotel booking just before midnight and the cash withdrawal the following day."

"We know Stephanie Harford was alive at six o'clock on Sunday evening," said Gus. "We can't be certain she booked the hotel room. Her card was used, but did anyone at Premier Inn speak to her in person?"

"If the booking happened online, they wouldn't have checked anything other than the bank details," said Geoff. "The killer could have made the booking. But why? If they had no intention of visiting the hotel?"

"Perhaps it was an attempt to persuade the family Stephanie was still alive," said Gus. "The cash was withdrawn on Monday. Even if Bethany had raised the alarm first thing, the police wouldn't have acted. Stephanie had only been missing for twelve to fourteen hours at most. If they did carry out cursory checks the following day when Doug Thompson returned to say she still wasn't home, what conclusions would they draw? They would have suggested Stephanie had met someone on Sunday evening, they'd planned to go to the hotel, but their plans changed. She withdrew cash on Monday and probably went away for a couple of days. No doubt, she'll turn up at home, sir, wondering what all the fuss was about. The police would have told him Stephanie was forty-three, single, and perfectly capable of looking after herself."

"I suppose so," said Geoff.

"Why did DI Flowers start to wonder whether the daughter and her boyfriend were involved?" asked Gus.

"When the family were interviewed, Gordon Flowers learned that Bethany knew the PIN for her mother's debit card," said Geoff.

"Not unheard of, I suppose," said Gus.

"It didn't seem an issue in the early days of the investigation," said Geoff. "When the mobile phone company coughed up the call records for Stephanie's phone, they realised that although Doug Thompson had tried calling his daughter's phone day-in day-out since Monday evening, Bethany had made no attempt to contact her mother."

"So, Flowers wondered whether the daughter withdrew the six hundred in cash on Monday," said Gus. "He thought Stephanie could already have been dead. Alice Venton hadn't met Stephanie after work on Sunday due to illness."

"Flowers and Lenham thought Stephanie worked all day on Sunday as normal. Then, she left the shop to cycle home on her bicycle. Adie Lawrence and Bethany intercepted her, strangled her, and disposed of the body," said Gus. "But what was their motive?"

"You're forgetting one thing, Gus," said Geoff. "The bank card."

"Of course," said Gus. "The card was found with the body. It had to have gone into the ground with her purse and mobile phone."

"Look, we've been here too long," said Geoff. "The girl on the counter keeps looking at us. She'll remember us if someone comes asking questions. I want to do some more digging to confirm my suspicions. Enjoy the weekend, and we'll fix a time to meet again. Where do you know that's quiet and very few people will recognise us?"

"The Plough at Sparsholt," said Gus. "I took Blessing there last week. The snack menu was good. When's a good time for you?"

"As I'm leaving at the end of February, Kenneth will need to get used to me disappearing from time to time," said Geoff. "I can use a visit to the solicitor as an excuse or a trip to Clench Common with Christine. Can you make it at one o'clock on Monday?"

"No problem," said Gus.

Geoff left the café first. Gus used the facilities and read the community noticeboard before walking to his car. He scanned the half-empty car park but saw nothing to concern him.

Monday, 17 December 2018

"WHAT ARE your plans for today, darling?" asked Suzie.

"I might tackle a couple of the outstanding items on that list of chores you compiled," said Gus. "Why, was there something else you had in mind?"

"You haven't mentioned Geoff Mercer since he called on Friday morning," said Suzie. "Did you see him at London Road after the press conference?"

"We had a brief chat," said Gus. "He's got more spade-work to do before he can let me loose on that investigation."

Suzie could tell she wasn't going to get the whole story. Gus had been preoccupied all weekend. They hadn't strayed far from home, just a visit to the supermarket on Friday night, then an hour at Worton Farm on Saturday morning. They'd enjoyed a meal with Brett and the Reverend at the Lamb in the evening. Then, yesterday had been spent at home, chilling out, apart from Gus making a trip to the garage for petrol.

Gus had been with her in body throughout, but Suzie could imagine those little grey cells were working overtime on something troubling him. So why didn't he want to share the puzzle with her? And if Gus wasn't working, why did he need to fill the tank on the Focus?

"Will you be home by five-thirty tonight?" she asked.

"I'm not going anywhere special," said Gus. "I'll have dinner ready by six, don't fret."

Suzie kissed him.

"Have fun," she said and left for work.

Gus waited for the Golf to leave before ringing Eve Northwood.

"What is it this time?" she asked. "Another clandestine lunch in Marlborough, perhaps? I rather enjoyed that."

"Not on this occasion, Eve," said Gus. "Have you worked for Gablecross lately?"

"No juicy murders on my list in the past few weeks. They have other names they can call if they need a coroner's input. Why?"

"If I were sneaky, I'd tell you I'm between cold cases, but actually, I'm on gardening leave."

"I see," said Eve. "You thought someone at Gablecross might have tipped me off, told me not to have anything to do with you. Was it something serious?"

"I kept poking my nose in, despite a senior detective in Salisbury telling me they could handle it."

"Were you on the right track?" asked Eve.

"I didn't have the right answer when I started, but yes, I did get to it before them."

"So, you're calling from home, not the office. What do you need to know?"

"I'm driving to Wootton Bassett in the morning," said Gus. "Could you spare me thirty minutes while I'm there? I'll explain everything then."

"Hold the line," said Eve. "Where will you be at ten-thirty? I can spare an hour."

Gus gave her an address on Lime Kiln, thanked her, and rang off.

After spending an hour in the second bedroom fitting a dimmer switch and proving yet again DIY wasn't his forte, Gus drove to Sparsholt to meet with Geoff Mercer. Gus checked his rear-view mirror throughout the journey. When he reached the outskirts of the village, he remembered the agricultural college had a visitor's car park. As he walked back towards the Plough, he spotted a dark saloon car idling close to the pub.

Gus waited and watched as the car reversed into a parking space. When the driver got out, he recognised him.

"When did you change your car, Geoff?" he asked when he crossed the road.

"A month ago," said Geoff. "Christine insisted we

bought something more economical for when we retired. I got a great part-exchange deal on my old one."

"I became suspicious when I saw someone passing the pub at five miles an hour," said Gus.

"I was looking for your car, you idiot. I wondered why you were late, considering you've got nothing else to fill your time."

"Cheeky," said Gus. "Suzie keeps me busy around the house. I parked at the college just around the corner. The wife of a guy who lives next door to the Plough works there. He's one of the musicians who played with Ash Harding in venues around Winchester."

"I see," said Geoff. "Well, we're here now. Let's hope it's warmer inside."

Geoff needn't have worried. The log fire was glowing brighter than when Gus had been here with Blessing.

They got their drinks, ordered food, and sat at a table near the window.

Gus scanned the faces in the bar and recognised several from last week. Nobody was paying them any attention.

"What have you learned since yesterday?" asked Geoff.

"Very little," said Gus. "I'm meeting Eve Northwood tomorrow morning. I want to get a feel for the place, and she's got an hour to spare, but if I want to visit Lydiard Millicent and the spot where Stephanie's body was found in daylight, it might pay to leave that trip until Wednesday morning. How much digging were *you* able to accomplish in one evening?"

"Fair point," said Geoff. "I haven't delved into the details yet, but two unsolved murders appear to fit the pattern. The first was a French woman with a brother working in Bath as a chef. She came for a two-week visit in 2001. Marie Legrand wanted to take the opportunity to improve her English while she was here. Unfortunately, she never reached Bath, and her body was discovered near Barbury Castle."

"That's the site of an ancient hillfort on the Ridgeway, isn't it?" asked Gus.

"That's right," said Geoff. "Off the beaten track, that's for sure. The body was hidden in undergrowth half a mile from the Castle, between some racing stables and the Barbury Shooting School."

"The North Wessex Downs are the perfect spot for country pursuits," said Gus. "I can imagine the class of customers they attract. It must have come as a shock to whoever stumbled across the body."

"Not one of the hunting, shooting, and fishing fraternity," said Geoff. "A married couple were out exercising their dogs early in the morning, hoping to catch sight of the racehorses on the gallops," said Geoff. "They let the dogs off the lead for a minute and found them standing like statues by a stretch of bramble and hawthorn. As they got closer, the couple realised they were looking at a naked body."

"How long had Marie Legrand been missing?" asked Gus.

"A month, almost to the day," said Geoff. "Marie was strangled. They dumped the body less than ten miles from where Stephanie Harford was found. Also, Marie Legrand disappeared after leaving a transport café at South Marston."

"I've been there," said Gus. "That's the truck stop where our serial killer used to park his trailer unit before visiting his father, Stan Jones. What was this French woman doing there?"

"When I find out, I'll let you know," said Geoff. "Can

you see why I think this death could be linked to that of Stephanie Harford?"

"The truck stop is less than ten miles from the farm shop where Stephanie disappeared," said Gus. "That's two similar deaths inside a relatively small circle. So, yes, it's possible."

Their snacks arrived, and conversation ceased while they ate.

"Would you like a coffee, Gus?" asked Geoff.

"You've got another potential victim, so we'd better keep the landlord happy by putting money in the till. Otherwise, he'll think we just came indoors to keep warm."

Geoff went to the bar to order, and Gus wondered who had handled the Marie Legrand murder. Flowers and Lenham had still been at Gablecross. They would have been the most likely candidates. Also, he needed to ask who carried out the autopsy.

"Right," said Geoff. "Fast forward to 2007, and Claire Dyke, a forty-year-old artist who lived alone in a cottage just outside Brinkworth, a village between Malmesbury and Royal Wootton Bassett. The official verdict was she died from asphyxiation. The murder took place in her home. The body was found by her parents, who hadn't heard from her for several weeks. They drove up from Brighton to check everything was okay and found the cottage locked and no signs of their daughter. Claire's body was found stuffed into the airing cupboard. Her VW Golf was later discovered in a multi-storey car park in Swindon."

"How old was Marie Legrand?" asked Gus. "Do you know?"

"About the same age, I think," said Geoff, "but don't quote me on it."

"So, in essence, the three victims have things in

common," said Gus. "They were much the same age, alone when they were attacked, and their bodies weren't found for weeks or months."

"All three were single when the killer struck," said Geoff. "Although Stephanie Harford was separated from Greg, her husband."

"I'm not sure that's the correct term, Geoff," said Gus. "They were living apart. I don't recall reading anything indicating they were in touch with one another or talking to solicitors about a divorce. As I see it, Greg walked out in 1988 and never got in touch. Doug and Mary Thompson told detectives they didn't know his whereabouts."

"Okay, but none of the three women was in a stable relationship when they died. How's that?"

"That will do for now," said Gus. "Did the other women have children?"

"No," said Geoff.

"Perhaps the killer saw Stephanie at the farm shop and didn't realise she had a twenty-year-old daughter at home. Remind me what happened to make the police switch their attention to the boyfriend."

"I don't know that Gordon Flowers didn't suspect the daughter and her boyfriend from the off," said Geoff. "We know the statistics. A family member, close friend, or near neighbour will often be the culprit. You must ask the detectives how many times they spoke to Bethany Harford and Adrian Lawrence in the first six months. Then, when they could confirm they were dealing with a murder, rather than an unexplained disappearance, the relationship between Stephanie and Adrian Lawrence and her daughter came under the spotlight."

"Was there ever any doubt about their alibis for Sunday night?" asked Gus.

"Nobody in Lime Kiln saw Bethany in the evening," said Geoff. "She left the house with Adrian Lawrence just after lunch, and they were seen watching a Sunday football match in town. Lawrence said they had visited a pub after the game, and he dropped Bethany at home at around nine-thirty. After the late night on Saturday, Bethany was tired and wanted an early night."

"Could Lawrence's parents confirm what time their son arrived in Wroughton?" asked Gus.

"They had gone to bed before he reached home," said Geoff.

"So, the couple didn't have alibis between maybe nine in the evening and early Monday morning."

"No, but what was their motive?" asked Geoff. "Plus, several people from the pub said they'd been there for three hours at least. They couldn't have been in Lydiard Millicent at six."

"Why on earth did Flowers and Lenham persist in chasing a lost cause then?" asked Gus.

"Because events took an unexpected twist after the body was found," said Geoff. "Bethany failed to show up for her mother's inquest, and Doug Thompson told the coroner his granddaughter was unwell."

"Did the detectives check whether she was ill?" asked Gus.

"The coroner had several questions he wanted to ask Bethany and Adrian Lawrence," said Geoff. "As Bethany was absent, he asked Lawrence whether he was responsible for Stephanie's death. Lawrence refused to answer, saying his legal counsel had advised him not to answer questions to avoid potential incrimination."

"The right to silence," said Gus. "Not something he would have thought of himself. Heaven knows what his legal counsel thought Lawrence had to hide. The more I see of this case, the less I think the youngsters had anything to do with it."

"The coroner then asked Lawrence whether he'd cooperated with another person in Stephanie's murder. But, again, he didn't respond."

"Once you hear the first 'no comment' in an interview, you know you might as well give up," said Gus.

"Doug Thompson pleaded with Lawrence to tell the court what had happened," said Geoff. "Lawrence shook his head."

"Within days, Bethany and her boyfriend were arrested on suspicion of murder," said Gus. "I read the article in the Swindon Advertiser, but the CPS decided no charges would be brought after mulling over the case for a further six months. Everything ground to a halt. Flowers and Lenham moved to another case, and the youngsters were left to get on with their lives. As were Doug and Mary Thompson."

"I'd better get back to London Road," said Geoff. "I'll continue gathering details for Marie Legrand and Claire Dyke. I can't be sure whether there was another one earlier than Stephanie Harford, but nothing since 2007 fits the profile yet."

"I'll talk with Eve tomorrow, and if I can fix a meeting with Gordon Flowers, that would be good. I can't fathom why they didn't pursue other lines of enquiry."

"Why don't you leave now and walk to wherever you parked the Focus?" said Geoff. "I'll deal with the landlord and treat us to lunch."

"Don't forget you can't claim for a pub lunch when you told Vera you were popping to Clench Common or seeing your solicitor," said Gus.

"Curses, foiled again," said Geoff.

"The gravy train is pulling into a siding, Geoff," said Gus. "Business lunches, Kassie's bacon baps and sticky buns will soon be history."

"Her bacon and sausage baps, maybe," said Geoff. "I've told Kassie I'll give her a weekly cake order, just like Kenneth. I'm retiring, not living like a monk."

Gus left the Plough and walked to the college. Geoff's new car was long gone when he drove past the car park fifteen minutes later. The dashboard clock on his Focus showed half-past three when Gus parked outside the bungalow in Urchfont.

Suzie arrived home at five-thirty and found him in the kitchen.

"Busy day?" she asked.

"It had its moments," said Gus. "Dinner will be ready in fifteen minutes."

Gus noticed Suzie did a bungalow tour before returning to sit opposite him at the table. She was checking up on him.

"The dimmer switch," she said.

"I tried it again just before you got home," said Gus. "There was no loud bang, and the lights didn't even flicker."

"I suspect you didn't spend all day at the bungalow," said Suzie.

"My legal counsel advised me not to answer to avoid potential incrimination," said Gus.

"Just as I thought," said Suzie. "You're up to something, and Geoff Mercer is involved."

"Did you tour the mezzanine today to check if anyone had left the office for a few hours?"

"I couldn't possibly comment," said Suzie. "Will you be doing something secretive tomorrow?"

"I'm meeting an old friend," said Gus. "Gardening leave has its positive side."

"That's all very well," said Suzie. "Please be careful."

Tuesday, 18 December 2018

GUS LEFT HOME five minutes after Suzie drove to London Road and headed for Wootton Bassett. Forty minutes later, he had negotiated the Beckhampton straight, reached Broad Hinton, and turned left onto a minor road. When he reached the town, he joined the Bath Road and was soon passing Lime Kiln House.

The imposing building was a restored Grade II listed property and must have been surrounded by many acres of land a couple of centuries ago. Now the area surrounding the property was filled with a housing estate. Gus knew what he was looking for and spotted it parked at the side of the road outside number fifty-seven.

Eve Northwood had arrived before him in her bright yellow Mini. He parked the Focus behind her and went to join her.

"What's so special about this place?" she asked.

"You don't like it, I take it?" said Gus.

"Little boxes," said Eve.

Gus explained who had lived there twenty years earlier.

"I imagine the daughter moved away," said Eve. "Twenty years; that makes her forty now. She's probably married with children. If someone asked me where I'd put my money, it would be on Bethany having moved on from the garage mechanic."

"I haven't got as far as tracing everyone connected to the case who's still alive," said Gus.

"From what you've told me, there wasn't enough evidence against the daughter and her boyfriend," said Eve. "They had means and opportunity, I suppose, but so did thousands of other people in the county that night. Fortunately, only a tiny minority ever take advantage of it. A motive is what reduces the number of murders we get. So what motive might they have had?"

"The obvious thing would be money," said Gus. "However, Stephanie Harford's husband had walked out ten years earlier. I can't imagine she was rolling in it, even if she worked a forty-eight-hour week in Lydiard Millicent. Thanks to the daughter's housekeeping contribution, I reckon she was barely keeping her head above water. Her parents have gone now, so we can't check whether Stephanie was getting help from that quarter."

"Where did her parents live?" asked Eve.

"Grange Park," said Gus. "They'd downsized a few years before the murder."

"Oh, it's nice there," said Eve. "Their daughter's death must have hit them hard, poor things."

"Her death was what I wanted to ask you about, Eve," said Gus. "I don't know who carried out the autopsy. DS Mercer was able to tell me Stephanie had been strangled, but when I asked about the time of death, Geoff told me that was tricky."

"Are you sitting comfortably," said Eve. Gus nodded.

"Then I'll begin. There are three different times of death: When the victim's vital functions cease. The legal time of death is the time recorded on the death certificate. Then the estimated time of death is when people like me *estimate* that death occurred."

"We don't know when Stephanie drew her last breath," said Gus. "Your unknown colleague will have recorded a time on the death certificate issued six months after Stephanie disappeared. What about the third option?"

"The estimated time of death can vary greatly from the legal time of death and the physiologic time of death," said Eve. "Most deaths aren't witnessed. Natural death may come during sleep, and accidental and suicidal deaths often occur when the victim is alone. The killer is often the only witness to a murder, and we can't rely on the killer to check his watch. Therefore, when we determine the time of death in circumstances like those of Stephanie Harford, we can only estimate the approximate time."

"Six months can do a lot of damage to a body buried in the ground," said Gus.

"The three times of death I mentioned can differ by days, weeks, and even months if the body is not found until well after the physical death. In your example, death occurred in April, but as the body was not discovered until October, the legal death would have been marked as October since that was when the corpse was discovered and the death legally noted. If I had a copy of the document before me, my colleague would have estimated the time of death as April, May, or June. He had to try to be as accurate as possible."

"You're saying Stephanie could have been held some-where for weeks, even a couple of months before she was killed," said Gus.

"The sooner after death the body is found, the more accurately a time of death can be assessed," said Eve. "Once the body reaches ambient temperature, all bets are off."

"Hang on," said Gus. "If Stephanie was still alive as late

as July, wouldn't that have been obvious when they removed the body? She was wrapped in thick plastic sheeting."

"I couldn't comment without seeing the autopsy report," said Eve. "There are all sorts of factors that determine the rate of decomposition. The skeletal remains were all retained inside the sheeting. Therefore, it wasn't hard for them to identify the broken hyoid bone. As for whether she was covered in bruising or had been restrained, that would have been impossible."

"There was no mention of Stephanie having been sexually assaulted in the press reports I read," said Gus. "That would have been impossible to determine, too, I imagine."

"I'm sorry, Gus," said Eve. "We can't work miracles."

"Do you know where you would find that autopsy report?" asked Gus.

"Gablecross will have a copy in their evidence store, I'm sure. But I imagine you can't ask them for a copy while on gardening leave."

"That's one reason," said Gus. "I was thinking of the report written by the police surgeon in October 1998. Who was doing that job back then?"

"Gosh, let me think. It was before Stuart Fitzwalter was in charge. Bruce somebody.... Bruce Marsh, that was the fellow. He was our police surgeon in the Nineties."

"Any chance you could sneak a look at that report and let me know what you think?"

"The reports are a matter of public record, Gus," said Eve. "You can apply for a copy."

"It's time I came clean, Eve," said Gus. "If DS Mercer or myself approached Gablecross or the Coroner, there would be a record."

Chapter Five

EVE NORTHWOOD CONSIDERED what Gus had said for a while.

"Look, I understand you've upset a senior detective by solving a case they bungled in the past, but why would anyone want to prevent you from viewing an autopsy report?"

"DS Mercer believes the killer was a serving policeman," said Gus. "Stephanie might not have been his only victim."

"How well do you know this part of Wiltshire, Gus?" asked Eve.

"Not very well," said Gus.

"There's a police station not half a mile from where we're sat," she continued. "The PCC announced only three weeks ago that it will be transformed into a facility fit for twenty-first-century policing. Wootton Bassett has been designated as a hub where the area's Community Policing Team are briefed at the start of each shift. They patrol Wootton Bassett, Cricklade, Malmesbury and the surrounding villages. Next summer, while three-quarters of a million pounds worth of work is being carried out, officers and staff will move to temporary accommodation at Burton Hill, the site of Malmesbury police station."

"So, even in 1998, Stephanie Harford had a station with several officers on her doorstep," said Gus. "I wonder how we could find out who was working there without tipping off the killer?"

"I can see why you called me now, Gus Freeman," said Eve. "You thought if I looked up an ancient autopsy report it wouldn't raise suspicions. I suppose I could cite a training exercise at the Great Western Hospital for post-mortem technical staff to explain my interest."

"I hadn't thought of that," said Gus. "That's an excellent idea,"

"Leave it with me, Gus," said Eve. "Are we done? No, coffee and toasted teacake? There's a delightful café not two minutes away, my treat."

"I haven't even knocked on a few doors here to discover whether they know where Bethany Harford lives," said Gus.

"I'm way ahead of you, Gus," said Eve. "The library is almost next door to the café. We can look at the electoral register and newspaper files after our snack. I want to hear how your partner is faring at six months. Are you taking good care of her?"

Gus could tell when he was beaten. He returned to the Focus and decided to go with the flow. Gus tried to keep up with Eve's Mini on the short burst to Borough Fields and failed. An hour later, they were saying goodbye outside the cafe, and he drove back to Urchfont.

The coffee and teacake had been as good as Eve promised, and without disturbing anyone in the library, they'd compiled a list of current occupants of houses Gus was interested in.

Doug Thompson died in his sleep in 2008, and his wife, Mary, died in the hospital three years later. When Eve checked local newspaper records, she learned that Bethany Harford had moved in with Adie Lawrence after the first inquest.

"That surprises me," said Eve.

"Why? Adie and Bethany *had* been seeing one another for fifteen months," said Gus. "It's not that much of a surprise."

"The newspaper article said the *first* inquest, Gus," said Eve. "Let's dig deeper into what led to a second inquest being ordered. The other item of note in the Advertiser was in July 1999, the house in Lime Kiln was to be sold. So further efforts were made to locate Stephanie's husband."

"Geoff Mercer told me nobody knew his whereabouts at the time of the murder," said Gus.

"He surfaced in response to a request to get in touch posted by the solicitor dealing with the victim's estate. Unfortunately for Bethany, Greg Harford was still legally married to Stephanie, and there was no will."

"So, Bethany wouldn't have got a penny," said Gus.

"We don't know what caused the marriage breakdown, Gus," said Eve. "What made Greg Harford walk away after twelve years? According to this article, he was in his early thirties, married with one child, working with a security firm in Bath. Then, for a decade, nobody knew where he was."

"I give up. Where had Greg gone?" asked Gus.

"The North Sea oil rigs," said Eve. "It was pure luck he spotted the solicitor's advert in the Aberdeen Evening Express. Greg's contract had ended, and he was flying to

Mexico at the end of the month to work on one of the rigs in the Nansen field."

"He had no intention of staying in Wiltshire to get to know his daughter again," said Gus. "How long after Stephanie's body was discovered did Greg arrive on the scene?"

"Nine months," said Eve. "You know how slow the process of dealing with a death can be when it's complicated by murder. The detectives had to wait weeks for forensic evidence. The post-mortem was carried out within seventy-two hours, but it was months before they held the first inquest."

"Then Bethany and Adrian's behaviour at the coroner's court triggered their arrest," said Gus. "DI Flowers was convinced they had a reason for acting the way they did and jumped to the conclusion they were guilty. However, he didn't have enough to hold them beyond the prescribed time, and they were released without charge."

"I've found what we were looking for. The second inquest was scheduled a month after the first," said Eve. "The coroner wanted to ask the same questions of both youngsters, but they didn't turn up."

"What was their excuse?" asked Gus.

"The same as before," said Eve. "I'm sure you've heard this during your illustrious career, but the Coroner & Justice Act of 1988 was in force back then. They couldn't force Lawrence to answer questions nor insist Bethany attend the inquest. Nowadays, there are financial penalties."

"I remember it being a factor in a case of mine in the dim and distant past," said Gus. "So, in late spring of 1999, the CPS concluded that, based on the evidence available, there was no realistic prospect of conviction."

"At last, Doug Thompson was able to arrange his

daughter's funeral," said Eve. "The search for Greg Harford and any other people who might have had a legitimate claim on Stephanie's estate then began. Greg contacted the solicitor in late September 1999."

"Once DI Flowers heard about Greg Harford turning up, he must have realised the folly of his pursuit of Bethany Harford and Adrian Lawrence," said Gus. "They had nothing to gain by murdering Stephanie. Bethany had everything to lose."

"I haven't seen any reference in the press about Greg Harford being interviewed by the police," said Eve.

"Someone must have spoken to him," said Gus. "Otherwise, how did they know Greg hadn't been on shore leave from the rigs when Stephanie died? I bet that sort of detail would be in the murder file somewhere. I'm working with one hand tied behind my back; it's frustrating."

"Where to next?" asked Eve.

"Was Bethany still living with Adie Lawrence one month after the first inquest?" asked Gus.

"They lived together for at least eighteen months," said Eve. "Both names appeared at the address in Wroughton in the April 2001 census."

"I wonder when they split up?" asked Gus. "Are there reports of any marriages?"

Eve started searching for Adrian Lawrence but found nothing.

"He's a mechanic," said Gus. "I'll try the Chiseldon garage first and see whether he's still there. Of course, any conversation will only be for background information, but he might remember seeing someone taking an unhealthy interest in Stephanie."

"Here we are, Gus," said Eve. "Bethany Harford married Andrew Cunningham at St Bartholomew's

Church, Wootton Bassett, on Saturday, the thirteenth of April in 2002."

"Her mother disappeared on her birthday, on the seventeenth of April," said Gus.

"If she had nothing to do with her mother's death, does it matter?" asked Eve. "People deal with things differently these days, Gus. Our diaries still contain the details of unfortunate events on a particular date. Years ago, people marked those days so the relevance wouldn't be forgotten. In a decade from now, it wouldn't surprise me if people had forgotten to remember things like Ascension Day, Epiphany, and Ash Wednesday."

"When I was at school, everyone in my class knew why October the twenty-first was important," said Gus. "Now people are only interested in Hallowe'en in October, and how many shopping days it is to Christmas. Because Horatio Nelson isn't an influencer or a rap artist, he can't be worth bothering about."

"Mr and Mrs Cunningham have two teenage children," said Eve. "They live in Chippenham, and Andrew works in a bank. I've made a note of the address for you."

"Thanks, Eve," said Gus. "That will be another fishing expedition, looking for clues as to who might have wanted to murder her mother. I'm not sure Bethany will even want to see me. Although, there are a couple of questions I'd like her to answer. After Mary Thomson died, did she inherit the house at Grange Park? Bethany was their only granddaughter. What happened to her father? Did he go to work in Mexico? Is Greg Harford still alive?"

"You could ask her one question from me," said Eve, "Why did she insist she was unwell for both inquests? It's as puzzling as the hotel reservation. There doesn't seem to be an explanation."

"We're running out of time, Eve," said Gus. "I don't want to get in your bad books by making you late for your next appointment."

"I can spare you five more minutes," she replied. "Did you have more for me to investigate on your behalf?"

"Geoff Mercer has identified two more deaths that could be linked to that of Stephanie Harford," said Gus. "Marie Legrand and Claire Dyke. They were around the same age as Stephanie and were strangled or asphyxiated. Unfortunately, their bodies weren't discovered for some time."

"Three's a pattern," said Eve. "Why didn't the cases get linked before? When did the murder of the French lady take place?"

"Marie Legrand died just over three years after Stephanie Harford," said Gus. "Claire Dyke died six years later in 2007. She was murdered in her home."

"There's been nothing since?" asked Eve.

"Geoff Mercer couldn't find anything to match the details of the other attacks."

"Serial killers don't tend to stop," said Eve. "If anything, the frequency at which they kill increases. Some experts say this is because they want to get caught, but I'm not sure I agree."

"They get a taste for it," said Gus.

"Exactly. I suppose the killer could have moved away from the Swindon area," said Eve. "Okay, leave it with me. I'll check who investigated these two murders and which of my predecessors dealt with the body."

"That would be great, Eve," said Gus.

"I'll call you at home when I've got something worthwhile to pass on," said Eve. "You can pop in to see me in my surgery if you like. By the sound of things, you'll be spending a fair bit of time in the Swindon area over the next few days."

"I plan to visit any address or location involved tomorrow," said Gus. "When you've driven back to the surgery, I'll try getting hold of DI Flowers or DS Lenham. Geoff Mercer told me they were long since retired but were still in receipt of a pension the last time he checked."

"I must get moving," said Eve checking her watch. "We'll talk soon, I'm sure. Gosh, this is more fun than listening to my patients giving me an explicit description of their aliments."

Eve grabbed her things and left Gus in the library. The look a member of staff gave him when he took his mobile phone from his jacket pocket made him stop. He winked at her and went outside to the Focus before making his first call.

"Flowers," came a gruff reply.

"Is that Gordon Flowers?" asked Gus. "This is Gus Freeman. I don't know whether you remember my name?"

"I'm not senile," said Gordon Flowers. "You worked at Bourne Hill, didn't you? What's this about? Are you after a contribution to the Police Federation Christmas raffle?"

"Not at all," said Gus. "I wanted to ask you about Stephanie Harford."

Gus wondered whether the silence meant the connection had been lost.

"I don't understand," said Flowers after thirty seconds. "That was twenty years ago."

"You didn't get a positive result," said Gus.

"Nobody solves every case they handle if they put in a full shift as I did, Freeman," said Flowers. "I don't fret about the ones that got away in my thirty years as a detective, unlike other old-timers I could mention."

"Why do you think you couldn't find the killer on that case?" asked Gus.

"What's it got to do with you, anyway? I've been retired for sixteen years, so you must be in the same boat. Get to the point, man. I've got money on the next race on TV."

"I've been out of retirement for nine months, working for Geoff Mercer at London Road," said Gus. "He asked me to take a look."

"Ricky Lenham worked with me on that case," said Gordon Flowers. "We did everything by the book. The Harford woman was mixed up in something. She had to be. Why book that hotel room? We couldn't find anyone she was dating, so Ricky asked around, you know, to see if any of our informants knew her name. A woman like that, on her own, not bad looking, might be tempted to earn a bit extra. We don't see many girls standing on street corners these days. Even twenty years ago, they had moved indoors to hotels and motels if they didn't have a place. So that was the angle we followed for a while."

"I suppose you stopped once her body was found," said Gus.

"Why?" asked Flowers. "They never made it to that hotel bedroom, did they? Harford must have given the guy a hard time. Maybe she was asking for more money or wanted too many restrictions on what she was prepared to do and pushed him too hard."

"So, it was her fault she died, is that it?" said Gus.

"I never said it was her fault," said Flowers. "We had to change tack once the inquest reached the coroner's court. The daughter and her boyfriend started playing silly beggars. She wouldn't attend the inquest, and he'd watched too many episodes of Kavanagh QC. Ricky hadn't found any evidence the mother was a working girl, so we focussed on the two kids. We couldn't fathom their game, and, in the end, the CPS pulled the rug out from under our feet."

"Had you found new evidence?" asked Gus.

"Not a scrap," said Flowers. "Our boss assigned us a new case, so we tidied up the paperwork and forgot it."

"You and Ricky were still working together in 2001, weren't you?" asked Gus.

"Of course," said Flowers. "I didn't want another partner. We were retiring in twelve months."

"Who investigated the Marie Legrand murder?" asked Gus.

"It wasn't us," said Flowers. "I don't remember who they handed that one to. It's so long ago. That was the French girl on her way to Bath, asking for trouble by trying to get there by hitching lifts with truckers. Ricky and I were working on an armed robbery. Criminals don't bother with those nowadays; they can screw enough money out of people online. Why chase around after bullion vans when you can sit at home and make a million with a keyboard?"

"Bruce Marsh was your Police Surgeon in those days, wasn't he?" asked Gus.

"He was the guy we dealt with on the Harford case," said Flowers. "Hold on. Typical, the horse I backed fell at the last fence. Ah well. Bruce Marsh would have been gone by the time that Legrand woman's body was discovered. Allen Bradbury was doing the job then. He didn't stay in Wiltshire long; within a year, he'd disappeared to New Zealand with his boyfriend."

Gus made a note to let Eve know what he'd learned. She could tell him about Bradbury and keep looking for the name of the person who dealt with Claire Dyke. Who could he ask at Gablecross about detective teams assigned to murders? Jake Latimer had moved from the area. Gus wondered whether to risk a phone call.

"Do you have any more questions, Freeman?" asked Gordon Flowers. "I've got better things to do than rake over long-forgotten cases."

"When I visited Stephanie Harford's home this morning, I realised there's a police station just around the corner," said Gus. "Did you and Ricky ever have cause to visit?"

"What do you think?" said Flowers. "We could always be sure of a cuppa and catch up on the latest gossip. The building was staffed with uniformed officers in those days. After we retired, the Community Support model spawned in the Met was rolled out across the country."

"You weren't a fan," said Gus.

"Toy soldiers," said Flowers. "About as much use as a chocolate teapot when dealing with real villains. They made the public feel safe, but the cardboard figures they placed in shopping precincts were just as effective."

"When you were working on the Harford case, proper coppers still crewed the station on Lime Kiln, didn't they," said Gus. "Can you remember any of them? Did anyone take an interest in the case? How did they help you with your investigation?"

"Surely you remember what a rural station like that worked?" said Flowers. "They had cars patrolling a stretch of the M4 and maintaining a presence in Cricklade and Malmesbury, as well as Wootton Bassett itself. We always started our day in the squad room at Gablecross, so we missed the roll call at Lime Kiln when the whole team was present. Our contact in Wootton Bassett was Geoff Bailey, a Sergeant who handled the front desk. He had his finger on the pulse of the small patch the team patrolled. We went to

Geoff for background on Stephanie Harford, her family, the farm shop where she worked, and the staff. Stephanie Harford had never been in trouble with the law, and there were no red flags on anyone connected to her family. We checked everyone connected to the farm shop: the manager, staff, and anyone who had left in the past year. Like I said, me and Ricky did things by the book. There was nobody with the slightest black mark against them to suggest they wanted to hurt her."

Gus realised Gordon Flowers had missed one set of people that could have felt differently. Now wasn't the time to mention it. As Geoff Mercer said, they didn't know how many could have been involved.

"It sounds like you did your best, Gordon," said Gus. "Sorry to keep you from your racing for so long. Better luck in the next race. By the way, have you seen Ricky Lenham much since you retired?"

"Every week," said Flowers. "We meet up for a pint at lunchtime on Fridays at the Prince of Wales in Shrivenham. It's been our local for forty years. In the old days, we'd drive out from Gablecross for a swift half whenever we needed a break. No doubt you had a favourite watering hole in Salisbury, Freeman. They were different days when a copper could enjoy a beer, smoke a cigarette, and have a proper conversation on any subject under the sun."

"Another development in modern policing you weren't keen on," said Gus.

"Don't tell me you enjoy thinking twice before opening your mouth, Freeman," said Gordon Flowers. "Do you know what I notice the most about people wherever I look in this country? Not their colour or whether they bat for the other side. I was never bothered about any of that. No, year after year, peoples' skins have become thinner and thinner.

It's not just the kids who are snowflakes; everyone's more sensitive, even senior citizens. People take offence over such trivial things these days. Yet they're prepared to let serious stuff go. The criminal fraternity hasn't changed, which means they can't believe their luck. I read the other day that a serious sexual assault was dealt with by an out-of-court disposal. The bloke was as guilty as sin, and didn't even get a suspended sentence. What's the world coming to, Free-man? In my day, he would have been banged up, and during the first few weeks of his sentence, he would have been recovering from injuries suffered in the custody suite. I remember the floors could be very slippery, and we didn't have cameras watching every square inch of the station either. Accidents happened a lot in the old days. Rough justice it might have been, but villains get it too cushy today."

Gus had heard enough about the old days.

"Is Ricky Lenham still on the same number?" he asked.

"We're not kids. We don't swap phones every five minutes for a new model," said Flowers. "Of course he is. Ricky won't tell you anything different. We were a team for years and watched one another's back. I hope you've got someone watching yours, Freeman. The detectives who dealt with those other two murders might not be as friendly."

Gus ended the call. If that had been a friendly chat, he'd hate to be around when Gordon Flowers was angry. As he had driven home to Urchfont, he remembered that in the days of the dinosaur, some were dangerous, and others were docile. Gus was content anyone who had worked with him in the past nine months would place him in the latter category.

His first job when he reached the bungalow was to send a text message to Eve Northwood.

He received a prompt response.

'Never met Allen Bradbury. DI Joe Gorse worked with DS Dave Frost on the Marie Legrand murder case. Gorse retired in 2010, and Frost left two years later. I will chase the details on the Dyke case. Gorse died last year. Frost lives in Southern Ireland.'

When Suzie arrived home, Gus had just finished speaking to newly-promoted DI Jake Latimer in Winchester. Gus didn't ask how he got on with his boss, Anna Cromwell.

"Jake Latimer. How may I help you?"

"Good afternoon, Jake. It's Gus Freeman here. Can you spare a minute?"

"Of course, Gus," said Jake. "I heard from Neil Davis at the weekend. He invited me to Beatrice's christening in the New Year. Perhaps we can share a drink that weekend?"

"I can't see any reason why not," said Gus. "I called because I'm taking a trip down Memory Lane. What do you remember of Gordon Flowers and Ricky Lenham?"

"Before my time at Gablecross. They were old-school and not in a good way, if you get my drift."

"So they were inclined to cut corners," said Gus.

"They were solid, without being spectacular, according to squad room banter. I don't recall anyone saying they would do anything illegal to close a case, though. But, on the other hand, Ricky Lenham had a short fuse and used his fists on a suspect more than once. As for Gordon Flowers, he thought putting women in uniform was madness. That's about all I can tell you."

"Joe Gorse and Dave Frost were a more recent pairing," said Gus. "Did your time at Gablecross as a Detective Constable overlap with that team?"

"The odd couple," said Jake. "Yeah, I remember them.

DI Gorse committed suicide not that long ago. Frosty had moved to the Dingle peninsula shortly after leaving the force."

"So, Joe Gorse retired, but his partner quit before retirement age," said Gus. "Any story attached to that? Why were they called the odd couple?"

"Joe took things to heart, Gus. Every case chipped away at his sanity. Dave was a happy-go-lucky sort. Nothing ever phased him, and nobody could understand how they stuck working together. So when we heard the news about Joe Gorse, nobody was shocked. Disappointed, maybe, but it seemed inevitable. He jumped from a road bridge over the M4. Dave didn't come over to attend the funeral. I don't think he even sent a card."

"I heard Gorse and Frost handled the murder of Marie Legrand, the French woman whose body was found near Barbury. Does that ring a bell?"

"We didn't get more than five murders a year to deal with, Gus," said Jake. "I remember that case. She accepted a lift from someone at the truck stop near South Marston and was never seen alive again."

"Nobody saw whether Marie left in a car, van, eighteen-wheeler semi-truck or one of the juggernauts," said Gus.

"That site is far better lit these days and covered by CCTV," said Jake.

"Not all murder victims are attacked when they're outside, minding their own business," said Gus. "What about the woman who died at her home in Brinkworth?"

"I was paired with Theo Hickerton when that happened, Gus," said Jake. "We were too green to get assigned a murder case. Sam Prince and Simon Rutty were running that one. They're still at Gablecross. Simon has his own team now, and Sam was promoted to DCI eighteen months ago."

"Anything you can tell me about those two, Jake?" asked Gus.

"Three pairs of detectives, each investigating murders of women," said Jake. "It doesn't feel like a trip down Memory Lane, Gus. What are you after?"

"Nothing concrete at this stage, Jake. Prince and Rutty, what were they like?"

"Solid as a rock. If they hadn't been, I'd like to think they wouldn't have continued to be promoted. Remind me what the victim's name was."

"Claire Dyke," said Gus. "She was a forty-year-old artist who lived alone in a cottage just outside Brinkworth. Claire died from asphyxiation, and her body was stuffed into the airing cupboard. Her car had been left in a Swindon multi-storey car park."

"Simon Rutty spoke more about the case in the squad room than his gaffer," said Jake. "They searched for her car on CCTV between Malmesbury and Swindon. She drove a Moonlight Blue VW Golf GTI. With something that conspicuous, they believed they had to see it entering the multi-storey. She lived in a village, and her home was some distance from the nearest property. It was impossible to give an exact time of death. Her body was in that airing cupboard for some time. Did the victim drive to Swindon for shopping, park in the multi-storey and get grabbed when she returned to her car? Was she then taken to Brinkworth and murdered? Or did the killer break into the cottage, choke the woman to death, and then drive the car to Swindon to confuse matters?"

"What did DI Price think?" asked Gus.

"The latter," said Jake. "Claire Dyke was an artist with

two finished paintings and one a work-in-progress. Her equipment wasn't valuable, except to her. Sam Prince thought the motive was robbery because Claire had a wall safe behind one of her paintings in the bedroom. In addition, Claire had several pieces of jewellery and an engagement ring from a previous boyfriend. That relationship ended years before. He was living in Germany and hadn't left Dusseldorf all year. The whole lot was worth no more than fifteen hundred pounds when the items were valued. That included her passport, a few certificates, and four hundred euros. Simon Rutty didn't believe that added up to a robbery."

"Three pairs of detectives, Jake," said Gus. "If you'd handled all three cases, might you have started to wonder? By the way, I think a different police surgeon handled all three deaths."

"Three middle-aged women in a vulnerable situation, with nobody to come to their aid," said Jake. "Do you think they attracted a stalker? Nothing pointed that way on the Brinkworth case that I remember."

"Stephanie Harford was leaving work on her bicycle," said Gus. "Marie Legrand was alone at a truck stop, and Claire Dyke was home alone in a remote cottage. Or possibly, alone in a multi-storey car park late at night. Does it make sense they would willingly go with a stranger or let him into their home?"

"These weren't naïve young girls, Gus," said Jake. "It had to be someone they knew, surely? Although, the French woman didn't know anyone in England except her brother."

"Which leaves us with one possibility," said Gus. "They trusted the person they met in the hours before they died."

Chapter Six

GUS SENT a text message to the Crime Review Team members inviting them to a Christmas drink at the Waggon & Horses on Friday night. Gus knew Lydia would see through the ruse. He wanted to hear whether she'd told Morris Beard she was accepting the job offer. The sooner he knew what he was dealing with, the better. Maybe there was a way he could protect Alex if he had a head start over the PCC.

As Gus prepared vegetables for their evening meal, wondering when he'd next hear from Geoff Mercer, he heard his mobile phone buzzing. Was it another text message from Eve Northwood, or could it be Geoff?

Gus retrieved the phone from the table in the hallway. Eve Northwood had found something. *'Ian Hughes. 2003- 2008. Gablecross used him exclusively. He would have performed the autopsy on Claire Dyke. Will check his report.'*

Gus had never heard anyone mention Ian Hughes before. He replied to Eve, begging her to be careful. They didn't want to be making waves.

Suzie was keen to talk when she got home at five-thirty.

"Did today live up to expectations?" she asked. "Where did you go, anyway?"

"I drove around the Lime Kiln estate and dropped by the library in Borough Fields."

"Did you and your friend find anything useful?" she asked.

"All mundane background stuff that might come in handy if I get the green light to work on Geoff's case. Before you ask, I haven't spoken to him today. Was he at London Road?"

"I was busy," said Suzie. "I didn't bump into him whenever I was out of my office. His door was closed when I was, as was Kenneth's. The PCC wasn't wandering about either, not today. I saw one familiar face as I walked to the car tonight."

"Do you want me to guess?" asked Gus.

"Friday night?" asked Suzie.

"Divya Yadav told you she'd just received a text message," said Gus. "I thought it was a good idea. Lydia put the idea in my head when she was here the other evening."

"You can be devious as well as incorrigible," said Suzie. "She can't avoid telling you what she finally decided. Clever. Dinner smells gorgeous. Do I have time to change?"

"There was me hoping you'd never change, darling," said Gus. "You've got ten minutes."

They spent a quiet night in the lounge, watching television. Suzie watched the programme while Gus blocked out the commentary and tried to make sense of all the threads he'd worked loose relating to the murders. So far, they hadn't produced any potential suspects.

Wednesday, 19 December 2018

GUS WAS outside the bungalow at twenty-past eight, standing beside the Focus with his car keys in his hand. He needed an early start to visit what he thought of as the kill zone.

"I'll see you at five-thirty tonight then," said Suzie. "Be careful."

She got into her Golf and drove through the gateway more quietly than usual. Gus followed her along the lane and risked a fine for breaking an often forgotten rule of the Highway Code by flashing his headlights as Suzie turned into the car park at London Road. He headed for the Beckhampton straight and drove into Wroughton at a quarter to nine.

Gus turned left and took Wharf Road past Butterfly World and Farm Park. It never ceased to amaze him how many unlikely attractions thrived in Wiltshire. Bert Penman always told him there was only a tiny percentage of butter-flies near the allotment now, compared to when he and Cora first married. Perhaps if there weren't so many animals and insects in captivity, more people would appre-ciate how vital they were in the wild.

When he drove onto the Lime Kiln estate, he stopped close to the police station. It wasn't wise to go inside and ask questions. Who was it Gordon Flowers had said was on the front desk? He phoned Geoff Mercer.

"Morning, Gus," said Geoff. "Where are you?"

"Sat just up the road from Lime Kiln nick. Don't worry. What can you tell me about a uniformed sergeant called Geoff Bailey? Gordon Flowers mentioned him when we spoke yesterday."

"How did that go?" asked Geoff. Gus could hear Geoff tapping on his keyboard.

"He was a man of his time," said Gus. "Racist, homophobic, and misogynistic. However, he had convinced himself that he was nothing of the sort. It was just banter."

"Almost the full set," said Geoff. "Did he stop spouting bile long enough to tell you anything useful?"

"One thing not in the headlines you gave me," said Gus. "They believed Stephanie Harford booked the hotel room to take a client there that night. Flowers thought she might have been a high-class hooker."

"Unbelievable," said Geoff. "I've got details on the other two cases now. When can we meet to discuss them?"

"It will have to be tomorrow, or Friday, Geoff," said Gus. "Let me see what I can learn today. I'll call you tonight at home to fix a time and place. So, Geoff Bailey?"

"Bailey was on the desk at Lime Kiln from 1998 to 2002. He retired at sixty and took a security job in Swindon. Then, in 2005 he started working for Highways England."

"A bunch of ex-coppers keeping our motorways open," said Gus. "Is he still on the major roads in all winds and weather at seventy-six?"

"No, Geoff Bailey died in 2012," said Geoff. "Sorry, Gus, another potential source of valuable information torn from your grasp."

"Such is life," said Gus. "I'll call you later."

Gus watched as two PCSOs left the building further up the road, got into a marked car, and drove away. He followed at a safe distance until they turned towards Cricklade. His first port-of-call was the address where he had sat outside with Eve Northwood yesterday morning. He wasn't stopping today. It was a start point for the farm shop in Lydiard Millicent. Gus wanted to follow the route

Stephanie Harford had taken so frequently. He took the A3102 out of town, crossed the busy M4 below him, and drove through Greatfield before turning right for Lydiard Green.

It was difficult to tell whether much had altered in the landscape since Stephanie had cycled these lanes. The narrow road was flanked on either side by high hedges for long stretches. Gus didn't see another car for two miles, and there were no solitary cyclists. He turned off the road into a small trading estate of six units. The farm shop stood in the far corner, and Gus counted seven vehicles outside.

He parked behind the row of early visitors or staff and walked towards the shop. Once inside the building, he looked for someone in charge. The teenage girl at the checkout wore a brown polo shirt with the business's name in orange lettering. She was engrossed in buffing her nails and didn't look up. Gus followed the painted white arrows on the concrete floor, hoping they led to an office.

A young lad, wearing the same brown and orange uniform, was replenishing stocks of twenty-five-kilogramme bags of fertiliser up ahead. He spotted Gus waving.

"What's up, mate?" he asked.

"Where's the manager's office?" asked Gus.

The lad nodded towards the automatic doors at the rear of the building.

"She'll be in the shed outside, next to the terracotta pots."

"Does she have a name?" asked Gus.

"Kathy, Mrs Pike."

Gus approached the doors, and they swung open swiftly when he was three feet away. They moved quicker than either member of staff he'd seen so far. The shed was three times the size of his at the allotment, and there was just enough room for Kathy Pike and her office equipment. Gus needed to stand in the doorway to speak to her.

"Mrs Pike?" asked Gus. "Can I trouble you for a few minutes?"

The lady sitting behind the desk looked up at him.

"What were you looking for, dearie?" she asked.

Gus knew he couldn't show her his glorified library card. There was nothing for it. He'd have to tell her who he was and hope she wouldn't check.

"Information," said Gus. "My name's Freeman. I was a Detective Sergeant in Salisbury, and since I retired, I've taken an interest in Wiltshire murder cases."

"Oh, are you an author? I enjoy reading murder mysteries," said Kathy Pike. "I know why you came here. A lady who worked at this farm shop years ago went missing. She cycled off towards Wootton Bassett one night but never reached home."

"Stephanie Harford," said Gus. "Yes, that case has interested me. You're too young to have been working here in 1998. Is there anyone left on your staff from that time?"

"I was still at school," said Kathy Pike. "Roy Wakeley was here, though. Roy's about your age, I reckon. He's been here since we opened. You'll find him in the vegetable department indoors."

Gus thanked Kathy Pike and returned to the main building. Signs indicating the various sections were suspended from the roof rafters. Gus reached the vegetable department by the most direct route, ignoring the white arrows. He got a few dirty looks from customers pushing trollies laden with products when he almost collided with them.

Roy Wakeley was a younger version of Bert Penman. Five feet six inches, sixteen stones on a good day, and bald.

His brown polo shirt stretched over an ample stomach, and the orange lettering was worn away in places.

"Kathy Pike said I'd find you here, Roy," said Gus. "She said you were around when Mrs Harford went missing. Did you work that Sunday?"

"Sorry," said Roy. "I didn't catch your name. Are you a reporter?"

"No, Roy. I worked for the police when Stephanie was murdered."

Gus crossed his fingers behind his back. It was only a little white lie.

"Oh, I see. Well, two of your colleagues came to speak to everyone who worked that day. I heard they contacted people who had retired or moved away, too, looking for clues as to who took Stephanie. It was a dreadful time. Not something you forget. I worked that Sunday, and I was on my way home when she pushed her bicycle along the path beside the building. I looked back and waved goodbye."

"Stephanie kept her bike in a lockable store behind this building, didn't she," said Gus.

"That's right, but it's gone now," said Roy. "Nobody cycles these days because the roads are too dangerous. Kathy's office replaced the store you're talking about."

"Did Stephanie wave back?" asked Gus.

Roy nodded.

"Did you know her well?"

"As well as I knew anyone who worked here. I knew Stephanie lived in Wootton Bassett, on the other side of the motorway. She was friendly, enjoyed her job, and that was the way the manager we had at the time liked it. The farm shop business has changed a lot in the past twenty years. Tastes have changed, and we stock varieties of plants and vegetables today we hadn't heard of back then, and to keep the customers coming to an out-of-the-way business like this, you need to offer something different. If you'd stuck to the white arrows, you would have reached the Christmas grotto."

"Did you know Stephanie was married with a teenage daughter, Roy?" asked Gus.

"Of course," said Roy. "When I said I knew her well, I meant when she was working in this building. I never saw Stephanie at any other time. She talked about her daughter now and then. My wife and I live in the village; a ten-minute walk away."

"Was there anyone who paid her closer attention? Someone, she didn't encourage?"

"There was nothing like that. We all told the police at the time. Stephanie got on great with everyone who worked here."

"There aren't many customers here this morning, Roy," said Gus. "But some can be awkward."

"They don't follow the arrows, d'you mean?" said Roy.

"You never heard Stephanie arguing with a customer or saw anyone outside watching her or speaking to her?"

"Nothing like what you're suggesting," said Roy. "We see families here, especially at certain times of the year. Women come here alone to get fresh vegetables and bedding plants. Couples visit at the weekend when the wife drags the husband along because she decides they need something for the garden. We don't tend to see a big percentage of younger men on their own. Senior citizens, maybe, who've lost their wives. Maybe I'm wrong, but whoever murdered Stephanie was younger than me and older than Shane."

Gus looked over his shoulder. The lad lifting fertiliser

bags earlier had progressed to filling trays with potatoes and cabbages.

"Why do you say that?" asked Gus.

"It stands to reason," said Roy. "Nobody knew when Stephanie was strangled. The police said it could have happened an hour after she left or days or even weeks later. Stephanie exercised a lot and cycled to and from work every day. She was fit, so whoever killed her had to overpower a healthy woman. It made me wonder whether there was more than one person involved. Especially when we heard her body had been found near the motorway six months later. You can almost see that spot from the corner of the car park outside. Whoever took her wouldn't have wanted to risk hanging around on that embankment, digging a grave, moving the body from a car, or whatever they transported her in. Speed would have been of the essence."

"You've thought about this, haven't you, Roy?" said Gus.

"I told you. It's not easy to forget."

Gus thanked Roy for his help and followed the arrows to the checkout.

"Have a nice day," said the young girl as Gus slipped past another customer unloading their trolley.

He returned to the car park and checked the maps on his phone. How could he reach that spot Roy mentioned? Would it mean using tracks or bridle paths? Gus was glad he'd thrown his wellington boots into the boot of the car before leaving the bungalow. Before he left the car park, he walked to the opposite corner to see which stretch of motorway Roy said was visible.

His eyesight was good for a man of his age, but whether the trees straight ahead were maple or not, Gus couldn't tell. The only thing for it was to drive as close to the burial site as possible and walk the rest of the way. But, of course, everything would have altered in twenty years. It would help if he knew how much those trees would have grown. Gus rechecked his phone. If he was looking at the same row of maple trees, they must have been six to eight feet high, at most, in 1998.

Gus made the return journey towards Wootton Bassett, and as he drove over the bridge crossing the M4, he looked at the hard shoulder below. Who carried out the maintenance of those embankments? Gus thought the local Council was responsible unless the land was privately-owned.

The Highways Department would have parked their vehicles on the hard shoulder to carry out the survey and remedial work. The killer couldn't risk doing the same, so they must have reached the top of the embankment from the Wootton Bassett side of the bridge. He'd noticed a turning on his left not long before he'd reached the bridge.

Gus slowed as he approached the junction. A sign beside the entrance informed him it was a private road leading to a farmhouse. Nobody was sitting on his rear bumper, so Gus signalled right and waited for a tractor and trailer to pass. He parked close to the high hedge on the left-hand side, retrieved his wellingtons from the boot, put them on, and started walking along the roadway.

Before the motorway was built, the map on his phone showed this lane connected with the village of Hook. Signposts for the homes of five hundred souls had been in evidence as he drove through Greatfield earlier.

Gus could hear no sounds of activity in the fields behind the hedges. Perhaps all that was left of the farm was the house itself. As he rounded a bend in the road, Gus could see the steep embankment a hundred yards ahead.

Nobody would risk moving a dead body along this road in broad daylight, even in a marked car, but it would be easy to come and go without being disturbed under cover of darkness.

"Excuse me," a female voice cried out. "Where do you think you're going?"

An older woman was now on the road behind him, walking a pair of Springer spaniels.

"Good morning," said Gus. "I'm from Health and Safety, madam. The Council asked me to check conditions leading to the embankment. It might be necessary to use your roadway to gain access to the particular stretch of the motorway ahead of us. We've heard they'll be resurfacing half a mile of the inside lane in 2019, preventing the Highways Department vehicles from using the hard shoulder. Every attempt will be made to reduce the inconvenience to yourself, Mrs?"

"Poulsom, Hannah Poulsom," she replied.

Gus wasn't sure whether his explanation convinced her.

"I can't see anything to cause them problems," said Gus. "I'll submit a report, and if the Council deem it necessary to carry out tree maintenance while the resurfacing is in progress, I'm sure you'll receive advance notification."

"I'll look out for the letter," said Hannah Poulsom.

"Have you lived here long, madam?" asked Gus.

"Eight years," she replied. "I'm surprised you didn't know that."

"You know what Councils are like, madam. They only tell us what they think we need to know. I had a phone call yesterday asking me to take a look. The only detail I had was a map reference, and Geography wasn't one of my best subjects at school. So I wasn't sure I was in the right place until I saw the fencing at the end of the lane."

Hannah Poulsom led her dogs towards a gap in the hedge behind them.

"You'll find your way back to your car, I hope?" she said.

Gus smiled and headed back to the Focus, returned his wellingtons to the boot, and drove towards Wootton Bassett. Fingers crossed; Hannah Poulsom wouldn't check with the Council at the lack of a mention of a budget for resurfacing in her 2019 Council Tax bill.

His trip to the truck park at South Marston meant driving past Butterfly World again. Gus didn't want to use the M4, even if it saved him ten minutes. He wanted to stop for coffee soon and try to work out how Marie Legrand reached her final resting place near Barbury. The route to the truck stop took him close to Coate Water Park and Dorcan. After working on the Stacey Read case, he was on familiar ground and recalled a supermarket café on Dorcan Way that would suit his purpose.

As he sipped his hot black coffee, Gus checked another map on his phone and scribbled calculations on a serviette. Geoff had mentioned there had been almost a month between Marie Legrand's disappearance from the truck stop and the discovery of her body near Barbury Castle. Eve Northwood had shown it was impossible to establish an accurate time of death in that situation.

Did the killer, or killers, murder the victim within hours of snatching them, or had they held the women for some time? Where might they have been kept? Had the bodies been found earlier, would evidence of torture and sexual assault have been forthcoming?

If Geoff was right, and the people they were searching for were in uniform twenty years ago, they would have been forensically aware. That would explain why great care was taken over the bag containing Stephanie Harford's body and the discarded items. But unfortunately, no traces of DNA were found, partly due to the delay in examining the body.

Gus had yet to read the details of the autopsies for Marie Legrand and Claire Dyke. No doubt, they revealed nothing to give the investigating detectives a solid lead. Finally, it was time to complete the trip to South Marston. He finished his coffee, threw his serviette into a waste bin, and ten minutes later, he stood by a wooden building opposite a row of trucks. There was no chance anyone inside would remember seeing Marie Legrand here in 2001, but a quick chat with the lady he could see behind the counter might prove beneficial.

When Gus opened the door, the smell of fried food hit him. The truck drivers dotted around the room carried on eating and reading their newspapers. Gus looked at the breakfast menu above the counter. It was tempting, but he didn't have time today. A buxom woman emerged from the kitchen with a large plate of food. She delivered it to a table behind him.

"Cheers, Annie," the trucker growled.

"No worries, Dusty," she replied as she returned to the counter.

Annie gave Gus the once-over. Perhaps she'd spotted he wasn't a trucker.

"Morning, love, what's it to be?"

Gus looked at the name tag on her ample chest. It read Annie Ovens.

"Have you seen any uniformed police around the truck stop today, Annie?" asked Gus.

"Lost your colleagues, have you?" said Annie. "No, luv, nobody's been in this morning. They stop here regularly enough, though. Spot checks on trucks and vans, looking for drugs, illegals, and alcohol and cigarettes that haven't had the duty paid."

"Where do most of them come from would you say?" asked Gus.

"I wouldn't know, love," said Annie. "Gablecross, I suppose, and because we're so close to the motorway, we see the Highways England vehicles in here, on occasion. Of course, they don't come so much for the cooked food or fuel, but they can't half put away tea, coffee, and cakes while playing pool in the other room."

"Thanks, Annie," said Gus. "Maybe I'll be back another day to enjoy one of your fry-ups."

Annie shrugged and went to serve a new customer.

Gus returned to the Focus, checked the clock on his dashboard, and set off for Barbury Castle. One mile from the truck stop, he joined the A419 and was soon crossing the M4 at the Badbury Roundabout. He took the exit for the A436 and Chiseldon and wondered whether he should drop into the garage for a chat with Adrian Lawrence before moving to his final kill zone site this afternoon.

Geoff was close to being right about the three bodies being discovered less than ten miles from where they were last seen alive. In the case of Marie Legrand, the distance was as the crow flies, but Gus was climbing the narrow B-road to Barbury Castle within twenty-five minutes of saying goodbye to Annie Ovens. Once he'd turned off the A436 at Chiseldon Camp, it was little more than a rutted track littered with potholes and puddles.

Gus couldn't think of many better places to hide a body. Everywhere he looked, on either side of the road, were a hundred dark corners that wouldn't see an inquisitive visitor for months on end. He knew there was nothing to see at the hillfort on the ancient Ridgeway route at this time of year. With perfect weather conditions, you could see the Cotswolds and the sunlight glinting off the River Severn.

Gus stopped before reaching the scheduled site. He needed to don his wellington boots again to get to the clump of brambles and hawthorn that had hidden Marie Legrand's body from view. The Barbury Shooting School Geoff mentioned was to Gus's left, towards the Ridgeway. Looking back from where he'd come, it confirmed what he thought. That road from Chiseldon was the only way to reach this spot without being on horseback.

So, whoever killed Marie drove up here, probably late at night, hoping they didn't bump into a poacher or a courting couple. Gus stood at the rear of the Focus, putting on his boots, and tutted. He was losing it. Why worry about meeting someone, even if they were in an unmarked car? They would scare the civilians to death by appearing out of nowhere, then take their details and send them packing. Then they had the hilltop to themselves to transfer the body from the car's boot to the hiding place of their choice.

Gus walked across the field from the gateway, trying to match a location to Geoff's reference points. Finally, he stopped at a spot halfway between the racing stables and the shooting school. He turned slowly to his right, and there it was, almost directly behind him, twenty yards away. The clump Geoff mentioned was now a dense mass of trees and bushes. You could hide a car in there, let alone a body.

Late at night, alone in the field, it would have been possible to dump the body in the bushes within a few minutes. Then they would have crept back down the hill-side, sticking to the B4005 into Wroughton. Once through the village, they could have gone anywhere in Swindon without anyone noticing.

Chapter Seven

GUS ARRIVED in Wroughton and continued to the B4005. The killer was in his comfort zone here. The road hugged the M4 for several miles and then morphed into the B4042 on the outskirts of Royal Wootton Bassett. Not long after he passed the town's Rugby club, Gus was crossing the M4 again and dropping down from Callow Hill into the village of Brinkworth.

He slowed as he passed the local pub, The Three Crowns. Breakfast had been ages ago, and he fancied a snack. Claire Dyke had lived in a cottage near The Causeway, which wasn't far from here. Gus turned into the pub car park and went inside.

Eleven years had passed since Claire's body had been found in the airing cupboard of her home. The rate at which pubs changed the landlord's name over the door had accelerated since then. There was little chance Glynn Whiteside, who was now authorised for the sale and supply of alcohol, and the provision of late-night hot food and drink had ever served Claire Dyke.

Gus perused the lunchtime menu.

"Good afternoon, sir,"

Gus reckoned the Welsh lilt to the voice meant the land-lord was on duty.

"BLT sandwich, plus a slimline tonic, ice and lemon, please," said Gus.

Glynn Whiteside took his food order and poured him his drink.

"We haven't seen you in here before, sir?"

"First time in Brinkworth," said Gus.

"We've been here seven years," said the landlord.

"It reminds me of another village near Chippenham," said Gus. "Kington Langley, that's strung out along the main road through the village too. Your pub is at the centre, with the church and several centuries-old properties. But then, more and more houses have been added at the side of the road. I'm not sure whether it helps create community. I couldn't tell where the last village ended and Brinkworth began. I imagine it will be the same when I look for The Causeway?"

"You sound more local than I am, sir. What line of busi-ness are you in?" asked the landlord.

"I'm a retired policeman from Salisbury, the other end of the county," said Gus.

"Very nice, sir. Were you looking at properties in this area? Not sure there are many on the market on The Causeway at present."

"Any idea who painted that view you've got hanging next to the menu?" asked Gus.

"We inherited that," said Glynn. "I've never looked closely at the signature. Could be *Claire Dyke '03*, but it's not easy to read."

"You've not heard the name?" asked Gus.

Glynn Whiteside shook his head.

"Not really my type of thing, sir. But the regulars seem to appreciate it."

Glynn went to serve another customer, and a young girl appeared behind the counter with his sandwich two minutes later. Gus finished his lunch, nodding to the landlord as he left. Glynn Whiteside was chatting with people sitting at a table in the corner. Perhaps the regulars appreciated the beautiful view from Callow Hill for its local connection. Gus couldn't afford to appear too interested in what happened near The Causeway eleven years ago. Did they know a murder victim had painted the landscape? Or were they newcomers like the landlord?

Gus drove away from The Three Crowns towards The Causeway. Traffic was heavier in the early afternoon, but he hadn't seen the same car in his rear-view mirror today. No point pushing his luck. The visit to the two-bedroomed detached cottage where Claire Dyke lived would be the last for today.

It was apparent most properties on The Causeway were well out of the artist's reach. A quick search on his phone while he ate his sandwich had told Gus he wouldn't get much change from three-quarters of a million pounds if he wanted a family home in these parts. Even the artist's tiny property sold for over a quarter of a million a year after her death. It had changed hands twice since that time, and as he slowed to take a closer look, he spotted an estate agency 'Sold – subject to contract' sign in the garden.

The cottage was set back from the road behind a high hedge. Gus turned into a lane leading to a row of older redbrick semi-detached houses. They looked to have been there since the Fifties. In those days, with fewer people owning cars, it was typical for a row of garages to be constructed nearby.

Those garages had long gone, but Gus could see reserved parking spaces for three properties on the main road had been put in their place. Owners of the semi-detached houses parked their vehicles on the driveway, while the rare two-car family also parked in the lane. Eleven years ago, Claire Dyke would have utilised her reserved space for that Moonlight blue Golf GTI of hers.

As he performed a three-point turn in the lane, Gus could see a six-foot wooden fence at the rear of the cottage and the gate she might have used to access the back of her property. Whoever killed Claire could have kidnapped her, late at night, from the multi-storey in Swindon and brought her home. Gus didn't like to think about what happened to the poor woman inside. How many neighbours, none of whom lived close to the cottage, would notice a different car parked across the road?

Elderly residents made up the majority of Brinkworth's population, and those occupying the properties on the lane were most likely asleep before Claire and her captor arrived. Gus sat in the Focus for five minutes before leaving the road and returning to Urchfont. He didn't see a curtain twitch nor a nosy neighbour come outside to put an item into a recycling bin. The lane was a quiet as the grave.

Gus steered the Focus through the gateway of the bungalow, parked under the rambling roses, and checked the dashboard clock. He had another two hours before Suzie would be home. Gus got out of the car and fetched his wellingtons from the boot. He walked to the rear patio, used his garden hose to wash away the mud, opened the back door and left the boots to dry on the coir mat.

As he waited for the coffee machine to work its magic,

Gus assessed the progress he'd made today. He had to admit there weren't many big positives, but he was happy with his appreciation now of the sites from which two of the three women had been taken. Once you've seen one multi-storey, you've seen them all, in Gus's opinion. There was little point in visiting another one. He was well aware of how Suzie had been grabbed in Leamington Spa.

A woman, alone, at any time of the day or night, should be able to go about their business safely, and that was one type of building where it was nigh on impossible. Gus could well imagine Claire arriving on the third or fourth floor looking every which way, praying she'd reach the safety of her car without incident. She may even have been holding her car keys in her fist, ready to defend herself.

Until he read the autopsy report, Gus didn't know whether Claire carried mace or an attack alarm. But if Geoff Mercer's fears were genuine, who could blame Claire for relaxing if she saw a marked police car parked next to her Golf?

Armed with a coffee, Gus started the next task for today. Geoff Mercer answered the phone on the second ring.

"How did you get on today, Gus," he asked.

Gus gave his friend the headlines of his trip around the critical section of the M4 corridor.

"You had to do some quick-thinking by the sound of things," said Geoff. "Nobody can accuse you of misleading them into thinking you were a police officer. Although, it was touch-and-go with Mrs Poulsom."

"Can we meet tomorrow afternoon, Geoff?" asked Gus. "Should we risk the café by the Wharf Theatre again? Or is there somewhere further out of town that might be safer?"

"I've got just the place, Gus," said Geoff. "Christine rang earlier. We've got a set of keys for the Clench

Common property so I can meet you there at two o'clock. Is that okay?"

"Perfect," said Gus. "Do you have a moving date yet?"

"The current owners are in Switzerland on a skiing holiday until the New Year," said Geoff. "How the other half lives."

"If you can afford to buy their place, then you live in the same half, Geoff," said Gus. "Have they agreed to you dropping in while they're away to measure up for curtains and the like?"

"That's what Christine wants to do at the weekend. I thought you and I could spend an hour there tomorrow without her knowing, and there's very little chance anyone else would know about it. I have to hope Vera Butler doesn't ask where I'm going if she sees me creeping out of my office at one o'clock. What have you got planned for the morning?"

"I'll call Ricky Lenham first after I hang up on you. Then I'll try Dave Frost in Ireland," said Gus. "My schedule in the morning will be influenced by what I hear."

"Have you given up on the idea of speaking to Adie Lawrence?" asked Geoff.

"I almost went to the garage in Chiseldon this afternoon but thought better of it," said Gus. "There are several questions I'd like to ask Bethany Cunningham first. By the way, I don't recall anything about her mother being a fitness fanatic."

"It wasn't in the file I read," said Geoff. "Do you think it's important?"

"Maybe not," said Gus. "Roy Wakeley still remembered it, twenty years on."

Geoff gave Gus the address in Clench Common and

contact numbers for the two retired detectives. Gus thanked him and ended the call.

Ricky Lenham lived within a stone's throw of the police station at Gablecross in Shrivenham. Gordon Flowers had told Gus they met every Friday lunchtime in the Prince of Wales pub. It was obvious his ex-boss had called Ricky as soon as Gus had spoken to him.

"Ricky Lenham?" asked Gus. "My name's Freeman. Can you spare five minutes for a chat?"

"You're still raking over dead coals then, Freeman," said Lenham. "Why you think I can help you, heaven knows. The Harford case is ancient history."

"I don't know why you're being so negative, Ricky," said Gus. "I'm happy you and Gordon did a decent job on the Harford investigation. Given the evidence available, and the lack of viable suspects, I don't think anyone could have done any better."

Ricky Lenham didn't have a reply for a change.

"I only have a couple of questions," said Gus. "How often did you and Gordon speak to Bethany Harford and Adie Lawrence?"

"We interviewed them a couple of times after the woman's father reported her missing," said Lenham. "You know the drill. Get them talking casually about every second of the day from when they awoke to when we got the call. Then go through it all again for the official state-ment. For example, we asked about the cash withdrawal and why the missing woman booked a hotel room. That was something which seemed dodgy to me."

"Gordon Flowers told me what you thought was going on," said Gus. "Did it seem likely, once you'd spent a few days talking to her family and people who knew her at work?"

"Easy to say with hindsight," said Lenham. "The woman was only missing at the time. We didn't know we were dealing with murder for months. Yeah, we suspected she'd come to harm, but we had to keep looking for clues as to where she might have gone. Her parents were clinging to the hope she was alive."

"What about the boyfriend?" asked Gus. "Did you interview him more often?"

"We asked Lawrence how well he knew his girlfriend's mother," said Lenham. "An attractive older woman whose husband walked out years ago. Well, these things happen, don't they?"

"You suggested he'd slept with Stephanie," said Gus.

"Lawrence swore nothing happened between them," said Lenham. "We never found anyone to tell us differently."

"How far into the investigation would that interview have occurred?" asked Gus.

"A month, six weeks at the most," said Lenham.

"Surely you spoke to the couple again before the body was discovered?" asked Gus.

"What for?" asked Lenham. "We had sworn statements from all interested parties. Every alibi had been checked and rechecked. Pictures of Stephanie Harford had been circulated in the Police Gazette. Every station in the country knew who to look for, but no reported sightings existed. So the investigation was on the back burner as far as Gable-cross was concerned. We were handling a dozen other cases for weeks. Odd jobs which we could drop if something new turned up."

"Then the embankment a few miles from where Stephanie disappeared suffered two weeks of torrential rain, and her remains were uncovered," said Gus.

"We were back on the case full-time after that," said Lenham. "While we waited for forensics, Gordon went through every statement again, checking whether we'd missed something. The autopsy showed she'd been strangled, but when the other results returned, forensics never threw up a potential suspect. So I spent a couple of weeks trawling through records of offenders with a similar MO, looking for a criminal in the area when she went missing. Unfortunately, that proved fruitless, too."

"Who spoke to Greg Harford?" asked Gus.

"The husband?" asked Lenham. "Why bother with him? Nobody knew where he was for years before his wife went missing. The family's solicitor got in touch to say Greg had turned up out of the blue months after the body was found. He'd been working on the oil rigs and had no idea his wife was dead. Gordon made a phone call to confirm his alibi with Aberdeen Police, and we were soon working on another case."

"I asked Gordon about Lime Kiln Police Station," said Gus. "What do you remember about that place, Ricky?"

"We only ever spoke to George Bailey at the front desk," said Lenham.

"I know, but what did you make of the crew working there? Were they a friendly bunch?" asked Gus. "I've visited Gablecross on several occasions in the past nine months, and the squad room has a warmth, you know, and a buzz when the whole team are in there. It feels like a good place to work. I remember times like that at Bourne Hill, too, when I was there, but now and then, there would be an element that soured the mood and made it not so pleasant to turn up for work every day. You must have had times like that in your career."

"How did you make things better when you had a square peg in a round hole?" asked Lenham.

"When I first started, my sergeant would knock the offending officer into shape, so he either fitted in or was on his way," said Gus. "Later on, we had to rely on our boss cutting out any cancer before it spread."

"Twenty years ago, things were very different in this part of Wiltshire," said Lenham. "Until ten years ago, the Chief Constable deployed as much as ten percent of our total strength on patrol duties. They were dedicated to the M4 and A-class roads dealing with situations that occurred. The large majority of those officers' work rate wasn't to do with traffic incidents at all. It was to do with major crimes being committed on the motorways or criminals using the motorway network and the A-class trunk roads to travel about in pursuit of crime, carrying stolen property. The number of arrests those patrols made was considerable and undoubtedly a potential deterrent to criminals. They certainly made criminals think twice before venturing onto a motorway or main road network."

"We've retreated from that brand of targeted policing now," said Gus. "I take it you feel that was a mistake?"

"Cameras and ANPR can bring results," said Lenham. "I don't deny that, but the Chief Constable would get slaughtered if he left the policing of the centre of Swindon, or Salisbury, to cameras, with no uniformed police presence. Unfortunately, that's what we've done with the M4. Our motorways are a vital part of our national transport infrastructure. They need to be better patrolled and supervised."

"Highways England is manned by many of your former colleagues," said Gus. "Surely they fulfil a worthwhile role?"

"Gordon told me you were retired," said Lenham. "Do

you have a warrant card with this consultant job you're doing?"

"No," said Gus, "and it's frustrating. I see where you're going. The Highways England guys don't have powers of arrest. Their role is to keep the traffic moving, assist other officers investigating the cause of accidents, get breakdown trucks on the scene to clear debris and so on. After thirty years with the police, that must rankle with some of them."

"Did you ever wonder what happened to those square pegs that wouldn't alter their ways?" asked Lenham. "Gordon reckoned Lime Kiln were a motley crew. He didn't want to ruffle their feathers, so we never spoke to any of them, just George Bailey."

"You're saying Lime Kiln was home to every square peg Wiltshire threw up," said Gus.

"They were a rule unto themselves," said Lenham. " They thought they were the elite. I wouldn't want to get on the wrong side of them."

"Gordon told me to watch my back," said Gus.

"And you're still asking questions," said Lenham. "It's only a matter of time before they get wind of it."

"Was there anyone at Lime Kiln capable of murder?" asked Gus.

"Everyone's capable of murder if someone pushes the right buttons," said Lenham. "I've said enough, Mr Freeman. Do yourself a favour, and quit while you're ahead. Oh, and lose my phone number. I don't want to hear from you again. Gordon's already blocked your number. We're enjoying our retirement and want it to continue that way for many years."

Gus heard the click as Ricky Lenham hung up on him.

Nothing ventured, nothing gained. Gus called Dave Frost in Castlegregory on the Dingle peninsula.

"Is that Dave Frost?" asked Gus. "Gus Freeman here, from Bourne Hill, Salisbury. Do you have time to answer a few questions?"

"Bourne Hill, did you say?" said Frost. "I've been out of the game for six years now. I can't imagine how I could help you with anything that far from my patch."

"We were looking at an old murder case near Swindon," said Gus. "A colleague at London Road, Devizes, spotted similarities to an investigation you worked on with Joe Gorse. What can you tell me about that case?"

"The only murder Joe and I worked on was a French woman. Marie Legrand was reported missing, I remember. But we weren't involved much while the search took place. There was always a chance she'd changed her mind and not visited her brother in Bath. The previous year, she'd worked at a hotel in the New Forest, and Joe asked the local police to check whether she had returned there. The French police were adamant she'd travelled on the ferry, so she was in the UK somewhere. Then her body turned up in the middle of nowhere, and Joe and I had to drop everything to pick up the threads. The trail was cold by then, and forensics yielded nothing. Finding witnesses who had seen Marie at any stage on her journey was tricky."

"Did Joe ask Lime Kiln for help?" asked Gus.

"He did, but he always wished he hadn't," said Frost. "That was the start of it, I reckon."

"I heard Joe died recently," said Gus. "You didn't fly over for the funeral, though."

"I thought it best to stay as far away from it as possible," said Frost.

"I need your help, Dave," said Gus. "My colleague at London Road is keeping this investigation off the books. We understand how sensitive it is. The Marie Legrand case was the second case to show a similar MO."

"Are you saying there were others?" asked Frost.

"At least one more," said Gus. "What happened when Joe Gorse spoke to patrol teams at Lime Kiln?"

"They stonewalled him," said Frost. "Every patrol team was the same. They were evasive or straight out refused to answer his questions. He'd arrange to meet someone at the station, and they wouldn't be there. George Bailey would apologise and say we'd just missed them."

"You had a job to do," said Gus. "You were on the same side. Why didn't Joe report the matter to his bosses?"

"Why do you think?" asked Frost. "I'm sure people will tell you Joe took things to heart and carried his work home at the end of the day. That's why he ended up on that motorway bridge last year. Joe wasn't like that before we handled the Legrand case. He cared about the job and wanted to do the best he could every day, but they got to him. There was so little to go on that we wrapped up the investigation a month after the body was found. I expect someone has dug the file out and gone through the motions every five years, but with dead ends everywhere, it would have been a thankless task."

"You said *they* got to him," said Gus. "What did you mean?"

"Joe would get home at night to find a car parked twenty yards from his front door. He had phone calls at odd times, day and night. Nobody spoke, but he could hear funeral music in the background. Joe walked into the office one morning and found a dead rat in his wastebin."

"How long did this go on for?" asked Gus.

"It never stopped while he worked at Gablecross and continued after he retired," said Frost. "I can't speak for what happened after I moved away in 2012. I was glad to be out of it and hoped they'd forget about me. But I could see the effect it was having on Joe. They dismantled him bit by bit."

"Why on earth didn't he speak to someone?" asked Gus.

"How could he? Joe received photos of his wife and two daughters in the post. They might have been out shopping, at work, or in a bar in the evening. Joe said his daughters went on holiday to Benidorm, and he received photos of them by the pool at the hotel."

"Were you ever threatened?" asked Gus.

"We weren't working together then. Joe asked his boss to split us up," said Frost. "Told him we weren't getting on. I couldn't believe it. We made a decent team and always got on great. But maybe they'd sent him a photograph of my wife and me somewhere. I don't know. Joe never said. Anyway, we never worked together after that."

"Would you be prepared to give us names?" asked Gus. "Which patrol teams do you believe were responsible?"

"Not a chance," said Frost. "They will still be in touch with one another, even if they're retired. The Lime Kiln crew were like the Three Musketeers—all for one and one for all. You have no idea what you're dealing with. Whoever you've spoken to at London Road, I should advise them to lose whatever evidence they've uncovered. That crew will protect one another to the grave."

Gus was about to ask another question, but Dave Frost had hung up. There was a pattern emerging. The sound of Suzie's Golf arriving outside prevented Gus from giving the matter further thought.

"What a grey day," said Suzie as she dropped her car keys on the table in the hallway.

"Alright for those sat in a warm office," said Gus. He'd left the lounge to return his empty cup.

Suzie followed him into the kitchen and spotted the wellington boots at once.

"Where on earth did you go today? Surely you didn't visit the allotment?"

"I wasn't sat inside the car all day," said Gus. "I've visited parts of Wiltshire that other detectives can't reach."

"What did you learn?" asked Suzie.

"Nothing I can share with you, I'm afraid, darling," said Gus. "Geoff Mercer would have my guts for garters if I breathed a word."

"I told you this morning to be careful," said Suzie. "Did you take my advice?"

"I'm not in any more trouble now than before," said Gus.

"I'm not sure if that's a good thing," said Suzie. "Right, I'm off for a shower. Can we have a conversation before we meet Brett and Clemency later?"

Gus hoped the conversation was about the wedding preparations or how to coax Bert into getting back into circulation. There was no way he'd endanger Suzie by telling her what they had revealed so far.

He needed to tell Geoff Mercer what he'd learned from Ricky Lenham and Dave Frost. The sooner Geoff uncovered the names of the people working at Lime Kiln in the mid-Nineties, the better.

Chapter Eight

WHEN SUZIE EMERGED from the bathroom twenty minutes later, Gus sat in the lounge with two cups of coffee.

"You're a lifesaver, sweetheart," said Suzie.

"I do my best," said Gus. "Now, what did you want to talk about?"

"I know you're busy," said Suzie. "But could you spare time tomorrow to visit Bert and Irene? You did promise to be available to drive Bert anywhere he fancied. So I thought it would help keep Brett and Clem's spirits up if we could tell them tonight that you're giving it another try."

"It would be best if I could say I was trying on Friday," said Gus. "I'm dashing around the county again tomorrow."

"Friday's better than nothing, I suppose," said Suzie. "Are you going anywhere special?"

"Nice try," said Gus. "Chiseldon and Chippenham for starters, and a trip to the countryside in the afternoon. What prompted you to ask if I could pop in to see Bert tomorrow?"

"You found time for a haircut in your busy schedule the other day, and that gave me an idea. Bert might agree to a trip to the barber before next Monday. He'll want to look his best when his grandson gets married."

"Okay, I'll call the chap I use in Devizes to see if he can fit Bert in on Friday morning."

"Thank you. Do you think Geoff Mercer will have the green light for your clandestine investigation by then?" asked Suzie. "He's been busy with something all week, and nobody seems to know what. It makes people nervous. They're worried another round of cuts are being lined up, so that Sylvia Robbins can give herself a flying start."

"Geoff hasn't said anything to me," said Gus. "As for the green light, I'm hoping to hear news very soon."

At seven-thirty, Gus and Suzie made their way to the Lamb for their mid-week meal with Brett and the Reverend. The Lamb wasn't likely to have a quiet night until the second of January, and the landlord was making the most of the higher level of customers. He knew lean times were just around the corner. December was no time for an attack of the miseries. He did everything he could to encourage the sound of laughter, and see that everyone enjoyed themselves.

The four friends may have had to wait a few more minutes for their main meals, and desserts, as the kitchen staff struggled to keep everyone happy, but the quality, and the quantity didn't suffer in the mayhem. When they walked along the lane together at closing time they were content.

"I enjoyed tonight," said Suzie. "Christmas can give you such a warm feeling, can't it?"

"The brandy helped in that regard," said Brett.

"Not long before all of us can enjoy an alcoholic drink," said Suzie.

"The season of goodwill crept up on Brett," said Gus. "He persuaded me to join him."

"If you can persuade Bert to go into Devizes for a trim, that would be terrific, Gus," said Clemency.

"I'm booked into a unisex salon just up the road from the surgery in the morning," said Brett. "Several of our girls go there, and they swear I'll survive the experience."

"There you are, Gus," said Clemency. "That's what you can slip into conversation when you see Bert. The bridegroom and best man will look smart, so it's only fair other family members do the same."

"Leave it with me, Reverend," said Gus. "I'll find the right words. Resistance will be futile."

They wished each other goodnight, and Brett and Clemency continued walking towards the Rectory.

"Did Brett get you a double?" asked Suzie as she watched Gus trying to get the key into the lock.

"Tonight was a precursor to his stag do," said Gus. "He's spending an evening in Wootton Bassett with his colleagues tomorrow night. Then we top it off on Saturday with a meal at the Fox & Hounds."

"That's because of his age, darling," said Suzie. "If he was twenty-five years younger, he would have flown to Ibiza for seven drunken nights. Heaven knows what the Reverend would have done for her hen night."

"I expect they do, darling," said Gus. "I'm off to bed. If I sit down in the lounge I'll be asleep before you've found something on TV worth watching."

Thursday, 20 December 2018

GUS FOUND Suzie in the kitchen when he surfaced. She had eaten already and was putting her breakfast things in the dishwasher.

"Will you be safe to drive first thing, darling?" she asked. Gus could tell he was in the dog house. Suzie rarely stood with her hands on her hips.

"I'll delay my departure by thirty minutes," said Gus.

"See you tonight then," said Suzie. She hugged him before leaving.

Gus slipped two pieces of bread into the toaster and poured a strong coffee.

He may be showing signs of a hangover, but the mystery faces from Lime Kiln kept him from sleeping last night. He'd thought Geoff Mercer was being overly dramatic with the precautions he took when they met at Caen Hill Locks. Since his phone conversations with Ricky Lenham and Dave Frost, Gus wondered whether Geoff had underestimated the threat these people offered.

Fortified by two coffees and marmalade on toast, Gus showered and dressed. He made two phone calls and left the bungalow at half-past nine. Neither party had been eager to speak to him, but they had relented in the end. He felt confident that by lunchtime, he could tick another two tasks from his list.

Gus drew up on the garage forecourt in Chiseldon forty minutes after leaving Urchfont. The lady at the front desk informed him that the mechanic he'd come to see was taking a coffee break.

"You won't keep him away from work for long, will you?" she asked. "Adie's got an MOT this afternoon, and the owner of the car he's finishing now expects to collect it at twelve."

"If he gives me the right answer to a couple of questions, I don't see a problem," said Gus. "Where can I find him?"

The receptionist pointed to a door marked 'Staff Only' on the back wall. Gus crossed the workroom floor, knocked, and walked into the restroom. The man sitting at the table finished a sausage roll, and a Coke can was beside his lunch box. Gus thought it more suited to a teenager than a man of forty-five.

"Mr Lawrence?" asked Gus.

"That's me," said Lawrence. "Are you Mr Freeman?"

"That's right. I'm checking a few details from the Stephanie Harford murder. You were involved in that investigation, I believe?"

"I was going out with Bethany, her daughter," said Lawrence. "I wasn't involved in anything, not like you said. I had nothing to do with her mother's death."

"You were seeing Bethany for over a year, weren't you? How often did you see her mother during that time?"

"Loads of times," said Lawrence. "She'd answer the door when I went to pick Bethany up. Sometimes, I'd get invited in when I took her home, and her mother would stay downstairs until I left."

"Did you ever see her socially?" asked Gus.

"Just once," said Lawrence. "On her birthday, the day before, she disappeared."

"If you drove from Wroughton to her house on Lime Kiln several times each week, you must have seen police vehicles driving around."

"I suppose so," said Lawrence. "The A3102 took me direct to Bethany's estate. The police station was further on, one junction beyond her road. I never needed to go that way unless we were driving towards Lyneham to visit a country pub in the summer. Most nights, we stuck to the pubs we liked in Swindon."

"Are you married, Mr Lawrence?" asked Gus.

"Never bothered with women after Bethany finished with me,"

"What happened?" said Gus. "You two lived together for a while, didn't you?"

"Her grandfather never forgave me for what I did at the inquest," said Lawrence. "He and his wife kept on at Bethany to stop seeing me."

"Why did you refuse to give evidence?" asked Gus.

"My solicitor told me it was my best option. He said that putting the onus on the police to prove I did it was safer than saying something I later regretted. I never really understood what the coroner was on about. Put me under a car bonnet, and I know what's what, but two minutes answering questions in that court and they would have had me tied up in knots. So, I refused to answer. Bethany wasn't happy. Within days, she'd moved out and gone to stay with her grandparents. The next thing I heard was her Dad had turned up and the house at Lime Kim was on the market, but Bethany and me were finished, so none of them spoke to me after that."

"I mentioned police cars earlier," said Gus. "Did you ever have any hassle with them twenty years ago? What about speeding tickets, or a random stop, late at night? Did you ever experience anything like that?"

"We got pulled over on the M4 one night when I drove back from Bath. I'd taken Bethany to a restaurant in Queen's Square. Posh place it was, for her birthday, the year before her Mum died. The coppers reckoned there was a problem with one of my rear lights, but it was fine. One bloke shone a torch in Bethany's face while his mate was chewing my ear by the boot of my car. When they let us go, Bethany said the bloke gave her the creeps. He never said a word, just kept the torch on her face, so she couldn't see what he looked like."

"Did you get a ticket?" asked Gus.

"Never heard a thing," said Lawrence.

"Could you describe the men who stopped you?" asked Gus.

"Sorry, but one copper in a hi-viz jacket and peaked cap pulled down over his eyes looks like another," shrugged Lawrence. "They were taller than me and built like a brick outhouse, so I kept quiet and hoped they'd leave us alone."

"You didn't get stopped by any other officers in the next twelve months?"

"No, I had too much at stake to behave like a boy-racer," said Lawrence. "I wouldn't be much use as a mechanic at this place if I lost my licence, would I?"

"Did Bethany's mother ever have run-ins with police from the station up the road?"

"What, riding a bicycle without lights? No, Bethany's Mum kept her bike in good nick. She had to rely on it every day for work."

"Was cycling the only exercise she did?" asked Gus.

"She loved swimming and keeping fit," said Lawrence.

"Where did she go for that?" asked Gus.

"The Leisure Centre, almost on her doorstep," said Lawrence.

"Thank you, Mr Lawrence," said Gus. "You've been most helpful. Good day."

Gus had a spring in his step as he returned outside to the Focus. It never ceased to amaze him when those conversations he thought would be meaningless threw up a golden nugget.

He left Chiseldon and headed towards Chippenham on the M4. It was the quickest route, and it was unlikely he'd need the services of Highways England.

Gus passed the sprawling Cepen Park North estate and turned off the main road into Frogwell Park. Andrew Cunningham, his wife, Bethany, and their two children occupied a five-bedroomed detached property. Gus wondered whether Bethany's husband was a manager with whichever bank he worked.

None of the local towns had a great choice of branches these days; they were closing as fast as pubs. Gus drew up on the road outside the house. It looked spotless on the outside and was in good company. So, this was where the well-heeled folks of Chippenham lived. He walked up the sloping driveway to the house, passing a Kia Sportage with a registration that showed it was three months old.

Gus rang the doorbell. As he suspected, even the ring-tone was refined. The lady of the house answered the door in seconds.

"Come in, Mr Freeman," she said. Gus wiped his feet, delaying his entry as long as possible. Bethany Cunningham didn't want the neighbours to see him loitering on the doorstep. Did he look like a policeman?

Gus studied the forty-year-old woman in front of him. Who did she take after? What was it Gordon Flowers said? Stephanie Harford was an attractive woman. He couldn't accept that she hadn't been in a relationship after her husband left. He'd suggested she used her good looks to persuade men to part with large sums of money to sleep with her.

Her daughter was confident and well-dressed. Bethany's

hair and nails suggested she was no stranger to the salons in the town centre. The quality of her clothing also told Gus her husband's salary was sufficient for her to be a stay-at-home wife.

Bethany led him along the hallway into the kitchen. Gus compared it to his bijou version in Urchfont. Even when all four members of the Cunningham family were gathered here, they still had room to spare.

"Thank you for agreeing to speak to me, Mrs Cunningham," said Gus.

"Call me Bethany, please," she said. "Would you like a coffee?"

"Black, please," said Gus.

Bethany prepared the coffee while Gus looked out of the picture window. The rear garden had been given a modern twist. Decking covered a large proportion, and there was a hot tub in the top-left corner, and a patio on the right-hand side contained a BBQ and a large picnic table.

Gus wondered whether someone in the Cunningham family was allergic to grass.

"Black, no sugar?" asked Bethany as she placed a cup and saucer on the table.

"That's correct," said Gus.

"What did you want to ask, Mr Freeman?" asked Bethany.

"How old were you when your father left home?"

"Ten," said Bethany.

"A difficult time," said Gus. "Your final year as a junior and all the pressures of moving to a new school. Greg and Stephanie had been together, man and wife, for twelve years. There appear to be no dramas for the first ten years of your life. Aged ten, you would have been aware of problems in the marriage, especially if there were plenty of arguments. What did your father do for a living?"

"He had been in the Army when they got married," said Bethany. "Dad did two tours in Northern Ireland. He left the Army in 1980 when I was two years old. That was when we moved to the house on Lime Kiln. Before that, we lived in married quarters somewhere on Salisbury Plain. I don't remember much about that time. Dad joined the police in Swindon. He wore a uniform and a helmet. You know, the style you don't see today. He became a sergeant just after I started school. Then he left the police when I was about seven and worked for a security firm based in Bath."

"Did he ever speak about why he resigned from the police force?" asked Gus.

"Not to me," said Bethany.

"Did your father ever work from the police station just up the road from your house?"

"At first, Dad was based in the town centre," said Bethany. "Then they built Lime Kiln to replace the building there since Victorian times. It became a pub called The Old Nick and was a popular place to go for years. Dad left the police within weeks of the move to the new building. He told Mum he needed a change."

"When did things start to go wrong in the marriage?" asked Gus.

"The hours Dad worked on security in the Bath area meant he came and went at odd hours. Mum thought he was seeing someone else, but Dad always denied it. That was the beginning of the end. There was always tension in the house when they were together. I tried to avoid upsetting either of them, then one day, I came home from school, and Mum was crying."

"That was the day your Dad left," said Gus. "Didn't he say goodbye to you?"

"I didn't think anything of it then, but the night before, he had come to say goodnight before driving to Bath to work. I was in my bedroom, reading. He never left without a word, but that night he stayed longer, told me he loved me, hugged me, and kissed me on the top of my head before he went. That was the last time I saw him until almost a year after Mum was murdered."

"I spoke to Adrian this morning," said Gus. "What was the real reason for you two splitting up?"

"What has he been saying?" asked Bethany. "We grew apart, that's all. I expect he's still living at home with his parents if they're still alive. Adie had no ambition, he was a mechanic, and that was enough for him. I wanted more and moved in with my grandparents."

"Did you meet Andrew Cunningham while living with Adrian Lawrence?"

"He was working for the bank where Mum had her account," said Bethany. "My grandparents banked there too, and we visited the branch several times after Mum disappeared. That was when we first met."

"The detectives involved in the search for Stephanie were interested that you knew your mother's PIN. Did you often use her card to withdraw money for yourself?"

"I never needed to use it," said Bethany. "After Dad left, Mum had to take responsibility for everything to do with money. When I reached eighteen, she showed me what was involved in managing our finances. Mum said it was preparation for the future. I teased her, saying I would have to give her pocket money when she was senile like she had when I was a child. She said that would be ages yet, but one day I'd be married and needed to be able to stand on my own two feet if the man in my life was no longer around."

Gus noticed a smartphone on the worktop beside the coffee maker.

"You had a mobile phone when your mother disappeared, didn't you?"

"Gosh, an old Nokia, I suppose. Why?" asked Bethany.

"The detectives asked why you didn't phone your mother after she went missing,"

"Grandad was ringing her number every five blessed minutes," said Bethany. "I remember wishing he'd leave her alone for a bit. I hoped she'd ring me to tell me she was safe if I left my phone on. I always thought Mum had only gone because the pressure had got too much. We were struggling with the household bills. I wasn't earning much at the supermarket, and Adie didn't want me working behind a bar in the evenings to earn a little extra."

"After six months, you must have started to worry," said Gus. "Then her body was discovered, and your worst fears were realised. So why didn't you attend the first inquest?"

"I was sick," said Bethany. "My stomach was in knots, and I didn't want to sit in that courtroom listening to details of what happened to Mum. Then, as the date for the inquest drew closer, I was physically sick and couldn't drag myself out of bed. Things improved in time, but I suffered a relapse when they wanted me to attend the second inquest. My grandmother cared for me. I heard my grandfather had shouted at Adie. Why he thought Adie had anything to do with Mum's death, I can't imagine. He wouldn't have the nerve."

"Did your father come to see you at your grandparents' house when he arrived in Wootton Bassett?" asked Gus.

"Dad visited them while I was at work," said Bethany.

"They didn't think he'd answer the advert from the solicitors. It had been so long they thought he must be dead or moved overseas. Grandad told me when I got home. He sat me down and explained that because Mum never made a will, everything went to her husband. I'd never asked Mum why she hadn't divorced him. I know she wasn't hoping he'd come home; she seemed content to leave things as they were. Daft, really. Even if she'd still been alive today, the house would still have gone to Dad unless he'd died."

"Has he been in touch?" asked Gus.

Bethany laughed.

"Dad came to Grange Park about three months after he'd put the Lime Kiln house on the market. He drove us to a pub in town for a quiet drink and a chat. Dad didn't want to speak in front of my grandparents. He said the house had been sold and gave me a cheque. I asked him why. Dad said he felt guilty about leaving me all those years ago but couldn't tell me why he felt forced to leave. There was no way he could stay in Wootton Bassett, so he was giving me the money now. Dad flew to Mexico the following month, and I've never heard from him since. He gave me no contact details, and so many companies are active in that area that it's been impossible to trace him. He could have moved elsewhere or been dead by now. I'll never know."

"Would you mind telling me how much your father gave you?" asked Gus.

"Fifty thousand," said Bethany. "About a third of what he got for our house."

"So, you had a decent sum to pay into your bank account," said Gus. "That must have come in handy when you and Andrew were looking for your first home. You were seeing one another by then, I imagine?"

"We were dating, yes," said Bethany. "There weren't

any objections to Andy from my grandparents as there had been with Adie. So we got engaged in the summer of 2001."

"And married in April 2002," said Gus. "When did you move to Chippenham?"

"Almost seven years ago, when Andrew became manager. The kids were small, the schools were better here, and after my grandmother died, I thought cutting my ties with Wootton Bassett was best. There were too many unhappy memories there."

"There must have been some happy times?" said Gus. "I know it wasn't ideal, just you and your mother, but because it was just the two of you, surely you grew closer? Did you do a lot of things together?"

"Mum couldn't afford to take us on foreign holidays," said Bethany. "We went on coach trips to the coast."

"You were fortunate to have the Lime Kiln Leisure Centre on your doorstep," said Gus. "Did Mum teach you to swim there?"

"Oh yes, we went swimming a lot. Mum loved to swim," said Bethany. "I took my two kids to the Olympiad here in Chippenham when they were tiny. I still go swimming twice a week. But, of course, they spend their spare time staring at screens."

"Someone from the farm shop told me your mother was as fit as a fiddle," said Gus.

"Mum signed up for keep-fit classes at Lime Kiln," said Bethany. "She didn't finish the course. I'm not sure why. When I went swimming with Mum when I was young, the sessions were for mothers and children. So we never saw any adult men. As a teenager, I was self-conscious about my figure as it was changing, and I didn't go with Mum as often."

"Mum found herself exercising alongside men in the open sessions," said Gus.

He knew little about how gyms, swimming pools, and fitness suites operated. The only exercise he got while he worked in Salisbury was the miles he walked every day and a quick sprint after a villain now and again. Since retiring, gardening constituted most of his exercise, and he only walked to the car and the pub.

"I got the feeling she felt less comfortable than in the past," said Bethany.

"The detectives asked you about stalkers or people taking an unhealthy interest in your mother," said Gus. "According to the statement you and Adie gave, there was nobody like that. You gave them the impression your mother had sworn off men after your father walked out."

"Well, can you blame her if she did?" said Bethany. "They suggested Mum had booked the hotel room to meet a man. That was laughable. Mum never forgave Dad for leaving us in the lurch as he did. I don't think she could ever have trusted a man after that. But she had male friends at work and on the street where we lived. I didn't see her every hour, but I never saw evidence of a stalker or anyone who fancied her."

"Did you return to swimming at the Leisure Centre with your Mum after you got older?" asked Gus.

Bethany thought for a while.

"I stopped going when I was about thirteen," she said. "So, maybe for four years, Mum went to the open sessions alone. I was getting interested in boys by then, although I hadn't met Adie. Mum kept asking if I'd go swimming with her again, and not long after my seventeenth birthday, I agreed."

"What was it like?" asked Gus.

"It was great to get back in the water and swim length after length together. I was shattered after that first session, but I returned the following week. Mum was over the moon."

"Was the pool busy?" asked Gus.

"You could swim a length without colliding with anyone," said Bethany. "There were signs everywhere warning people not to dive in. There was no bombing allowed."

"What sort of men did you see there? Were they young or old, on their own, or in groups?"

"The age range was incredible," said Bethany. "Eighteen to eighty, possibly. There was always a group of middle-aged men that swam together. Then they stood chatting at the side of the pool."

"No big surprise, I suppose," said Gus. "The police station was less than half-a-mile away. I expect some of them visited the centre after the end of a shift. Did you ever recognise anyone?"

"Not really," said Bethany. "I didn't meet any of Dad's police colleagues when he worked in town. He might have known the men at the Leisure Centre, but how would we have known whether they were policemen? Unless they had to wear Speedos with a logo when they're off-duty."

"I wasn't thinking of people your Dad might have worked with," said Gus. "Adie mentioned an occasion on your nineteenth birthday when you were returning from Bath late at night."

"Oh yes, I remember that night," said Bethany. "The police on the motorway stopped Adie for no reason and kept us hanging around on the hard shoulder for ages. I told the guy shining his torch at me that my Mum would be worried. We promised to be home by eleven. It made no difference."

"Adie said the officer made you feel uncomfortable," said Gus. "He couldn't describe either of the men who stopped you except that they were tall and muscular. Would that fit the description of any of the men you saw at the Leisure Centre?"

"They were as tall as you, if not taller," said Bethany. "That matched with the motorway police. To say they were muscular might be being kind. I'd say the group of men by the pool were about thirty, and a regular swim kept a middle-aged spread at bay, not getting their weight back to what it was a decade earlier. The ones who stopped Adie and me were tall and about the same age."

"Did they have local accents?" asked Gus.

"One of the motorway policemen sounded like he came from Swindon, but I don't remember the guy with the torch saying a word," said Bethany. "It's more difficult with the men at the Leisure Centre because of the background sound. The water, people having fun, other people at the side of the pool talking, and in a large hall like that, every-thing echoes, doesn't it? So I can't recall hearing what they said clearly enough to identify an accent. I'm sorry."

Gus had finished his coffee. Another interview appeared to have concluded without something to offer a way to split this case wide open.

Chapter Nine

"NOT TO WORRY, BETHANY," said Gus. "If you remembered something you were confident of, that's fine, but I don't want you to hazard a guess. They can do more harm than good. I'll be off now."

Bethany Cunningham walked with Gus to the door. He thought it best he let her down gently.

"I'll say the same to you as I did to Adie," said Gus. "You've been very helpful."

"I can't see how," said Bethany. "The detectives never found any suspects, no matter how hard they looked. Perhaps the uniformed officer was right."

"Which officer was this?" asked Gus.

"He came to the house in Lime Kiln with the detectives," said Bethany. "That would have been their first visit after Grandad had reported Mum missing. Two detectives came on Tuesday with other officers in uniform. One man stood outside the front door, and another went upstairs while I spoke with the detectives in the front room. I asked what he was doing, and the detective in charge, Mr Flowers, said he was looking for evidence in Mum's bedroom, the bathroom cabinet, and the kitchen. They were checking whether Mum had packed a suitcase, taken her toothbrush, and gone away for a few days. I said that was a crazy idea, but they said it was standard procedure."

"It would have been, Bethany," said Gus. "They didn't find anything, did they? So, what was it the officer who was upstairs said that stuck in your memory?"

"Because I was going to be alone in the house, the detectives called in the officer on the doorstep and asked him to get a WPC from the local station."

"Someone we call a Family Liaison Officer," said Gus, eager to hear about the man. "You were twenty, but with your mother missing, you needed support. I expect someone visited your grandparents too. Go on."

"The other man was still upstairs, and then a van arrived."

"A forensic team," said Gus. "They didn't know what they were dealing with less than forty-eight hours after Mum went missing. So they did everything by the book."

"Two men, dressed in white overalls, worked upstairs for at least four hours. The detectives returned to Swindon after telling me when they wanted to see me next. They promised to get in touch if they had any news. I suppose it was thirty to forty minutes before the WPC arrived. Her name was Janet. I didn't catch her surname. She came into the front room to sit with me, and I heard someone come downstairs and go into the kitchen. I wanted to see who it was and what they were doing, but Janet told me to sit still. She said it was one of her colleagues looking for clues. She walked into the hallway, and I heard her whispering to someone. I got up and listened by the front room door. The officer who'd been upstairs and was leaving had a thick, Scottish accent. There you are, Janet, he said, another woman who didn't understand how things work around here. I heard him leave, and then Janet returned to sit with me. She looked different, frightened, somehow. The officer on duty outside tapped on the door, and asked if there was any chance of a cup of tea. Janet jumped up, went to the kitchen, and filled the kettle. She seemed okay when she returned. I didn't think anything of it afterwards."

"Interesting," said Gus. "What did you think the Scotsman meant?"

"I thought he was talking about me," said Bethany. "Because I kept asking the detectives why they were asking silly questions instead of organising a search party. Things got worse because the money was taken from her bank account, and they discovered the hotel booking. All their attention was on Adie and me instead of going out looking for Mum. Or at least that's how we felt. That Scottish policeman thought we didn't understand the procedures they had to follow. That was what he meant, wasn't it?"

"If I could ask him, Bethany, I would," said Gus. "I'd like a word with that woman, Janet, if we could trace her. Thanks again. I'll let you get on with the rest of your day."

Bethany Cunningham had closed the door before Gus reached the car. At last, he finally had something tangible to tell Geoff Mercer when they met in Clench Common. Perhaps this morning hadn't been fruitless after all.

Gus took the Calne road out of Chippenham. He passed Avebury and its standing stones, arriving in Marlborough thirty minutes later. A glance at his watch showed he had an hour to kill. Geoff wouldn't arrive until two o'clock. He was familiar with Marlborough and decided to try the same café he and Eve Northwood had visited several weeks back. The usual song and dance of finding a parking spot on the main road followed, but he persevered.

As Gus sat with a chicken wrap and a black coffee on a table by the window, he pieced together all the jigsaw pieces he'd gathered from Adie Lawrence and Bethany Cunningham. When he'd finished lunch and visited the Gents, he stood outside the café on the pavement. The traffic lights to his left turned red. The gods were on his side today; there was no need to take his life in his hands trying to cross the road.

He quickly reached the Focus, filtered back into traffic as the lights turned green, and headed for Pewsey. Ten minutes later, Gus reached the picturesque village that would soon be home to Geoff and Christine Mercer. He parked some way from the address Geoff had given him. There was no point in drawing attention to two strange vehicles in the village. The locals might be friendly, but there were dark forces around, based on everything he and Geoff had uncovered.

At two o'clock, Gus spotted Geoff's new car in his rear-view mirror. Geoff turned off the lane, parking in the driveway of his cottage. Gus got out, locked the Focus, looking around him as he walked across the common to join his friend. So far, so good.

Geoff had already unlocked the front door and was standing in the hallway when Gus arrived. He quickly closed the door behind them.

"I wasn't followed," he said. "Did you take precautions?"

Gus nodded. He was interested in a quick tour, but Geoff was all business for a change.

"I can't stay long," said Geoff. "The only way I could get free of Kenneth's clutches was to claim a dental appointment. I brought the headlines from the two murder files I told you about, and I'm fairly confident I've found another. Let's sit in the lounge, where it's more comfortable, and we've got room to spread out."

Gus followed Geoff into the lounge. The room was smaller than he'd expected, but the joys of an old country cottage were thick walls, small windows, and low ceilings. Even though the skiers had minimised the central heating while they were on holiday, the temperature in the room was still adequate for late December.

"Right," said Geoff. "Marie Legrand was born, just outside Paris, on the fourth of June in 1961. Marie had two brothers, Emile, and Pierre. Emile was a chef working in Bath, who she was planning to visit. Pierre was a hotel manager who lived near Lyndhurst. Marie had worked at the hotel during the summer of 2000, and then a year later, she came to England by train. The plan was to spend two weeks in Bath, improving her English. She reached St Pancras in the early evening and accepted a lift from a married couple heading for Southampton. Police traced the couple after Marie's disappearance, and they confirmed they'd met her on the train, wanted to help Marie save money, and had driven to Swindon on the M4 before dropping her at the truck stop. They travelled to Southampton on the A34 after saying goodbye and reached home within ninety minutes."

"They wouldn't have got home that much quicker if they'd gone direct," said Gus.

"Detectives analysed Marie's mobile phone logs and those of her two brothers," said Geoff. "Marie tried to call Emile in Bath, but his phone was switched off. It was much later now, and although she did speak to Pierre in Lyndhurst, the connection was poor. He told Marie to phone for a taxi."

"Why did the Southampton couple drop Marie at the truck stop?" asked Gus. "If they'd gone that far out of their way, why not drive a few extra miles into Swindon? Late trains were running in those days, and there would have been easy access to a taxi rank."

"Marie seemed happy to be dropped there," said Geoff. "The husband of the couple thought it was all about the money. Marie hoped to hitch a ride with a truck travelling to Bath or Bristol."

"I visited the truck stop yesterday," said Gus. "It's better than the cafes on the A4 in the dim and distant past, where the sugar spoon was nailed to the counter on a length of string, but it's not the Ritz. Marie may have spotted a female trucker in 2001, unheard of when the greasy spoon was the only option for a thirsty trucker. That's not easy to say. Did anyone report seeing Marie hanging around outside the main building? Or did she venture inside, asking drivers if anyone was going her way?"

"As you can imagine, Gus," said Geoff. "Joe Gorse and Dave Frost weren't swamped with calls from truckers admitting they had seen Marie, let alone spoken to her that night. However, the handful of drivers they did speak to helped create a possible picture of what happened. Marie spoke to two truck drivers in the yard soon after being dropped off. Unfortunately, they must have been heading in the wrong direction because she entered the café. One eye witness saw Marie sitting at a table with a coffee. Another man saw her get a snack from a vending machine. Sometime later, approaching midnight, Marie was seen speaking to a man outside the building. She had her back to the window, and the man was behind her, hidden from view. The eyewitness couldn't be sure whether the man had been inside the café, left, or just arrived. That was the last time anyone saw Marie. Gorse and Frost believed the man she was speaking to around midnight offered her a lift."

"When I spoke to Dave Frost, he confirmed they hadn't been that involved when the police thought they were dealing with a missing person," said Gus. "Rather like the Harford case, after an initial burst of activity, everything cooled until the body was discovered. By then, the trail was cold, forensics gave them nothing to bite on, and as you've just said with Marie Legrand, it was tricky getting an accurate account of everything that happened to her from the moment she set foot in the truck stop."

"If people imagined every random incident leading to a tragic event and committed every second to memory, in case they needed to recall it, we would save a lot of time," said Geoff.

"Dream on, Geoff," said Gus. "I don't suppose any of the eye witnesses connected to Claire Dyke's case had heard your fanciful suggestion either. Anyway, I'm ahead of you on this one after speaking to Jake Latimer. Simon Rutty told everyone in the squad room at Gablecross that they searched for her car on CCTV between Malmesbury and Swindon. She drove a Moonlight Blue VW Golf GTI. Because they were dealing with murder from the outset, the case differed from the other two. Prince and Rutty reckoned they had to see he car entering the multi-storey car park. It was a shiny blue number that stuck out in a crowd. I visited Claire's cottage in Brinkworth, and the property stood some distance from the nearest group of buildings. Eve Northwood confirmed that an exact time of death was impossible because Claire's body was shoved in the airing cupboard for a month. Ian Hughes did the autopsy on that occasion.

Unfortunately, he was only around for a couple of years, between 2006 and 2008."

"The brief notes I read suggested Claire drove to Swindon for shopping, parked in the multi-storey, and was grabbed when she returned to her car," said Geoff.

"I agree. That seems the most plausible scenario," said Gus. "We can't be sure about when or where the fatal attack occurred with either victim. All we know is they were grabbed, taken somewhere, and in other cases, their bodies disposed of later.

"Although various sums of money were taken during each attack, robbery was never the prime motive, was it," said Geoff.

"True. Claire Dyke had a wall safe behind one of her paintings in the bedroom, containing several pieces of jewellery and an engagement ring from a previous boyfriend. The entire contents of the wall safe would have yielded less than a thousand pounds through a fence. Stephanie Harford's cash card enabled her killer to gain a few hundred pounds. Meanwhile, Marie Legrand didn't have much money, based on how she planned to cover the distance between St Pancras and Bath. No, money was never the motive. One point Jake made struck home, Geoff. These women were in their late thirties or early forties and far from naïve. Whoever persuaded them to move from a place of relative safety had to be someone they knew or trusted."

"Like a police officer," said Geoff.

"You mentioned another possible victim," said Gus.

"Susannah Buxton," said Geoff. "A forty-two-year-old mother of two who died in 2014 in Newbury. Susannah was a nurse who married young. She had two kids before she was twenty-one and split from her husband six years before she died. Both her kids were at university, one in Leeds and the other in Durham. Susannah was security conscious as she lived alone for long periods, yet everything at the scene indicated she opened the door to let someone into her house late at night on Saturday, the twenty-ninth of March. Her body was discovered on Monday afternoon when her son, Jordan, arrived home at the end of the spring term. Susannah had been strangled. There was no evidence of sexual assault, and the police were open-minded regarding the motive. It could have been a burglary gone wrong, and they thought the person responsible was most likely a local man, familiar with the area."

"I admit there *are* several similarities to the other cases," said Gus. "Perhaps the killer didn't realise Susannah had children? If they'd watched her since Christmas, they wouldn't know two youngsters would bring loads of dirty washing home for Easter. Was there something else that attracted you to this murder?"

"The detective team engaged the help of a forensic psychologist," said Geoff. "He suggested that although Susannah hadn't been sexually assaulted, the killer may have become aroused by inflicting fear and being able to dominate his victim. So he reckoned their focus was to humiliate and control Susannah."

"Now, that does ring true with elements from the other cases," said Gus. "Given what I heard from Bethany Cunningham. Sorry, Geoff, but you might be here for a while yet."

Gus summarised everything he'd learned since they last spoke.

"Bethany revealed several things Gordon Flowers either didn't check or buried in the murder file. You certainly never mentioned in your highlights that Greg Harford was a serving police officer in Wootton Bassett."

"I had no idea," said Geoff. "How on earth was that missed?"

"Harford served in the Army after leaving school and met Stephanie Thompson while he was stationed on Salisbury Plain. They lived in married quarters, Bethany was born, and Greg Harford left the Army in 1980 to join Wiltshire Police. He was based in the old police station in the town centre, and the family moved into the house on Lime Kiln. But, as you know, a new facility was built up the road from their house in the mid-Eighties, and the old station closed. Greg Harford left to work for a security firm based in Bath within weeks of the move to Lime Kiln. Bethany was only ten when her father walked out, but she sensed a change in her father's behaviour."

"Was he cheating on Stephanie?" asked Geoff.

"That was what her mother feared," said Gus. "That led to a series of arguments, but I'm more interested in why Greg didn't want to work at Lime Kiln. Why did he feel the need to quit when the move was so beneficial? Greg could have walked to work in five minutes. Instead, he took a job paying less money in Bath. After a couple of years, even the move to Bath wasn't enough distance between him and Lime Kiln. Greg disappeared to the oil rigs off the Scottish coast without telling anyone where he'd gone."

"You think that move was connected to the motorway patrols?" asked Geoff.

"Bethany never mentioned her Dad ever working on the M4," said Gus. "But some crews covering the M4 had to have been working in the town's old station in 1984. Regular patrols were a big part of the uniformed police role back then. What struck me was the influence the bad apples must have had on those that didn't conform. I believe Greg Harford was a straight arrow, and what was being said and done by a minority of his colleagues at the old station sickened him."

"You reckon they forced him out," said Geoff.

"I think Greg escaped to Aberdeen because he was scared of what they'd do," said Gus. "Look at what happened when he finally heard about his wife's murder. He surfaced long enough to sell their house and give Bethany fifty thousand pounds, before leaving for Mexico. Greg knew too much about what had happened in the past to hang around."

"Stephanie Harford was targeted," said Geoff. "Is Bethany Cunningham in danger?"

"Quite possibly," said Gus. "If that forensic psychologist you mentioned was on the right track, the killer among the Lime Kiln crew has something against women of around forty years of age."

"We don't know who or what Greg Harford was afraid of," said Geoff.

"Moving on," said Gus. "When I spoke to Gordon Flowers, it was clear his attitude to women hampered the original investigation. He focussed on Stephanie having booked the hotel room. Once that angle became a dead end, he accused Bethany and her boyfriend. I've spoken to both of them, and they weren't involved. I can't prove Flowers deliberately steered the investigation away from Lime Kiln, but although he checked the alibis of everyone connected to Stephanie and her family, he never considered a police officer a suspect."

"Why would he, though, Gus?" asked Geoff.

"I'll come to that in a minute," said Gus. "Let's talk about Joe Gorse first. Dave Frost told me Joe was another officer who had fallen foul of the Lime Kiln crew. When they were investigating the Marie Legrand murder, a motorway patrol car could have seen her at the truck stop. Of course it was worth an ask. After all, the crews spent hours on the M4, and even today, the Highways England guys frequent the truck stop café. Annie, the lady serving there yesterday, told me they were renowned for drinking gallons of tea, stuffing their face with cake, and playing pool. They're still a tight bunch, twenty years on."

"Did Joe Gorse ask the question at Lime Kiln?" asked Geoff. "Had anyone seen Marie?"

"He tried, but George Bailey was always at the front desk, and he would tell Joe they'd just left or weren't available. Finally, Bailey offered to pass on messages, but Joe never heard back."

"It sounds like Bailey was involved," said Geoff. "Not that we can ask him."

"Joe was warned off, in not too subtle ways," said Gus. "Late-night phone calls, a police car parked near his home. Photos of his wife and daughters when they were out and about were posted to him. The mental torture carried on for years. Dave Frost believed that was what led to Joe committing suicide. According to Frost, the rumour Joe always cared too much, and carried his work home with him was rubbish. The brotherhood started the rumour."

"Is that what they called themselves?" asked Geoff.

"I'm not sure anyone knows how they viewed what they were doing, Geoff," said Gus. "They were certainly a law unto themselves. No way was every officer in that building guilty of murder, but I'm convinced they thought they were untouchable if they stuck together."

"If there was never a weak link, then it was possible to maintain the image," said Geoff. "How did they latch onto

Stephanie Harford? It sounds like Greg tried to protect her by disappearing. The problems must have started between 1980 and 1984 when Greg was in the old police station."

"I agree," said Gus. "As for how they latched onto Stephanie, it was Roy Wakeley at the farm shop who pointed me in the right direction. He told me Stephanie was a keep-fit enthusiast. She didn't just cycle to and from work to keep fit; she visited the local swimming pool and fitness centre."

"That's on the same estate as the police station and her home," said Geoff. "I'm starting to get the picture now."

"Ricky Lenham suggested Lime Kiln was a dumping ground for misfits from police stations across Wiltshire," said Gus.

"He meant men with a poor disciplinary record, those resistant to change, and officers likely to cross the line when arresting a suspect. I hope that isn't the case today, but twenty years ago, it's possible the square pegs were sent to an isolated outpost where their bad influence could be minimised."

"Adie Lawrence and Bethany were pulled over on the M4 as they returned from a night out to celebrate her nine-teenth birthday," said Gus. "Adie told me the officers thought he had a problem with a rear light. He hadn't long had the car checked over and reckoned they were being picked on. Bethany told me the guy speaking to Adie was local. His colleague never spoke; he just shone a torch in her eyes so she couldn't identify him."

"Did Lawrence get a ticket?" asked Geoff. "That's something we might be able to trace."

"Nothing came of it," said Gus. "Bethany had more to say about the swimming and keep-fit, though. Stephanie taught Bethany to swim at the local pool, and they went there regularly until Bethany was a young teenager. Stephanie continued to go there a couple of times a week and kept asking Bethany to join her. Finally, Bethany relented when she was about seventeen, and she said whenever they were in the pool, there was always a group of men, perhaps in their early thirties, who swam beside them and then hung around watching."

"Did she think they were police officers from Lime Kiln?" asked Geoff.

"I think it most likely, don't you?" said Gus. "The clincher for me was when Bethany told me her Mum had started a keep-fit course on a weekday night when Bethany didn't go with her, and Stephanie never finished the course. She wouldn't say what had upset her, but I would put money on it being unwanted attention from that group of guys around the pool."

"How would we identify these men?" asked Geoff. "If they were police officers, how would we prove they were connected to Stephanie's murder?"

"Bethany told me something just as I was leaving," said Gus. "I didn't think I'd moved our investigation forward with what I learned from her and Adie. Then she remembered someone in her house when Flowers and Lenham paid her their first visit. They were dealing with a missing person's case, and uniforms went with them to check Stephanie hadn't simply packed a suitcase and gone on holiday. Flowers called out a forensic crew, too, to check for evidence of a string of male visitors in her bed, no doubt. Whatever, all they did was confirm Stephanie had disappeared on her way home from work. Flowers remembered to arrange for a WPC to sit with Bethany before they left Lime Kiln to return to the station. The FLO was called Janet, but Bethany never got her surname. Janet spoke to the uniformed officer, searching for evidence in the other rooms in the house, and Bethany overheard them speaking in the hallway before he left. The man had a thick, Scottish accent, and Bethany was convinced that what he said had frightened Janet."

"What did he say?" asked Geoff.

"There you are, Janet, another woman who didn't understand how things work around here."

"I can see how a Glasgow accent might make that sound sinister," said Geoff. "Are you sure Bethany wasn't reading too much into it? She was distressed. Her mother was missing."

"That's just it, Geoff," said Gus. "Bethany didn't think those words referred to her mother. She thought the bloke was talking about her because she'd been confused when several police officers arrived on her doorstep and started to check it wasn't just a misunderstanding. Bethany wanted the police to be scouring the countryside looking for her Mum. Flowers told her it was procedure, and you can imagine how patronising he would have been. Don't worry your little head about it, sweetheart. Leave it to the men."

"I think you're onto something, Gus," said Geoff. "There's plenty more to do yet, and we need to be extra-careful. Good work."

"So, we're agreed," said Gus. "One of the teams of motorway patrol cops operating out of Lime Kiln Police Station in the mid-Nineties is responsible for all four murders. Two men, as yet unidentified. One of them from Swindon, the other from Scotland, possibly Glasgow."

"The other teams of two that formed this brotherhood, or however they styled themselves, were equally as racist, homophobic, and misogynistic," said Geoff. "However, there's nothing to suggest any of them crossed the line to the same extent."

"Okay," said Gus. "But they've stuck together like glue throughout. Whether the others realised what they were covering up, we won't know until we catch them, but you can bet they're rotten to the core. When the model changed in 2008, the brotherhood was split up, but they still kept the psychological torture going for poor Joe Gorse, and Dave Frost is scared stiff they'll travel to the far side of Ireland to silence him. Some of those men will have retired, died maybe, but the rest will still be working the motorways."

"Those men are employed by Highways England and not affiliated with the police force in any way," said Geoff. "The primary job of a traffic officer is to patrol the UK's motorways and help keep traffic flowing smoothly."

"I get that," said Gus. "They keep motorists informed by passing on information through electronic signs, assist if you breakdown or are involved in a collision, remove abandoned vehicles, and organise temporary road closures."

"Traffic officers can't stop you for speeding or any driving offence," said Geoff. "They can't issue you with a ticket or search your vehicle. However, they can pass details to us if they witness dangerous driving or other offences. Not so many options to kidnap a victim."

"Although they've moved on from Lime Kiln," said Gus, "the crew we're interested in could still work together somewhere in the country. They have the power to stop a vehicle if they're in uniform and have a valid reason. So they could still be targeting women today."

"We would need to extend the search nationwide once we've identified them," said Geoff. "Our priority must be to catch them first."

Chapter Ten

"YOU NEED to get back to London Road, Geoff," said Gus. "I'll leave first to drive back to Urchfont. Could you give me a five-minute head start? What do you think our first step should be?"

"Somehow, I need to find someone prepared to talk about what was going on at the old police station in Wootton Bassett," said Geoff. "Who was WPC Janet, and how many other women worked alongside her? How many uniformed officers were there on site, and how many pairs covered the M4 patrols? If there were no risks attached, that would be straightforward enough."

"Dave Frost insisted we didn't know what we were dealing with," said Gus. "Ricky Lenham didn't want to have any further contact with me after we spoke. Even Gordon Flowers, who was far from squeaky clean, warned me to watch my back. Greg Harford put as much distance between himself and Lime Kiln as humanly possible, and poor Joe Gorse suffered for years before cracking under pressure. That's at least five men who rubbed shoulders with these characters and became frightened of what might happen if they stepped out of line. You were right to keep your cards as close to your chest as possible. There could be someone at London Road who was stationed in Wootton Bassett keeping a weather eye on activity connected to this outfits' activities. So far, we've been fortunate, and there's no clear sign someone is aware of our investigation."

"I propose we step back for a few days," said Geoff. "If we've kicked up dust, it might be wise to behave as they would expect in the lead-up to Christmas. I'll call you tomorrow. Here, take this phone."

"A burner phone?" asked Gus. "Should I ask where you got it?"

"Rank has its privileges," said Geoff. "Divya Yadav had an older model the Hub used when training their whiz-kids in the dark arts. I remembered signing the request form a couple of years ago, and she hadn't ditched it. It's clean and untraceable."

Gus put the phone in his coat pocket. If there was any doubt about how dangerous this case could get before he'd arrived in Clench Common, it had gone. He needed to keep this latest development from Suzie.

Geoff checked there were no cars parked on the road except for Gus's Focus. He held the door open for Gus to slip outside. The light was fading fast, and he knew he wouldn't return to London Road until after four o'clock. Would the Chief Constable accept that his standard dental appointment resulted in a ninety-minute root canal procedure?

Gus reached the Focus and scanned the nearby proper-ties for signs of life. Lights had appeared in windows, and curtains were drawn here and there. Other homes were in darkness. Maybe their owners were still working or enjoying their retirement in some far-fling foreign destination. Nobody in Clench Common was aware of cancer eating away at the organisation designed to keep them and their properties from harm.

Twenty minutes later, Gus was home. His first task was to charge the mobile phone. He didn't know what excuse Geoff had given Divya, but it was unlikely a discarded training tool had been regularly charged and updated since it was last used. Whatever needed to be done before tomorrow's chat with Geoff had to be finished before Suzie arrived home. Once he was satisfied everything was ready, he stashed the phone in the glove box of the Focus and waited.

Suzie reached the bungalow a few minutes after half-past five.

"Hello, darling," she said as she found him sitting in the kitchen. "You don't look like a man who was pulled over for drink driving, yet there's concern etched on your face. Spill the beans."

"Any criminal facing you in an interrogation room has no chance," laughed Gus. "No, I waited an extra thirty minutes before driving this morning, as you suggested. I negotiated the roads between here and Chiseldon, then Chippenham, without bumping into anything. After a snack in Marlborough, I drove home and have been gathering my thoughts here in the kitchen for the past hour and a half."

"Marlborough again," said Suzie. "Do I need to have a quiet word with Eve Northwood?"

"I dined alone," said Gus. "Talking about food, what would you like this evening?"

"I'll find out what you're up to soon enough," said Suzie. "Anything with fish will be fine. First, I'll shower and change, and perhaps after we've eaten, you'll be ready to talk."

They talked for several hours, but not about the Lime Kiln cowboys. Gus steered the conversation towards weddings, christenings, Christmas, and New Year. He resurrected stories from his time in Salisbury as a young detective that he'd long forgotten—anything to keep Suzie from the truth.

Friday, 21 December 2018

"GOOD LUCK WITH BERT TODAY, SWEETHEART," said Suzie as she headed for the front door.

Gus walked outside with her and waved her off. Once the Golf was in the lane, he rescued the burner phone and returned inside.

His hairdresser, Julian Yorath, had been working since seven-thirty and was taking a brief break before his next customer. Their negotiation wasn't quite on a par with those he'd had with mechanics and plumbers, but eventually, Gus got Julian to agree to squeeze Bert Penman in for a trim at eleven o'clock.

Who knew that although it said 'appointments not always necessary' on the noticeboard outside, today's younger men wanted far more pampering than they had in the old days? Gus didn't mind the extra fiver he'd had to offer to secure Bert's spot in the barber's chair. All he had to do now was persuade the old devil to get in the Focus and go into town.

Gus called Irene North on the landline in the hallway and told her he would collect Bert at a quarter to eleven. He heard an unfamiliar sound from the kitchen. Divya Yadav had a wicked sense of humour. She'd chosen 'School's Out' by Alice Cooper for the training phone's ringtone.

"Good morning, Geoff," said Gus. "I've checked for bugs in the bungalow. You're clear to proceed."

"Trust you to retain a sense of humour," said Geoff. "That might not be such a daft idea."

"My security cameras haven't caught any suspicious activity, Geoff," said Gus. "There have been times when I thought they were superfluous, but I examined them closely while I waited for Suzie to get home yesterday. Nobody'd been near here. Right, go ahead."

"First thing I did when I left Kenneth's office after mumbling my excuses was to run through the background to the changes in 2008," said Geoff. "When each constabulary patrolled its own proportion of the motorway, it was inefficient. We gradually withdrew from regular patrolling as the networks grew and vehicle numbers increased. Today, you can drive from Bristol to London without seeing a police car. That isn't to say there are no police available, but nowadays, we respond to calls, often from long distances and often not even from places on the motorway. That inevitably increases response times."

"With four thousand cameras available to them, they shouldn't miss much," said Gus.

"True, and virtually every vehicle entering the motorway system these days is observed by a camera of some kind or another," said Geoff. "A registration number comes up on a computer, and those vehicles can often be intercepted for an expired MOT or a lack of insurance."

"It's been said if highways officers were to be of real value, they needed more power," said Gus.

"Most are retired police officers," said Geoff. "Maybe

they could be re-enlisted as community support officers. At the moment, genuine traffic officers are something of a wasted resource. Meanwhile, we have our rogue officers to find and eliminate."

"Do you have a plan, Geoff?" asked Gus.

"I'll make a couple of phone calls at the weekend to retired colleagues," said Geoff. "People who will be invited to my retirement do at London Road if they're fit and well. My getting in touch shouldn't raise any suspicions. They're trustworthy individuals, and neither had a direct connection with Wootton Bassett between 1980 and 1984. However, they will have an insight into personnel who worked there."

"Why don't you just say they were at Gablecross, Geoff?" asked Gus.

"Okay, one of them was, but the other used to work in HR at London Road. She retired around twelve years ago. I haven't spoken to Lily Griffin for a while, but her mind was still as sharp as a tack at the last retirement party she attended."

"I'll keep this burner phone safe," said Gus. "When will you call again?"

"Next Thursday," said Geoff. "You weren't rushing off to the January sales, were you?"

"I don't think they bother with them these days, Geoff," said Gus. "Some companies seem to have a sale throughout the year. The TV adverts say 'must end soon', but they keep churning them out. Have a good Christmas. I look forward to hearing what your ex-colleagues give you."

Geoff echoed Gus's sentiments and rang off. Gus took the burner phone with him when he went to the car at twenty to eleven. He wondered what he'd find when he drew up outside Bert's house.

He needn't have fretted. Irene North was standing

next to Bert on the doorstep, holding his coat sleeve. There was to be no sneaking back indoors. Bert wore a winter overcoat, scarf, and flat cap. He wasn't likely to catch a cold, even if the barber was a little enthusiastic with the scissors.

Gus walked up the driveway to greet his old friend.

"Good morning, Bert. Let's get you settled in the car, and we'll be in The Brittox in no time. I've made an appointment, so you won't be kept hanging around."

"It's very good of you to bother, Mr Freeman, Gus," said Bert.

Gus knew better than to offer an arm for him to lean on. Bert sauntered down the slope to the car, using his stick to steady himself.

"You're a bit rusty," said Gus. "It stands to reason after that bout of flu. A few more trips like today, and you'll be back in the swing of things."

"Has she gone indoors yet?" asked Bert.

Gus looked back to see Irene standing in the doorway.

"Don't worry. Irene won't let the house get cold."

Bert lowered himself carefully into the passenger seat. Gus helped him secure the seat belt and waved to Irene as he walked behind the Focus to reach the driver's side.

"I don't remember a barber shop in The Brittox," said Bert. "Is it one of those fancy places? I used to go to Joe, the Italian fellow who had a lock-up shop in the village until a couple of years ago. There weren't enough customers to make it worthwhile for him to renew the lease. Then my next-door-neighbour mentioned a woman who tended to what little hair she had left. I asked if her mobile lady would trim my hair when she was passing."

"I can tell she hasn't been passing your house for a couple of months, Bert," said Gus as they entered Devizes.

"I should have asked for that lady's number," said Bert. "My next-door-neighbour passed in September."

"Got it," said Gus. He parked the Focus and helped Bert lever himself up from the car.

"Here we are," said Gus. "The chair's vacant, and Julian's ready to give you a trim."

Bert took a look around the salon. He realised there was no escape with Gus between him and the door, so he took off his hat, scarf, and coat and hung them on a stand in the corner of the room.

"Just a trim, sir?" said Julian when Bert was seated.

"My grandson's getting married on Monday," said Bert.

"Very nice, sir. Where would that be?"

Gus took a seat and picked up a magazine. He could relax for ten minutes because Bert was in safe hands. Another ten minutes of banter that Julian had perfected over twenty-plus years in the business, and they'd be in the car and returning to Urchfont.

"What's the damage, Julian?" asked Bert when his trim was complete.

"All taken care of, sir. Mr Freeman saw it as part of his duties as best man. Would you like to make another appointment, sir? Shall we say in six weeks?"

Bert looked at Gus for help.

"I can run you into town if you like, Bert," said Gus. "Or Irene can ask around the village to see if that mobile hairdresser calls at other addresses."

"No offence, Julian," said Bert. "It's a long way to come for a trim."

"None taken, sir. My wife, Connie, covers the villages around Devizes. I'll add you to her list."

"Connie," said Bert. "That was the lady's name. It's a small world, isn't it?"

"It certainly is," said Gus.

Bert made his way slowly back to the car. As Gus drove them out of Devizes, Bert had a question.

"When did they stop asking whether you wanted anything for the weekend, Gus?" he asked. "Joe always asked, even when I was in my seventies."

"Times have changed, Bert," said Gus. "Why don't we stop at the Lamb on our way home? One pint of cider won't put you in Irene's bad books."

"You're a good friend, Gus," said Bert. "But you must let me buy you a drink. My eyesight isn't great, but I could make out the price of a haircut for a senior citizen. I'm surprised Julian needs to send his wife out to work."

Gus smiled. It was satisfying to have Bert on good form again. Long may it last. He dropped Bert by the entrance to the public bar and parked in the car park. When he got inside, Gus found Bert sitting on his usual stool, chatting to the landlord.

"I got you a glass of Malbec," said Bert. "Just a small one. I don't think I could manage the walk home just yet."

"Ease yourself back in gradually, Bert," said the landlord. The bar was getting busier, and food orders were emerging form the kitchen. He was needed elsewhere.

"Good health, Gus," said Bert, raising what was left of his pint of cider.

"Don't worry, Bert," said Gus. "I had no intention of leaving you here to walk home. Good health."

It was like old times. They chatted about the weather, the wedding, and Irene's cooking. The allotment wasn't mentioned until they were leaving.

"Can we stop by the allotment to see what state my plot's in, Gus?" asked Bert.

"Okay, but I think you might be in for a surprise," said Gus.

Two minutes later, they were standing by the gateway. It wasn't easy to see much difference between the patches of land worked by the Reverend and Bert.

"Someone has been busy," said Bert.

"Clemency and Brett have worked in unison," said Gus. "Preparing for the future, she called it. I've tried to keep pace with them, but the weather was against me when I suddenly had the free time available."

"That's your excuse, and you're sticking to it, I suppose," said Bert. "You're not far behind, Gus. Once we're past February, you'll catch up. Unless you're working full-time again."

Gus didn't comment. He helped Bert back to the car, drove him home, and handed him over to Irene at the front door. She must have been standing by the window.

"Bless you, Mr Freeman," said Irene. "That trip will have done him a power of good. I'm almost ready for Monday and the wedding. Are you busy this weekend?"

"I haven't given it much thought, Irene," said Gus. He returned to the bungalow, made himself a sandwich, and fell asleep in the lounge by half-past two.

Suzie arrived home at the usual time, and they raced into Devizes to do the weekly shop. Gus told her about Bert's haircut and the visit to the Lamb as they each pushed a trolley around the supermarket. Suzie agreed everything was going to plan.

"Takeaway tonight?" she asked as they loaded their shopping into the boot of the Focus.

"We'll stop to pick up a Chinese on our way home," said Gus.

"I'm looking forward to our first Christmas together, darling," said Suzie.

"Our last together with just the two of us," said Gus.

They reached the bungalow at a quarter past seven and spent fifteen minutes storing away the extra provisions for the holiday period. Then they sat in the kitchen eating their Chinese meal.

"Roll on Tuesday afternoon," said Suzie, "when we can relax. We're off to the Waggon & Horses in an hour."

"Irene asked whether we had a busy weekend planned," said Gus.

"We need to visit Worton," said Suzie. "Our cars need cleaning and valeting. We've still got to pick up a tree, and we've done nothing to decorate the bungalow. I haven't bought a single present yet, and we're out with the happy couple at the Fox & Hounds tomorrow night."

Gus sighed. Geoff Mercer had put everything on hold for a few days. If he could forget about the case for the next six days, Gus should too.

They left the bungalow a little after half-past eight and drove to Harrington End. Grass verges close to the Waggon & Horses had suffered with the volume of rain and extra traffic due to the festive season. There was far more mud than grass. The emergency services would struggle to reach the pub with the number of cars double-parked on the lane tonight. Gus prayed they weren't required.

Suzie led the way into the back bar. They were the first to arrive. Gus ordered their drinks, and as they stood discussing whether it was naff to have lights simulating snow hanging from the eaves of the bungalow, they were joined by Neil Davis.

"You made it, Neil," said Gus. "Happy Christmas. How are Melody and Beatrice?"

"They're doing fine, Gus," said Neil. "We're all better, now mother-in-law has gone home. How have you been?"

"Secretive," said Suzie.

"I've been checking out a few things on behalf of Geoff Mercer," said Gus. "Nothing worth mentioning."

"Which means it is," said Suzie. "Have you heard from the others, Neil?"

"I spoke to Alex," said Neil. "That early-intervention scheme was kicked into touch today. They won't want either of us back in the New Year. Alex said Raj Sengupta told Lydia she'd done a great job clearing the backlog of records he'd amassed. Raj thought he could cope in January for the short period before his assistant's maternity leave was up."

"They'll be here soon," said Suzie.

Gus took a large sip of his glass of Malbec.

Suzie was right; Alex and Lydia entered the back bar minutes later, followed by Amazing Grace and Blessing.

Gus watched as his four colleagues paused at the bar to order drinks. Lydia looked across and waved. Not long to wait now. Blessing was the first to come across to speak to him.

"Evening, guv. Jamie's working tonight, so Grace brought me in the Batmobile."

"You can let your hair down, Blessing," said Neil.

"Did you come by taxi, Neil?" asked Suzie.

He shook his head.

"Melody couldn't come, so she suggested I drove. I can see her point. Beatrice will wake up every few hours. She's no respecter of hangovers at this stage."

"You're in good company, Neil," said Suzie. "That's four of us on non-alcoholic drinks. Not much of a party, is it?"

"As we've been separated for the past couple of weeks, there isn't much to celebrate," said Blessing.

"Here comes Divya," said Neil. "You need to make that five, Suzie. Arjun must be busy at the hospital."

Alex and Lydia had reached Gus's side.

"Are you two ready for your trip to Scotland?" he asked.

"We're on the train to Edinburgh tomorrow," said Lydia. "Do you have a minute, guv? Let's find a quiet spot."

They stood at the end of the bar, next to an inflatable Father Christmas.

"I called Morris Beard this morning," said Lydia.

"I appreciate you letting me know," said Gus.

"No, you don't understand," said Lydia. "I thanked him for considering me for the position, but I realised what excited me about getting out of bed every morning for the past nine months. I want to continue working with you as long as they let me. If they're stupid enough not to ask you back in the New Year, I'll suffer working for the likes of Raj Sengupta until I get to work with a proper detective like you."

"I was convinced they'd persuaded you to accept, Lydia," said Gus. "I can't promise what will happen in January. Although Geoff Mercer is speaking to me again, I haven't heard from the Chief Constable."

"Common sense will prevail," said Lydia. "As for the job with the PCC's team, when you translate their mission statement into plain English, it's impractical and idealistic. I want to make a real difference, not attend meetings which never result in lasting positive actions."

"I'm surprised, and humbled, Lydia," said Gus. "I'm sure you'll find the right move for you in time. So enjoy Christmas with your mother, and I'll ask Geoff Mercer to let everyone know if there's any change in the CRT situation before Wednesday, the second of January. In normal circumstances, that would be the day we return to the Old Police Station office."

"Got it, guv," said Lydia, kissing him on the cheek.

They returned to the far corner of the room. Suzie was deep in conversation with Neil and Alex, and Lydia caught up with Blessing and Divya, who were heading for the Ladies. That left Grace on her own.

"Good evening, Grace," said Gus. "How was it this week with Bromham's farming community?"

"Most of them are like John Ferris," said Grace. "Working hard from dawn to dusk, drowning in paperwork, and still managing to greet you with a smile. It's not a job. It's a way of life."

"Have you heard anything about what lies beyond?" asked Gus.

"I'm as much in the dark as you, Gus," said Grace. "Blessing and I completed our stint with the Farm Watch initiative today. The silence from London Road over what we do next is deafening. Unless someone tells me differently, I'll be at the office with Blessing on Wednesday week. How have you kept yourself occupied?"

"Suzie gave me a list of chores," said Gus. "Earlier this evening, she coolly added to that list. So my feet won't touch the ground between now and Christmas."

"Suzie told me you had an early morning call from DS Mercer one day this week," said Grace. "She wondered if I had any idea what was behind it. I didn't, of course. If it concerned the team, I'm sure you would have said."

"Of course, I would, Grace," said Gus.

"Was it something I could help with?" asked Grace.

"Geoff uncovered a couple of anomalies, Grace," said Gus. "He's only got until the end of February before he retires, and he needed another pair of hands to help him put those anomalies to bed."

"Suzie made it sound more important than that. She told me you were excited about getting stuck into an investigation once Geoff gave you the green light."

"Perhaps I overreacted," said Gus. "I'm not enjoying being on gardening leave, and the prospect of a few days checking arcane facts felt like manna from heaven."

"I've known you long enough to know when you're feeding me a load of bull, Gus," said Grace. "The fact you can't tell Suzie what's behind it suggests it's serious, am I right?"

"I couldn't possibly comment," said Gus. "Tonight was supposed to be a social occasion, Grace. Who knows, it might be the final time we meet as colleagues. I fully expected to learn Lydia would be working with the crowd at the other end of the office from the New Year, but she's sticking with the CRT."

"Lydia called me earlier this evening," said Grace. "The news didn't come as a shock to me, Gus. I couldn't understand why you were such a formidable outfit when I joined you, but I soon found out. You've tried to steer the conversation from what you and Geoff are working on, but no dice. Surely, with the five of us working on it, we'll get a result quicker?"

"Nothing will happen in the next ten days, Grace," said Gus. "So, do yourself a favour, forget about it, and go home to your family. Christmas is a time for burying hatchets, settling grievances, and building bridges. That should be enough cliches to tide you over until the New Year."

"I can tell you're not going to tell me anything," said Grace. "Which scares me. Suzie's worried too, and that's not what she needs right now."

"Are you ready for another drink?" asked Gus.

"I'm drinking cranberry and apple juice," said Grace. "I've got to carry Blessing upstairs later, by the looks of it."

They walked to the bar, and Gus ordered another Malbec plus Grace's soft drink.

"How's Blessing's boyfriend?" asked Gus.

"Jamie's fine; they're fine," said Grace.

"You haven't found anyone yet?"

"Jamie threatened to bring one of his mates to the farm after Christmas. I've agreed to drive home on Sunday to spend four nights with my parents. If it's a disaster, I'll drive back to Worton earlier, and maybe four of us will spend a night out in Devizes before New Year."

"What about Blessing?" asked Gus. "What's she doing for the holidays?"

"Her and Jamie are off to Englishcombe for Christmas dinner with Kelechi and Maryam. Jamie's working on Boxing Day, so if she returns to Worton, Blessing will be getting spoiled rotten by Jackie Ferris."

"Everyone's having a break for a few days. So that's good," said Gus. "Suzie and I will drop in to see her parents on Boxing Day, I imagine. I've forgotten the details. It's all so different this year."

Grace laughed.

"Will you promise me something, Gus?" asked Grace. "Remember, teamwork has been the cornerstone of everything you've achieved this past nine months. We're ready and willing to help in any way we can."

"I know, Grace," said Gus, "and it's much appreciated."

The others gathered in the corner of the bar when they returned to join them. Gus realised Neil was getting ready to leave.

"Off so soon, Neil?"

"This is a first, guv," he said. "My eyes are dropping, and the broken nights are taking their toll."

"The truth is you're missing Beatrice," said Divya, "and Melody, of course."

Neil said his final goodbyes and left.

"I haven't had a chance to speak to you yet, Divya," said Gus. "Everything okay?"

"We were busy in the Hub this week," said Divya. "It never stops. I've got a skeleton crew in over the holiday period, praying there's no major incident, at least until New Year's Eve. Arjun feels the same in that respect. Suzie tells me you have a wedding to attend on Christmas Eve. How wonderful."

"I'm looking forward to it," said Gus, and then he had a thought.

"We're very grateful for everything you do for us, Divya. Was there anything in particular that caused a spike in the Hub's activity this week?"

"Not especially. We had a few technical issues, and several file records disappeared. No doubt it was a glitch my team can rectify."

Gus was glad he'd asked, and he wasn't sure it was a glitch. Someone at London Road with access to the Hub was intent on sabotaging Geoff's search for the identity of the rogue officers.

Chapter Eleven

Saturday, 22 December 2018

GUS AND SUZIE hadn't been late home from the Waggon & Horses. Neil had been first to make tracks, with Alex and Lydia not far behind them. That was understandable, with a long day's travel ahead.

Grace managed to persuade Blessing not to dance around the bar with the inflatable Father Christmas, and Divya wanted to get to work early to help locate those missing files. It wasn't the party they had planned, but Gus knew there had been a positive side. Lydia's decision gave him a warm feeling. Unfortunately, Divya's revelation only served to reinforce the threat the group he'd termed the brotherhood posed.

While Suzie showered and got ready to hit the shops, Gus went outside to the Focus to send Geoff Mercer a message. Geoff replied before Gus could get the burner phone back in the glove compartment.

'If Divya believes the attack occurred inside the Hub building, that

drastically reduces the number of possible culprits. Based on Bethany's assessment, the men we're after would be between fifty and fifty-five.'

Gus replaced the burner phone and returned indoors. Geoff was right. Only a handful of people at London Road would have the correct access code on their security pass and be in the suitable age group. The net was closing.

THE REST of Saturday morning was spent searching for a Christmas tree to fit into the corner of the lounge. Gus hadn't bothered with decorations of any kind since Tess died. That gave Suzie free rein to purchase tree ornaments and lights, plus all manner of colourful items that would make the place look festive. Finally, they brought the tree and trimmings home and paused for a coffee and a sandwich.

"We'll dress the tree before we visit my parents tomorrow morning," said Suzie.

Suzie drove them into Devizes after lunch to buy last-minute presents for family and friends. After battling the crowds for two hours, Suzie handed Gus half-a-dozen bags.

"Lock those in the boot of my car, darling," she said. "You'll pass a couple of shops on the way to the car park. I'm sure you'll think of something."

Gus checked his pocket. He'd remembered to bring his wallet. What a relief. Suzie disappeared in the opposite direction, promising to meet him at the car in twenty minutes. Gus didn't panic when she hadn't materialised thirty minutes later. As he waited in the Golf, he wondered whether next Christmas would be more manic or less. How could he tell? He had nothing to compare it against.

When Suzie eventually joined him ten minutes later, he wondered what she had bought. Whatever it was fitted inside her bag. Then again, the Dagenham Girl Pipers could have been hiding there for months.

"I bought a choice of wrapping paper," said Suzie as she drove away from the car park.

"Very thoughtful," said Gus. Suzie sighed.

Gus tried to remember when he'd last seen wrapping paper in the bungalow. It came to him as they entered the village and passed the allotment. He'd used several half-used rolls for birthdays, anniversaries, and Christmas to start a bonfire a couple of years ago.

Everything was put on hold until the morning. The longer-than-planned afternoon shop meant they needed to shower and change, ready to collect the Reverend and Brett from the Rectory.

As they left the bungalow, Gus remembered Suzie was driving the Focus tonight. He couldn't think of a reason for her to root about in the glove compartment, but stranger things had happened. There was nothing to be done now.

Clemency and Brett were waiting outside the Rectory when they arrived.

"Sorry if we're a couple of minutes late," said Suzie. "We've had a busy day."

"Tell me about it," said Brett. "I thought we were ready for the wedding, but Clem suddenly panicked and thought of several 'must have' items."

"My parents are arriving tomorrow lunchtime," said the Reverend. "I'm off-duty on the Sunday before Christmas for the first time in a decade. I couldn't let my mother have a minor detail to complain about. Everything has to be perfect."

"We owe you guys a lot," said Brett. "Bert hasn't stopped talking about his haircut, the two pints of cider he had in the Lamb, and the coincidence that he's had his hair cut by a husband *and* his wife. Irene wondered whether Bertie should call the Guinness World Records people."

"I enjoyed yesterday morning as much as Bert did," said Gus. "You seem on top form, Brett. How did Part Two of your stag do go last night?"

"A good time was had by all," laughed Clemency. "I heard about it at three o'clock this morning when he got home."

"Really?" asked Suzie.

"Brett phoned me from his place, silly," said the Reverend.

The Fox & Hounds was packed to the rafters with revellers. The four friends made their way to their reserved table and ordered food and drinks. As they made their way outside again three hours later, the Reverend invited them to the Rectory tomorrow afternoon to meet her parents.

"The rest of my gang will travel to Urchfont on the day," said Clemency. "My parents wanted to stay at a hotel in Devizes until the day after Boxing Day."

"When will you and Brett get away for a honeymoon?" asked Suzie.

"I couldn't persuade the Bishop to let me have two weekends off," said Clemency. "So we're off to the coast for three nights after we've said goodbye to my parents."

Brett and Gus were nodding off in the back seat of the Focus while Suzie and the Reverend were chatting. They had enjoyed the double brandies so much on Wednesday night it only felt right to continue the tradition in the Fox & Hounds.

Sunday, 23 December 2018

GUS DIDN'T GET MUCH of a lie-in. His head was still thumping when he set about getting the Christmas tree in the exact spot Suzie wanted. An hour later, the inside of the bungalow had been transformed.

"Just the outside left to decorate," said Suzie.

"We told Jackie we would be at the farm by eleven," said Gus.

"Okay," said Suzie. "But we'll do it next year, for definite."

Gus didn't argue. Perhaps Suzie would be so busy with the baby she'd forget. They drove to Worton, exchanged presents to be opened on Christmas Day, and then Jackie insisted they stayed for brunch. Gus was feeling more like his usual self by the time they left to drive to the Rectory in the late afternoon.

Clemency answered the door and invited them inside.

"Brett's made himself scarce," she whispered. "My mother doesn't think he should see me until tomorrow."

"He can always phone you," said Gus. "I've heard that can be quite entertaining."

"Stop it, Gus," said Suzie.

Clemency introduced them to Douglas and Elizabeth Bentham. The Reverend's father looked to be from a military background, while her mother was an older, fuller version of her daughter.

"How was your trip from Dorchester, Mr Bentham?" asked Gus.

"The usual roadworks and potholes. Don't know what the country's coming to."

"Where are you staying in Devizes?" asked Suzie.

"The Bear," said Mrs Bentham.

Gus knew it well. He hoped Elizabeth didn't bump into any members of the FEW while they were staying there.

"Elizabeth read about it a few months ago," said Douglas Bentham. "A maid was outside the rear of the hotel some years ago and noticed a grey figure closing the curtains in a room she knew was unoccupied. She entered the hotel and went straight to the room to double-check. She was correct; the room was empty."

"Yet you still decided to stay there?" asked Suzie.

"Oh yes," said Elizabeth. "We asked to sleep in that particular room."

Gus expected the Reverend to offer to lend her Mother a Bible, but she never said a word.

"What time will Richard and Ruth arrive tomorrow?" asked Suzie. "I can't wait to meet their twins."

"Richard knows he needs to get here by ten o'clock at the latest," said Douglas. "Weddings always produce a late drama in my experience. Olivia and Sophie will need to behave better than they usually manage. Richard lets them get away with far too much."

Tomorrow will be fun, thought Gus. Thank goodness he and Suzie weren't keen on getting hitched.

"Come on, Gus," said Suzie. "Clemency wants to spend time with her parents. They'll see enough of us tomorrow. We've got things to do."

As soon as they were in the car outside, Suzie remembered the car wash and valeting she'd thought vital before tomorrow. She drove them back to the bungalow.

"We'll take the cars to the garage close to the supermarket," she said. "While you're moving through the car wash, clear out any rubbish from the footwells, the centre tray, and the glove compartment. Then we'll stand back while those Lithuanian lads do their thing."

Gus sighed with relief. He could grab the burner phone while the Focus was covered in foam and water. An hour later, the two cars looked a picture, inside and out. It wouldn't last, there was rain forecast for Boxing Day, but it's the thought that counts. They drove back to the bungalow, parked the cars under the rambling roses, and went indoors. Suzie turned on the lights on the Christmas tree. Gus crossed his fingers, but they didn't disappoint.

"We're ready," she said. "What shall we do now?"

"Tomorrow will be another long day," said Gus. "I vote for a snack, a quiet night in front of the TV, followed by an early night. And hope there are no ghosts."

Christmas Eve, 24 December 2018

DOUGLAS BENTHAM'S concerns were misplaced. Although Christmas Day would bring persistent rain showers, there were no significant dramas during the morning. The weather behaved in Urchfont, and Gus showered and shaved without incident. He was suited and booted by eleven o'clock.

Suzie had already left after an early breakfast. She drove to the Rectory to meet the bridesmaids, calm the bride, and open the front door to Connie Yorath, the mobile hairdresser.

"I've got my daughter, Jasmine, with me," Connie told Suzie. "She can handle any requests for nails and make-up. We'll make sure everyone looks their best."

Ruth, the twin's mother, had delivered them to the Rectory and returned to the Bear Hotel, where her husband and in-laws were waiting for the off.

Elsewhere in Urchfont, Irene North had managed to get Bert into his best suit and attached his buttonhole.

"You look smart, Bertie," she purred.

"Thank you, Irene," said Bert. "You do, too. Frank would be proud of you. Now, what time's the car coming?"

"Mr Freeman will be here at twenty to twelve, Bertie. He wants an extra five minutes with your grandson before the church bells drown out conversation."

"I expect he wants to tell Brett it's not too late to make a run for it," said Bert. "That's what my best man did. Last chance, he said, as the bus pulled up outside the pub."

"It's been a long time since a bus did that," said Irene.

Gus collected Bert and Irene at twenty to twelve on the dot and drove along the lane to St Michael's church. Brett was standing in the porch chatting with the vicar.

"Have you got the rings, Brett?" asked Gus when they'd walked up the long path to the church.

"All present and correct, Gus," said Brett. "I can't believe how many villagers are inside already."

"The Reverend is a popular lady," said Gus. "She's thrown herself into village life, and they've accepted her as one of their own."

Brett handed over two ring boxes. Gus put them into his suit pocket while Brett went inside with Bert and Irene. Gus watched from the aisle as Brett introduced his grandfather to members of Clemency's family. The vicar welcomed more people as they filed into the small church. Gus joined Brett in the front row of the pews. The bells began to chime.

"Clem only paid for five minutes," whispered Brett. "She can't stand much more than that. They can scrape together six ringers, but two are deaf, and timing has become an issue."

Outside, several villagers stood by the wall on the lane, waiting for the bride to arrive. At one minute to noon, the wedding cars drew up at the entrance. Suzie stepped out of the first car, followed by two excited young girls, Olivia, and Sophie. The bridesmaids and matron of honour looked radiant. Connie and Jasmine Yorath could be proud of their handiwork.

Clemency, in her ivory gown, got out of the second car and was escorted to the entrance by her father. Douglas Bentham's back seemed straighter than ever. Today was a day he'd prayed for but never thought would happen.

The stand-in vicar was hovering, making sure everyone was where they should be, and after a brief word with his colleague, led the way to the church door. The strains of the Wedding March by Mendelssohn brought the congregation to their feet.

"The organist is good," said Gus.

"They haven't had one for years," said Brett. "Thank goodness for compact discs."

Forty-five minutes later, Brett and Clemency Penman stood in the church porch for the first of many photographs.

Gus and Suzie walked beside one another from the chancel steps.

"It went without a hitch," said Suzie.

"I'm sure that augurs well for the future," said Gus.

They followed the happy couple down the path to the lane. There was no need for cars to take anyone to the reception. It was only a short walk to the Lamb. Safer all round, considering the champagne the landlord had on ice. The fire had been lit soon after he got out of bed, so the wedding party was sure of a warm welcome.

Everyone was soon indoors and toasting the bride and groom. Brett and Gus had spent valuable time chatting with the landlord at closing time on Wednesday to finalise the menu. When the covers were removed to reveal the spread, even Elizabeth Bentham was impressed.

Gus performed his duties as best man well, despite his lack of experience. The speeches were kept to a minimum, and the Reverend only offered a few words of thanks to everyone who had dashed away from Christmas preparations to be there. She promised to keep the sermon she'd prepared until Sunday.

Gus spotted Bert and Irene in a corner, with refreshments in front of them. Bert was chatting to regulars that hadn't seen him for a while. Irene looked happier than she had for weeks.

It was five o'clock before anyone left and almost seven before Gus called for a taxi to take Bert and Irene home. Richard and Ruth Bentham rounded up their daughters and said their goodbyes to family and new friends before heading back to Weymouth. Brett and Clemency thanked the landlord for a fantastic day and walked to the Rectory with her parents. Douglas Bentham shook Gus by the hand before he left.

"We'll have a hot drink with Clemency and Brett and then get a taxi to the hotel," he said. "Hope everything goes well with the baby."

"Thank you, Mr Bentham," said Gus. "I hope you get another undisturbed sleep tonight."

"We should get home, darling," said Suzie. "It's been a long day, and I would love to get out of this dress and these shoes."

The bar was filling with another round of partygoers, so Gus had a final word with the landlord. He wished him a Happy Christmas and walked with Suzie to the bungalow.

"The clouds are masking the stars tonight," said Suzie.

"The security light over the front door is good enough to find our way," said Gus.

"It's not as pretty as the string of lights we've stored in the second bedroom," said Suzie.

"Nice try, sweetheart," said Gus.

Thursday, 27 December 2018

GUS COULDN'T BE sure when Geoff Mercer would be in touch. He'd mentioned trying to get information from Lily Griffin but hadn't given details of his other contact. The burner phone was still in the glove compartment of the Focus.

"I was wondering whether to drive to Bert's house," he said. "Just to check that they had a good Christmas. Irene was cooking dinner, and with Brett and the Reverend otherwise engaged, they were on their own."

"If you give me fifteen minutes, I can come with you," said Suzie.

"That's okay; it will only be a flying visit. I'll be back before you know it."

Suzie watched Gus dash out of the bungalow and heard the Focus go into the lane. What was he up to? She was resting on the settee in the lounge with a coffee and a piece of shortbread.

They had slept late on Christmas morning and had a slice of buttered toast with their first coffee before exchanging presents. Suzie was wearing the necklace Gus had purchased, and he had several new shirts and sweaters in the wardrobe. Nothing pink on this occasion.

After visiting her parents on Sunday, Suzie realised

turkey with all the trimmings wasn't necessary. Instead, Jackie had insisted they spend most of Boxing Day at the farm. So, before going to bed on Monday night, they located the lamb joint that had worked its way to the bottom of the freezer. Slow-cooked lamb was just what they needed when they sat down to dinner at six in the evening.

The whole day wasn't the traditional way of celebrating Christmas, but they had watched enough mindless TV shows for the year. They listened to music, watched the lights sparkling on their first Christmas tree, and didn't feel guilty about going to bed at ten.

Boxing Day at Worton Farm was just as Suzie knew it would be. Her father was tending to the animals when they arrived at noon. Her brothers had already paid their regular brief visit and left. They had work to do on their farms too. Jackie was busy in the kitchen, as ever, and when Gus and Suzie entered the kitchen, they found Blessing Umeh helping her.

"I wondered whether you would come back," said Suzie. "What rotten luck Jamie's on duty today. How was Englishcombe?"

"We had a lovely Christmas," said Blessing. "Jamie drove us down on Christmas Eve, and then...."

"Go on, Blessing," said Jackie. "Wash that flour off your hands first."

Suzie had guessed what was coming. Gus was clueless, of course.

Blessing was soon wiping her hands dry and taking something from her purse.

She showed Gus and Suzie her left hand.

"Jamie asked me to marry him on Christmas Eve," said Blessing. "I said yes, of course, and then he had to ask for my father's blessing in the morning. My parents were over the moon. I'm so happy."

"What a beautiful ring, Blessing," said Suzie. "The sapphires and diamond combination is timeless."

"Congratulations, Blessing," said Gus. "Has Grace heard the news yet?"

"I rang her on Christmas morning," said Blessing. "Grace's parents gave her a frosty reception, as she expected, but her brothers persuaded her to stick it out until tomorrow. Grace will be back at the farm by lunchtime. We were working on her vegan treats when you arrived. Jamie's free on Friday night, and we're going into Devizes for a meal and a few drinks."

"Another celebration," said Gus. "I hope Grace is going with you."

Blessing giggled.

"She has no idea what Jamie has in store. He threatened to bring one of his mates along, and she dreaded getting stuck with a military policeman talking shop. Jamie also has friends in the Army, people he plays sports with. Major Marcus Sanders is Grace's blind date. He's with the Armoured Infantry Brigade at Bulford camp."

"A hunk?" asked Suzie.

"Oh yes," said Jackie. "Jamie showed me his five-a-side football team photo. Marcus is a thirty-five-year-old hunk, alright."

"He's a keeper," said Blessing.

"It's too soon to say that, surely?" said Gus.

"A goalkeeper, Gus," tutted Jackie.

John Ferris returned to find them still laughing.

Their afternoon had been spent eating, chatting, and laughing. It was late before they drove back to the bungalow. Today, all she wanted to do was chill out. She'd offered to get ready to accompany Gus to Bert's, but she was happier relaxing here with her shortbread selection. There was one thing missing: another cup of coffee.

As soon as she reached the kitchen, Gus came through the front door.

"Everything okay?" she asked. "Do you want a coffee?"

"Bert and Irene are fine, and I've just had a coffee with them."

Gus didn't tell Suzie Bert had added a generous slug of Irish whiskey to his mug.

He kept the news he'd received from Geoff Mercer quiet, too.

Geoff had spoken to Ned Milkins, a retired Detective Superintendent, who had worked at Gablecross in his late twenties as a DS and most of his thirties as a Detective Inspector. Gus calculated that meant his spell in Swindon covered the closure of the old police station in Wootton Bassett, the transfer to Lime Kiln, and the first murder investigation.

Gus had asked Geoff where his mate was working during the Marie Legrand and Claire Dyke murders. For the first murder, Milkins was at Polebarn Road in Trowbridge. Then, when Claire Dyke was killed in 2007, he was at London Road, in what was now Suzie's office.

Geoff had too much to tell Gus in the brief conversation they had. They had agreed to meet tomorrow at lunchtime at the Raven in Poulshot. Gus knew it was a country pub about eight miles from Urchfont with a stellar reputation for its food. Geoff wasn't putting as much distance between them and the enemy as Gus would have liked. He had to hope his friend knew what he was doing.

"A penny for them," said Suzie.

"I might drive into Devizes tomorrow," said Gus. "I

can't imagine we're in a rush to visit the supermarket. We haven't made a dent in what we bought last Friday yet. If you have a couple of items that we need, give me a list, and I'll pick them up on my way home."

"Home from where?" asked Suzie.

"Nowhere special," said Gus. "Geoff Mercer texted me while I was at Bert's, that's all."

"I see," said Suzie. She was positive Gus's mobile had been in the lounge when she sat in there earlier.

Friday, 28 December 2018

GUS LEFT the bungalow at a quarter to twelve to drive to Poulshot. Geoff Mercer's car was already parked in the small car park when he arrived. Gus left the Focus in a spot as far away as possible and had to step across several puddles to reach the pub door.

Geoff was sitting at a corner table with a white-haired lady. He hadn't asked where Lily Griffin, the former HR lady, lived.

"Gus Freeman, this is Lily Griffin, an ex-colleague from London Road."

"Pleased to meet you, I'm sure," said Lily. "I remember your name."

"Yes, I worked at Bourne Hill for years," said Gus. "I'll get a drink and join you."

"We'll order food now you've arrived, Gus," said Geoff. "Grab a couple of menus from the bar, could you?"

Gus was soon back with menus, and a slimline tonic, ice, and lemon.

"Lily was able to tell me a lot about the men we're after,

Gus," said Geoff. "Perhaps it's no big surprise, but they had various disciplinary issues."

Geoff went to the bar to place their food orders. Lily Griffin told Gus what she'd heard when she interviewed officers at London Road who were leaving the force.

"One of the WPCs who worked at the Wootton Bassett station told me she tried to report a colleague for making inappropriate remarks," said Lily. "I won't reveal her name. She's married with children now and left before the move to Lime Kiln. Several of the boys on the motorway patrols would joke about female victims of rape and sexual offences. One officer, in particular, would openly admit his connections with the National Front and bragged about intimidating women when he was on patrol. The poor girl waited months before hearing back about her complaint. Meanwhile, she bumped into the man almost every day. Eventually, George Bailey told her there was no case to answer. The matter had been dealt with ages ago. She asked why nobody bothered to tell her. Bailey shrugged and said nobody else had a problem working with Mick Reynolds, so the fault must lie with her."

"Did Reynolds transfer to Lime Kiln?" asked Gus.

Lily nodded.

"He came to us from Cambridge. I think we both know why they moved him on. The WPC had believed any complaint she made was anonymous, but Mick Reynolds' colleagues made her aware he knew who was responsible."

"That would have made things a darn sight worse when they came across one another in the station building," said Gus.

"Reynolds treated her like dirt, made snide remarks as they passed, and his mates put her in the 'difficult' pile," said Geoff. "We've heard that term before from several police stations. The women involved felt it impossible to encourage victims of domestic abuse or sexual assault to come forward and report incidents when so many of them had lost faith in the system. In the end, many quit because they realised there would never be any support from their superiors."

"The women who were termed 'difficult' often reported having been passed over for advancement, despite having the relevant qualifications," said Lily. "They would tell me there was no point staying if a man was always going to get the promotion, regardless of what a bigot he was."

"How old is Reynolds now?" asked Gus.

"Fifty-three," said Lily. She got up and went to the Ladies.

"I know what you're thinking, Gus," said Geoff. "Don't forget Lily worked in HR until 2008. That was two years after what they called the new Police Pension Scheme was introduced. Several of the men we're discussing had joined at eighteen, which meant they could retire before they reached fifty, provided they had completed thirty years of service. Others who have since gone to work with Highways England had joined young enough to complete twenty-five years of service, which enabled them to also retire at fifty."

"So, how many men who fell in the right age bracket were at Lime Kiln between 1998 and 2007?" asked Gus.

"Six," said Geoff. "One of those was Mick Reynolds."

"Hold on," said Gus. "We've been keeping our cards close to our chests so far. Everything we know about these six men suggests they'll stop at nothing to keep their past crimes hidden. I don't like the idea of putting Lily in danger."

"Well, Lily thought it was a risk worth taking," said Geoff. "I'll let her tell you why when she gets back."

Lily Griffin arrived back just as their pies arrived. When Gus saw the dishes of vegetables that followed, he sighed. The chef here would rival Jackie Ferris for quantity if nothing else.

"Tell Gus what you told me at the weekend, Lily," said Gus.

"I'm going to live with my sister," said Lily. "She's on her own too, and she's begged me to join her for a few years. I thought I was too old to start a new life in Australia, but she's the only family I have left."

"When do you leave?" asked Gus.

"The middle of January," said Lily.

"Fair enough," said Gus. "Right, who have we got?"

Chapter Twelve

GEOFF SHOWED Gus the list of names Lily Griffin had provided.

"I'm afraid this won't be every officer that committed offences or made inappropriate comments working in the county at the time," said Lily. "I'd like to believe things were at their worst thirty years ago, and we've got rid of the vast majority of the problem. I've not been close to the situation for several years, but I fear we've got some way to go."

"We're well aware of that, Lily," said Geoff. "There are still young women in our police stations suffering this behaviour daily. It can't be right for it to be normal for them to deal with unwanted sexual attention or advances."

"We must bring the men on this list to account," said Gus. "Every successful prosecution improves the situation for the officers targeted, and the culture within each station has to be better once the rotten apples are thrown out."

"Our biggest battle will be regaining public confidence," said Geoff. "When we finally get these men to court, we'll be getting justice for people like Bethany Cunningham and the families of Marie Legrand, Claire Dyke, and Susannah Buxton. But unmasking their killer as a serving police officer or a Highways England employee will be damaging. There's no escaping that."

Gus studied the list. Geoff had added footnotes gathered from Ned Milkins.

Mick Reynolds, the racist bully from Cambridge, was at the top.

Frank Pickering from Exeter, fifty-three years old, had earned a reputation as both a racist and a homophobe. Reynolds and Pickering had been young PCs paired on the M4 patrols operating out of Wootton Bassett and Lime Kiln. They continued to work as a team after the patrols stopped, and until they retired, aged fifty, they covered the Cricklade area.

"Do we know where these two men are now?" asked Gus.

"Reynolds returned to Cambridge to live," said Geoff. "He's been doing security work at football stadiums in East Anglia and London. Pickering went to Highways England and now works on the M5, anywhere between Bridgwater and Exeter, his home town."

Mervyn Hill was born in Swindon and joined Wiltshire Police at eighteen. There were no recorded complaints against him, but Ned Milkins had marked him as a weak character, easily led, someone who wanted to be accepted as one of the lads. So he'd been paired with Keith Nicholls from Bristol. Hill was now fifty-two, one year older than Nicholls. Their work pattern followed the same path as that of Reynolds and Pickering. When they no longer patrolled the M4, they left Lime Kiln each morning to cover the Malmesbury area.

"Nicholls is a piece of work," said Geoff. "Lily remembers him."

"He was in his late twenties when he came to my attention," said Lily. "Nicholls had been married for around six years, the marriage broke down, and he started seeing a WPC from Wootton Bassett. Her name was Sonia Jackson. I heard that six months later, she reported him for actual bodily harm after he refused to accept the end of the relationship. He turned up at her home late at night. Hill sat outside in the car, while Nicholls forced his way inside and attacked her. Although her crime report was registered, the matter was never referred to the Directorate of Professional Standards, and no action was taken. Two years later, Nicholls was arrested on suspicion of rape and placed on restricted duties. A female officer from Malmesbury withdrew her statement after being shunned and verbally abused by her colleagues. One month later, Nicholls had his restrictions lifted; there was no case to answer, so he returned to work."

"Nicholls and Hill left Lime Kiln three years ago," said Geoff. "Hill moved to Spain and was last heard of playing golf near Murcia. So he escaped from Keith Nicholls after the best part of thirty years. His nemesis has been with Highways England in the Midlands. The motorway Nicholls covers stretches from Junction 19 of the M1 at the Catthorpe Interchange, near Rugby, the start point for the M6, and then covers the roads around Birmingham, Staffordshire, and Stoke-on-Trent. Nicholls is single and lives in Wednesbury."

Gus realised the final pair was what he was most interested in.

John Pearce, fifty-one, from Shrivenham, had joined straight from school at eighteen and worked in Wootton

Bassett. He'd covered the M4 patrols with Gerry McLean, four years his senior and a man who had moved south from Glasgow.

"What disciplinary records do these two have?" he asked.

"They sailed close to the wind at Wootton Bassett and then Lime Kiln. Ned Milkins only found a handful of colleagues prepared to speak about them. Let's say McLean was from the same school as Gordon Flowers, and Pearce looked up to him."

"Based on what we heard from Adie Lawrence and Bethany, these two were the ones who stopped them on the M4 when they were returning from Bath," said Gus. "Pearce gave Lawrence a hard time for no reason while McLean hid behind the torch beam leering at Bethany Harford. Then, after her mother went missing, McLean turned up at the house and was heard speaking to this WPC, whose first name was Janet."

"That would have been Janet Gerrish," said Lily. "She lives in Cricklade now, married with grown-up children."

"Would that be the female officer you referred to earlier, Lily?" asked Gus.

"I'm afraid not," said Lily. "Several women worked at Wootton Bassett, both uniform and civilian staff. People like Mick Reynolds didn't differentiate."

"We can place McLean and Pearce in the right area for the first three murders," said Gus. "What about Susannah Buxton?"

"McLean had more than enough service under his belt to retire at fifty, Gus," said Geoff. "He moved to Highways England in 2013 and has worked on the M4 between Swindon and London ever since. Pearce resigned three months after his pal retired. He joined the same outfit, and

Newbury would have been right in the middle of their patch."

"When will they be arrested?" asked Lily.

"We haven't enough concrete evidence yet, Lily," said Gus. "The dots on the map suggest McLean and Pearce worked on the M4 during the four murders. We need to join the dots and add more incriminating facts. If we could get one of these men to talk, it would aid our cause."

"Nothing we've heard so far suggests there's a weak link," said Geoff.

"In that case, we might need to attack their stronghold from another angle," said Gus. "Have you spoken to Divya Yadav since last weekend?"

"I have," said Geoff. "She's a clever girl, that one. After speaking with you on Friday night, she went to work on Saturday to check what CCTV coverage there was of the main car park. Although it wasn't designed to watch staff members entering or leaving the Hub building, the angle from one camera enabled Divya to catch sight of someone she recognised. They came out of the Armed Response Unit complex."

"Was this person in their fifties?" asked Gus.

"Yes," said Geoff. "Divya had two problems. She couldn't tell where they had gone next. When they disappeared off-camera, they could have been heading for the main gate, and the person she saw didn't have the correct accreditation to enter the building. Unless they had stolen another swipe card, they wouldn't have been able to get in."

"So, although we might be able to connect this character to the six men on our list, we can't prove it was him who removed the missing files."

"I told you Divya was a clever girl, Gus," said Geoff. "After living with Arjun for several years, Divya has adopted his belt and braces policy. Nothing to do with his wardrobe, but she had back-ups of our older records in the Cloud."

"You've lost Lily altogether, Geoff," said Gus. "You almost lost me too, but Suzie tried to explain it to me a few weeks back. So, just in case some historical records got deleted by mistake, Divya stored them in digital format on servers in off-site locations. The servers are maintained by a third-party provider responsible for hosting, managing, and securing the data stored on its infrastructure."

"I'm impressed," said Geoff. "Not a dinosaur, after all. Long story short, Divya identified the main file from which the records had been removed, compared it to the Cloud version, and isolated the missing items. I don't profess to understand how she did it, but Divya has eighteen records that someone deemed too incriminating for us to find."

"Six of which you already know," said Lily.

"The six names we have in front of us were all the subject of an individual file," said Geoff. "Those men also had group complaints made against them by people inside and outside the police. The only new name was Derek Calderwood."

"Derek is ARU, is he?" asked Lily.

Gus remembered when he'd worked with the ARU team leader, Jared Hawkins, when they raided The Haven in Avoncliff. Had Derek Calderwood been with them that weekend? Was Annie Matthews still Jared's second-in-command?

"Calderwood worked at Wootton Bassett; I take it?" asked Gus.

"No, only at Lime Kiln, Gus," said Geoff. "He moved to Wiltshire about twenty years ago. Calderwood wasn't involved in the motorway patrols, but he did mix with the crowd that spent time together socially. He switched to firearms about a decade ago, after Lily retired."

"What do we think?" asked Gus. "Calderwood had something to hide, which the brotherhood exploited, or was he a closet racist and woman-hater?"

"I hope we aren't giving men who think like that access to guns," said Lily. "None of us could ever feel safe. Thank goodness I'll be thousands of miles away from it in a few weeks."

"Divya is trying to locate which swipe card was used when she saw Calderwood on CCTV. With only a skeleton crew in that weekend, it should be possible."

"We finished eating ages ago," said Lily, "and nobody seems keen on a dessert. Why don't I say goodbye and walk home? My place is only up the road, and I can't add anything to what you already know. It's over to you two to join the dots."

"We can't thank you enough, Lily," said Geoff. "Gus and I will carry things forward from here. We mustn't draw attention to how far we've got. The fact Calderwood removed those records suggests they know something's going on, but it could have been a precautionary measure."

"Better safe than sorry," said Gus. "Geoff can arrange for surveillance to keep you safe until you catch your flight. We've not spotted anyone tailing us over the past ten days, but we mustn't be complacent."

"When you get to my age, a bit of excitement is rare. So take care, and Happy New Year."

Lily Griffin stood up, wrapped her coat around her and headed to the door, looking left and right before she stepped outside.

"Lily missed her calling," said Geoff. "I suppose it's too late to give MI5 a call?"

"She was right about one thing," said Gus. "We've been here long enough. When do you want to meet again?"

"It will have to be next week," said Geoff. "Look, Kenneth hasn't said anything yet, so I'm going to make an executive decision. It could be one of the last ones I make. You and the team can return to the Old Police Station office on Wednesday. I'll make an excuse to drop in to see you."

"Because you've been out of the office so much, did you hear about Lydia?" asked Gus.

"Everything was up in the air the last time we spoke," said Geoff. "I know she finished working with Raj Sengupta last Friday. Will Lydia be accepting the job with Morris Beard?"

"She told me on Friday night it wasn't what she wanted," said Gus. "Lydia wants to work with a team of detectives."

"That's fine," said Geoff. "Worst case scenario, Lydia's got a couple of months with you, and once we find a team for her, she can move on after Sylvia Robbins gives you the Spanish archer."

Geoff went to the bar to settle the bill, and Gus walked outside to the Focus. It was still raining, and the puddles were deeper now, but as he stepped over the one nearest the driver's door, the penny dropped: the elbow.

Gus drove back to Urchfont keeping a lookout for anyone tailing him. All was quiet on the western front. Susie hadn't thought of anything they needed from the supermarket, but Gus had eaten a meat pie Desperate Dan would have struggled with. No way did he need another meal tonight. He stopped at the supermarket and searched the shelves for something that would tickle Susie's tastebuds.

Susie was still chilling in the lounge when he walked into the bungalow.

"The wanderer returns," she said. "Can I ask where you've been?"

"The Raven at Poulshot with Geoff Mercer," said Gus. "Our main meal was excellent, and we had to stay seated for a while to let it go down. Geoff's given me the green light to return to work. He's contacting the others to tell them to be in the office on Wednesday, when he will come and brief them.

"I didn't expect that," said Lydia. "Has Kenneth spoken to him?"

"Geoff said something about a final executive decision," said Gus.

"Your mobile phone is next to the album rack, if you were looking for it," said Suzie.

Awkward, thought Gus. Perhaps it was time to come clean.

"Look, when Geoff called last week, he told me he suspected a murder committed twenty years ago had been the work of a uniformed police officer."

"Gosh," said Suzie. "Why didn't you tell me?"

"We've been investigating it on the quiet because it's sensitive. Unfortunately, Geoff's found more than one death with a similar MO."

"How many?" asked Suzie.

"Four, so far," said Gus. "It could be more, but Geoff didn't want to go public."

"What did I say about staying out of trouble?"

"We've been ultra careful," said Gus. "Nobody's followed us, and apart from a few records going missing in the Hub, there's nothing to suggest the killer is onto us. If we're right, he doesn't work for Wiltshire Police any longer. Geoff believes he retired and moved to Highways England."

"You know who is responsible?" asked Suzie.

"We believe so," said Gus.

"You can't arrest him, remand him in custody, and then begin the search for evidence to charge him," said Suzie. "How do you stop him from committing another murder while you're finding it?"

"I have an idea, but we need to learn more about the victims," said Gus. "The first murder was twenty years ago. Since then, others that Geoff thinks we can tie to him happened in 2001, 2007, and 2014."

"There's no suggestion of a time-related pattern," said Suzie. "Perhaps the victims mean something to the killer. What do they have in common?"

"They were all a couple of years either side of forty," said Gus. "At the time they died, neither was in a stable relationship. Oh, and they were all strangled, and it's unlikely they were sexually assaulted."

"Were they tall, leggy blondes or buxom brunettes?" asked Suzie.

Gus realised that he hadn't a clue.

"Because we've tried to keep our activity quiet, I've not seen photos of all the victims," said Gus. "Geoff will have them in the murder files he's studied. Perhaps we need to see the four women's photos, side-by-side, on a whiteboard to spot who the killer favours. That's a job for Wednesday."

"Why the uncertainty about a sexual motive?" asked Suzie.

"The first victim had been buried for six months before she was found. The second wasn't found until a month after she went missing. Any DNA evidence was long gone. There's one more common element which is why we were able to home in on our killer. Our four victims were snatched close to the M4, and while he was working for

Wiltshire Police, our prime suspect worked on motorway patrols."

"That might explain the long gap between the last two murders," said Suzie. "You said he moved to Highways England as a traffic officer. Perhaps the opportunities didn't appear as frequently in his new occupation."

Gus had already told Suzie more than he would have liked. He held back the information about the band of brothers formed at Wootton Bassett. The fact they had terrorised several female officers, intimidated male colleagues, and even driven one detective to commit suicide might be too much.

"We'll dig deeper into the victims on Wednesday," said Gus. "Perhaps that will point us towards the quickest way to end his reign of terror."

"All this excitement after a quiet day has made me hungry," said Suzie.

"I've taken care of that, darling," said Gus. "If you can survive another forty-five minutes, I'll dish up a sweet potato, spinach, and lentil dahl for one."

"Wonderful," said Suzie. "What are you having?"

"A few pieces of the shortbread you've been scoffing will suffice. Jackie intended us to share that selection."

Suzie handed over the half-empty tin.

"We'd better make the most of the weekend if your gardening leave is ending. Brett and the Reverend won't be interested in a night at the Lamb on Saturday, and she's got a double dose of church services on Sunday."

"Which leaves us with New Year's Eve on Monday," said Gus. "Do you plan to welcome in 2019 without a drink?"

"We've got good things to look forward to in 2019 as a couple," said Suzie. "Things might not be so rosy for you, but we'll cope with whatever Sylvia Robbins dishes up. Yes,

I'd like to sit here with a hot chocolate, watching the lights sparkling on our tree and the fireworks from London on the television as they count down the seconds. Everything will be fine as long as you're sat next to me."

Gus couldn't mount an argument. So instead, he took a piece of shortbread from the tin and went to the kitchen.

Wednesday, 2 January 2019

GUS AND SUZIE had spent a quiet weekend together. Perhaps it was the usual lethargy that sets in after the anticipation and excitement of the lead-up to a holiday period, but both of them were nervous about what lay beyond this morning.

"The condemned man ate a hearty breakfast," sighed Suzie.

"My first day back seemed to warrant sausage, egg, and bacon," said Gus.

"And a second cup of coffee?" asked Suzie.

Gus nodded.

At eight-thirty, they stepped outside the front door and walked to the cars.

"I'll see you at half-past five, darling," said Gus.

"Say hello to the gang for me," said Suzie. "Tonight, perhaps you'll feel able to tell me why you and Geoff have been running scared of one man."

They didn't promote Suzie to DI just because she was a pretty face, thought Gus.

Suzie led the way through the gateway and into the lane. She waved as she turned towards London Road, and Gus drove down Caen Hill for the first time since he'd visited the locks. It was good to return to the old routine, even if it might last only a few weeks.

The Church Street car park was busy with several town centre businesses re-opening after the interminable Christmas break. Gus thought it unwise that productivity and customer service took a ten-day hit in the UK every year. Whatever next? A four-day week?

Morris Beard and his team's new cars filled three reserved parking bays. They had clearly made themselves at home since Gus had been on gardening leave. Gus parked his Focus in a vacant spot and headed for the lift.

Gus spotted Grace's Smart car as he waited for the lift to descend. The newly engaged Blessing Umeh was riding shotgun. Grace parked the car, and the two girls joined him at the door.

"Happy New Year, guv," they said in unison.

"It's good to be back," said Grace.

"I'm interested to hear what we're going to do," said Blessing.

"We won't have long to wait," said Gus. "There's a convoy of vehicles just turning into the car park."

Neil Davis and Geoff Mercer were alone in their cars, but the red Mini bringing up the rear contained Lydia Logan Barre and Alex Hardy.

"This should be fun," said Grace. "Three into one won't go."

"If they've got any sense, they'll defer to DS Mercer," said Gus. "He won't want to risk his new car getting scratched by a member of the hoi polloi. Lydia and Neil can fight over the spare space after Geoff has left us."

Gus and the girls rode to the first floor. None of them knew what the new office layout would look like. But, when the doors opened, their worst fears were sent packing. The PCC's hit squad was hidden behind a row of free-standing partition screens. Blessing could hear a low buzz of voices and equipment, but where they sat was a mystery.

"Our desks and cabinets are occupying just over half of the space we had before, guv," said Blessing.

"We'll cope," said Grace.

Gus sent the lift to the ground floor.

"We might not have time to catch up until later," said Gus. "I know Blessing had a good Christmas. How about you, Grace?"

"I survived, Gus," she replied. "Things improved when I got back to the farm."

"I've never known Grace smile as much as she has since Friday night, guv," said Blessing. "It suits her."

"Am I right in thinking Friday night was a major success?" asked Gus.

Grace gave him the familiar stare. Her transformation wasn't quite complete. The lift doors opened, Geoff Mercer emerged, followed by three subdued characters. It wasn't like Neil or Lydia to arrive without a wisecrack or a loud greeting.

"Good morning, Gus," said Geoff. "Good to see you two ladies as well. I'm sure you have things to say to one another. But first, I'll check in with Morris to see how they're settling in, and then we'll get to why I wanted to get you back in harness. Back in five minutes."

Geoff disappeared behind the screens, and the buzz of conversation faded.

"We'll have to be quick," said Gus. "Neil, you go first."

"No dramatic change since last Friday night, guv," said Neil. "Beatrice continues to put on weight, and we're coping with the night feeds. I wouldn't claim we've got a system yet, but things get less frantic every day. I won't deny it wasn't welcome news when Mr Mercer called."

"We had a super time in Edinburgh, guv," said Lydia. "My mother had a video call from Chidozie and Rosa in Dubai on Christmas Day. We're flying out again at Easter for a short break. My father is keen to show us the improvements he's made to the restaurant."

"When did you get back to Chippenham?" asked Neil.

"Yesterday," said Alex. "Hogmanay was hectic, and we were in no fit state to face a long train journey the next day, so we arrived home late yesterday afternoon."

"Then the evening was spent shopping and getting clothes ready for work," said Lydia. "We could have done with another day off to recover. What did we miss while we were away?"

"Blessing has news," said Grace.

Blessing showed Lydia her engagement ring.

"Wow, what a rock," said Lydia. Alex didn't comment.

"Does that warrant another trip to the Waggon & Horses, guv?" asked Neil.

"I'll bear it in mind," said Gus.

"What about you, Grace?" asked Lydia.

"Jamie twisted my arm into a blind date with one of his friends," said Grace.

"I want all the details," said Lydia.

Gus wished her luck with that.

"How did your enforced break go, guv?" asked Alex.

"Nothing different to what I mentioned on Friday night, Alex. After the wedding we attended on Christmas Eve, Suzie and I had a quiet Christmas and, apart from a few hours at the farm, didn't venture far from the bungalow."

"Never mind, guv," said Lydia. "Next Christmas will be busier, and it promises to be amazing."

Geoff Mercer returned from his chat with Morris, Sarah, and Rosie.

"Right," he said, sitting at Gus's desk. "Grab a chair and gather round. I don't want what I'm about to tell you to go beyond these four walls. Is that understood?"

Gus saw a sea of nodding heads on his right as he took a seat.

Geoff held up the file he'd brought to his first meeting with Gus.

"A few weeks ago, I stumbled on something in this murder file that didn't feel right. Ever since I started to dig, it felt like I'd removed the pin from a hand grenade, and I needed to cling on to avoid it from blowing up in my face."

Geoff had the team's attention now, right enough.

"Gus and I have done some of the spadework, and so far, we believe we haven't alerted the people involved."

"How many people are involved, sir?" asked Alex.

"We can't be certain," said Geoff, "but a minimum of seven."

"How would anyone know what you were suspicious about, sir?" asked Neil. "Unless they had someone working at London Road."

Geoff told them the whole story, from when Stephanie Harford went missing to the lunchtime meeting with Lily Griffin. After he finished, nobody spoke for thirty seconds.

"Time for coffee, I think," said Lydia. "That was a lot to take in."

Blessing joined Lydia in the restroom while Neil and Alex followed Geoff's instructions.

The CRT half of the office had been transformed when the girls returned with seven hot drinks. The whiteboards and outer walls were covered in maps of the M4 corridor, crime scene photos, and brief histories of every leading player, including the detectives and police surgeons involved. In pride of place, in the centre of the room, next to Gus's desk, was a whiteboard containing four photographs.

"What do you see?" asked Geoff.

"All four victims looked a couple of years younger than their age, sir," said Alex. "If I'm allowed to say that."

"We'll forgive you, just this once," said Lydia. "It wouldn't be right to say they could be sisters, sir, but if we had a headshot of someone close to the killer, we might notice the features that incited him to attack these women."

"That's an excellent observation," said Geoff. "I checked the height and weight of each victim, and they differed in every respect."

"We need more background on Gerry McLean," said Gus. "Grace, can you handle that, please?"

"Got it, guv," said Grace.

"Do you intend to interview the men on the whiteboard simultaneously, sir?" asked Neil.

"We can't pick them off one by one," said Gus. "As soon as the others realise we've got one of their number in custody, they'll be on their toes. So my suggestion would be that we go for the biggest prize first."

"With McLean under lock and key, his brothers might feel ready to speak to us," said Geoff. "That's a thought. What about Derek Calderwood?"

"Call Jared Hawkins as soon as you get back to London Road," said Gus. "Get Calderwood assigned to duties that mean he can't get access to weapons. I don't want our witnesses or anyone in this room getting shot."

Geoff called the ARU team leader and asked him to be in his office at eleven o'clock.

"I'll leave you to get on with things, Gus," said Geoff. "I

don't want to antagonise the Chief Constable by being out of the office all morning. He's got his replacement arriving tomorrow."

Geoff did a quick tour of the material the team had available to them before he said goodbye, and headed for the lift.

"Cover those boards before you leave," he said as the lift doors closed.

"We won't be popular, guv," said Neil. "Who would have thought we had so many rogues in our midst?"

"Come on, Neil," said Alex. "We've all heard the rumours. Your Dad was the subject of a couple in his time. The only people who won't like what we're doing are those with something to hide. Every honest copper will back us to the hilt."

"I've found information on McLean, Gus," said Grace. "How did you intend to remove him from the game, anyway?"

"Unless our intel is screwed, he's spending his days on the M4 with John Pearce. A quiet word with Highways England will allow us to learn their exact location. Their superiors need to be briefed by DS Mercer or the boss. What have you learned?"

"Born in Dalmarnock, Glasgow, in 1963, McLean had a troubled childhood," said Grace.

"Dalmarnock's close to Parkhead, Celtic's ground," said Lydia. "Dalmarnock was a thriving industrial centre after WWII, but the boom only lasted until the end of the Fifties."

"McLean's father moved south looking for work, never to return," said Grace, "He left his wife, Jennie, with three young children. The youngest two infants were taken into care in 1968, but Gerry stayed with his mother. Police were called to the home on several occasions. Neighbours weren't happy about Jennie's choice of employment."

"So, Gerry's mother was a prostitute," said Alex.

"Gerry had to make himself scarce when a client arrived," said Neil. "A troubled childhood is an understatement."

"What happened to Jennie?" asked Blessing.

"She died of a drug overdose in 1973," said Grace. "Gerry found her when he got home from school. He was only ten and, therefore, was taken into care and was never reunited with his siblings. Gerry left the children's unit at eighteen and moved south to Wiltshire, searching for his father. He joined Wiltshire Police at the end of 1981. His first posting was to Wootton Bassett."

"Dalmarnock's in the east end of Glasgow," said Lydia. "If Gerry went to the children's unit there, his troubles had only started. It was the centre of abuse allegations in the early years of this century. Former residents alleged sexual and physical abuse in the 1970s by staff and claimed they were kept hungry or fed pet food. The home closed in the mid-Eighties."

"Do we think Gerry was abused during his time in care?" asked Neil. "On top of his life with his mother, that would be enough to mess with anyone's head."

"It doesn't excuse what we think he's done since, Neil," said Blessing.

"How old was Jennie when she died?" asked Gus.

"Forty," said Grace. "She died on her birthday."

Chapter Thirteen

"DO we have any chance of finding a photograph of Jennie McLean?" asked Lydia.

"We can try the local newspaper," said Blessing. "There may have been a report of her death."

"That local paper would have been the Glasgow Herald back then," said Lydia. "They dropped the Glasgow around the time I was born."

Gus wondered whether they were clutching at straws— an abandoned mother from a rundown part of Glasgow whose kids had been taken into care. Jennie McLean sold herself to pay for drugs, and when she reached forty, she ended it all. It didn't sound like it would have made headline news.

They continued to work on joining the dots throughout the rest of the day.

Geoff Mercer called back to confirm that Jared Hawkins had agreed to keep a close watch on Derek Calderwood and ensure he didn't have access to a gun.

Divya Yadav rang Gus to say she'd discovered whose

swipe card was used to gain access to the Hub building. The details belonged to Annie Matthews, but she wasn't working that morning. Divya believed Calderwood had cloned Annie Matthews' card. Gus asked Divya to sit on the information for the time being.

At a quarter to five, Gus was ready to go home. They would have to dig deeper tomorrow.

His phone rang. It was Vera Butler at London Road.

"Gus, can you be in Kenneth's office at nine in the morning, please? I tried getting you at home. What's going on?"

"Ask Geoff Mercer," said Gus. "I'll see you tomorrow."

As Gus ended the call, Grace got up and hurried to his desk.

"I've got a photograph, Gus," she said. "I was hunting through advertisements online from funeral directors. You know the things they can recommend. Where to get the floral tributes, and which printer offers the cheapest Order of Service. I struck gold when I spoke to someone at the fourth firm on my list. They used a black-and-white photo of Jennie McLean, provided by her parents, in one of their early brochures. Jennie was twenty-six at the time the photo was taken. They've sent me the original. I've used an online app to age Jennie by ten to fifteen years to see what she might have looked like if she'd stayed clean and been alive when Gerry got home on her birthday."

Gus took a long look at the photograph.

"I'm not seeing it yet," he said.

Grace took it from him and moved the photographs of the first two victims to the left, leaving room to place Jennie McLean in the middle.

Lydia and the others stopped what they were doing and watched.

"The eyes," said Lydia. "Just concentrate on the eyes."

"You're right," said Gus. "The brown eyes, the width of the nose at the top, even the eyebrows; they're not identical, but with Gerry McLean's warped mind, as soon as he clapped eyes on these poor women, he saw his mother. The mother whose lifestyle had caused him grief from infancy and delivered him into the hands of predators working at the children's home."

Finally, at one minute to five, Gus believed there was a sliver of hope.

"Tomorrow is another day," said Neil. "Melody will be waiting for me to start my shift with Beatrice."

"You love it, Neil," said Alex. "Same time tomorrow, guv?"

"Grace will be in charge, to begin with," said Gus. "The Chief Constable wants to see me at nine. DS Mercer could be for the high jump, too. Not a great start to the day with Ms Robbins arriving from Durham."

"We'll see you when we see you then, guv," said Lydia. "Despite everything, it's been grand being back in the office."

Gus couldn't argue. He followed Grace and Blessing to the lift, and thirty-five minutes later, he was parking the Focus beside Suzie's Golf.

Thursday, 3 January 2019

GUS WAS first up this morning and stood by the waffle maker while Suzie was in the shower. He had almost finished his first cup of coffee.

Suzie had grabbed him as soon as he got through the

door last night. They had spent an hour in the lounge, where he filled in the gaps in her knowledge. She wasn't a happy bunny.

"You implied this McLean character acted alone," she said. "When I warned you not to take risks, you told me not to worry. Geoff uncovered a group of perhaps a dozen police officers conspiring to cover up a litany of crimes—some involving attacks on females working in the police and four murders, for heaven's sake. McLean even had an accomplice. What was his role in all of this?"

"We don't know," said Gus. "But we'll find out once we've got them in custody."

"When we talked before, you said you didn't have the evidence to arrest McLean. Has that changed today?"

"Not in any material way," said Gus. "We understand his motivation better now, though."

"I don't like it," said Suzie.

"I don't think Kenneth does either," said Gus. "I've been summoned to his office in the morning at nine. I'll follow you into town."

"Well, at least you can drive home if he puts you on gardening leave again."

"Or drive to the office and get my thinking cap on. The photos of the four victims with Jennie McLean gave me an idea."

"Are you going to share something with me on this case, at last?" asked Suzie.

"Too soon, darling," said Gus. "I've got to beg for someone's help first."

Suzie joined Gus in the kitchen. Their waffles were ready, and he poured her coffee.

"What am I going to do with you?" she tutted.

"Congratulate me on a job well done if things work out.

Look, Sylvia Robbins will find a way to kick me out of the Old Police Station office regardless of what happens. If my idea goes pear-shaped, I'm done; and if we take a serial killer off the streets and identify six or seven ex-officers who brought shame on their uniform, we can expect the proverbial to hit the fan. Ms Robbins won't thank me for that."

"It's the right thing to do, darling," said Suzie. "I can see why Geoff wanted you to help him. He needed someone he could trust implicitly, and he couldn't have picked a better man."

They left the bungalow together, and today, Suzie was followed to the London Road car park. She kissed him before dashing upstairs to the mezzanine. Gus signed in at Reception, walked up the stairs, and paused by Vera's desk. The clock on the wall read one minute to nine.

"How are you and Kassie?" he asked.

"I'm fine," said Vera. "Kassie and Noah are still very much an item. She moved in with him before Christmas."

"I hope to get an invitation to the wedding," said Gus. "Kenneth might wear a kilt as he walks her down the aisle. What do you think?"

"I think you'd better get to his office," said Vera.

Gus knocked on Kenneth's door. There was no grunt, just a quiet female voice inviting him to enter. Kenneth Truelove was standing by the window. Sylvia Robbins was seated beside the Chief Constable's desk. Gus recalled a line from a poem:

We shall meet, but we shall miss him. There will be one vacant chair.

"Mercer tells me he asked you to return to the CRT office," said Kenneth, returning to his seat.

"Geoff spoke to me, sir, and told me he would contact the others," said Gus. "We met him yesterday morning, and he told us about a case he'd been working on. He asked for our help, and we set to work at once."

"How can you say that, and keep a straight face, Mr Freeman?" said Sylvia Robbins.

Years of practice thought Gus.

"We are aware of your success with the triple murder case in Salisbury," said Kenneth.

"The way it was achieved doesn't fit with how I intend to operate moving forward," said Sylvia.

"Do you have any comments you wish to make about DS Mercer's handling of this latest case?" asked Gus.

"Mercer explained his theories in detail yesterday evening," said Kenneth.

"We would like the case to be swiftly concluded," said Sylvia. "Every effort must be made to prevent any leaks."

"I don't think DS Mercer planned on speaking to the press, ma'am," said Gus. "We're not keen on letting the suspects know we're on their tail."

"Get to it, Freeman," said Kenneth. "I find the pain doesn't last as long if you rip off the plaster as quickly as possible."

Gus nodded to his boss; they understood one another. Sylvia Robbins looked like she'd swallowed a wasp. Gus couldn't resist a smile before he turned to leave.

Vera looked at the clock as Gus passed her desk.

"Bad news?" she asked.

"Far from it," said Gus. "They've fired the starting gun. Watch this space."

Gus trotted down the stairs, returned to the Focus, and drove to the office.

He turned into the Church Street car park and remembered he had to park in an unreserved spot. Why is it that when something good happens, it's swiftly followed by a kick in the teeth?

Gus found the team beavering away under Amazing Grace's supervision.

"How did it go, Gus?" she asked. "Are we good to continue?"

Gus soon had everyone's attention and relayed the message from London Road. He told them of the idea that came to him when they studied the array of five photographs.

"That could be dangerous, guv," said Lydia. "How would we ensure the arresting officers reach the car in time?"

"We will get full cooperation from Highways England," said Gus. "GPS trackers are fitted to their vehicles to follow the target's movements. Our vehicle will also be traceable and fitted with extras. So the initial stop, and what follows, will be captured in sound and vision."

"How do we deal with the other group of men, guv?" asked Blessing.

"Highways England can monitor and locate their vehicles on the M5 and M6 or at home. After we've grabbed McLean and Pearce, the others will be arrested the minute they return to base or at home. Once the operation is underway, we'll have our targets under twenty-four-hour surveillance. The only one we won't have eyes on will be Mervyn Hill unless one of you plays golf?"

"How long do you think it will be before we get our ducks in a row, guv?" asked Neil.

"There are a lot of things to organise, Neil," said Grace. "We only get one shot at this. There's no point rushing things. We have days, maybe weeks of work ahead of us before we can nail McLean and Pearce for all four murders."

"Exactly," said Gus. "There's little point preparing an elaborate trap unless we have the necessary evidence. The Met tried that approach, sending vanloads of officers, armed to the teeth, to arrest innocent men. We won't be arresting first and hunting for evidence later. Not on my watch. So, start digging, but don't let anyone get wind of what you're up to."

"Alex and I should visit the Gablecross storage facility, guv," said Neil. "It could take weeks, but these officer's note-books should be available for part of the period we need. I doubt we can go back to 1998, but 2007 when Claire Dyke was killed, should be traceable."

"Who could tell us what shifts these men worked while they were at Wootton Bassett?" asked Blessing. "Can we prove where McLean and Pearce were on Sunday, the day of Stephanie Harford's disappearance? After all, McLean was at her home on Tuesday morning."

"Shift patterns get altered at short notice for a murder investigation, Blessing," said Gus. "McLean and Pearce might have been driving near Lydiard Millicent at six on Sunday evening at the start of a shift, but they would have been contacted and told to report in at once."

"Got it, guv," said Blessing.

"It wouldn't have come as a big surprise to them," said Alex.

"Quite," said Gus. "I need to make a call. Wish me luck. Our trap can't be set without securing the right bait."

THE CONVERSATION WAS LENGTHY, and although Gus knew he'd asked the right person for the task, he was asking a lot of her. Somehow, her experiences in the past three years had steeled her resolve, and Gus promised that a successful outcome would bring her dream closer. She would be living in the early days of a better world.

Four days later, Gus received a text message.

'Contact made.'

Monday, 21 January 2019

A FEW MINUTES AFTER FIVE, Suzie was preparing to drive to the bungalow at the end of a quiet day at London Road. The weather was foul, and she couldn't wait to get home. Traffic was busy when Suzie pulled out of the car park. Then, as she turned off the main road towards Urchfont, she passed a dark van parked in a layby one hundred yards beyond the junction. Its headlights were on, and Suzie sensed the engine was idling.

It wasn't uncommon to see a vehicle parked there, but as soon as she passed the layby, the van pulled out behind her. Suzie slowed before the approaching bend in the lane because there was always the risk of oncoming traffic cutting the corner. Country lanes were dangerous places on dark, rainy nights in winter.

The dark van suddenly accelerated past, mounting the grass verge, and then the driver swung his vehicle to the left, causing Suzie to stand on her brakes to avoid a collision.

"Idiot," shouted Suzie.

The van doors opened, and two men got out. Suzie covered her eyes with one hand as two torches were aimed at her windscreen and locked her doors with the other. The first man to reach her driver's door rapped on her window with a baton.

"Don't be stupid. Open the window, or I'll smash it open."

Suzie could see both men wore hi-viz jackets, but the glare from the intense torch beams prevented her from seeing anything more. All she could tell was the man's voice sounded local, and the baton was a police issue. She pressed the button to lower the window an inch.

"It would be a shame if you didn't live long enough to have that baby. Get Freeman to quit. Final warning."

The man backed away slowly, and Suzie concentrated on the passenger. He kept the beam on her face while his colleague jumped in the van. Then the torch went out, the passenger was gone, and the van slowly disappeared down the lane. Suzie tried to get the registration, but it had been removed. She sat in her Golf, shaking.

Gus arrived in Urchfont minutes later. He saw Suzie's Golf ahead of him stopped at the side of the road. Had she broken down? He parked behind her and hurried forward. As soon as he saw her, he knew something was wrong.

"What's happened, darling?" he asked.

"They threatened to kill our baby and me," said Suzie. "Someone must have told them what you were doing."

Gus called Geoff Mercer and told him what had happened.

"Is Suzie okay?" asked Geoff.

"Badly shaken, " said Gus. "I'm concerned about the baby, so we'll get Suzie checked out tonight, and I'll stay home with her tomorrow. Grace can keep our investigations on track tomorrow."

"I'll try to trace the leak, Gus," said Geoff. "Do you want to step away from the investigation?"

"Not a chance," said Gus. "It's personal now."

Tuesday, 22 January 2019

GUS AND SUZIE had spent several hours at the Great Western Hospital, where staff reminded them extreme stress could trigger an early birth. However, the baby's heartbeat was regular. Nothing at this stage suggested the shock of the near accident would be serious.

Suzie was calmer by the time they left Swindon. However, this morning her calm demeanour had turned to anger.

"Who the heck do they think they are?" she said as she stormed into the kitchen.

"I told Geoff everything you could remember last night about the van and the two men," said Gus. "Surveillance will be in place from this morning, not just here, but at Lily Griffin's house in Poulshot and each of the people who gave us statements. The Gablecross storage facility has been locked down to prevent anyone from destroying evidence. Alex and Neil found much of what we sought in the first ten days of our investigation. Someone must have twigged they were signing in more often than the locals."

"I'm positive the man who spoke to me came from Swindon," said Suzie. "But now I've had a sleepless night; I don't think he was old enough to be Pearce. The angle of the torch beam suggested the other man was shorter than his colleague. He was less than six feet tall. What part of the world he came from, I have no idea."

"That rules out McLean; he's taller than that," said Gus. "I'll pass the information on to Geoff. It will be a great help. Now, sit down, and try to stay calm. You're not going anywhere for the next forty-eight hours. We'll leave others to keep joining the dots. They're almost there."

"If my dates were right, then tomorrow will be thirty-one weeks," said Suzie as she held her stomach.

Gus hoped the case would be wrapped up successfully within a week. Their baby needed to stay where they were for another eight weeks. At least, that's what he'd read somewhere. He called Geoff Mercer with the update.

IN THE OLD Police Station office, Amazing Grace checked the facts they had gathered in the past two weeks.

She had driven to Royal Wootton Bassett with Lydia to talk to ex-WPC Janet Gerrish. Janet was nervous about discussing the past, but Lydia had assured her she wouldn't be alone. They were talking to everyone who worked at Lime Kiln and the old station. They left the house with a written statement detailing the inappropriate language and behaviour she had suffered from over a dozen male uniformed officers. Three of those men were dead, and four were retired. The rest were still actively employed, mostly with Highways England.

Armed with Janet's statement, they had visited Sonia Jackson. Grace asked about Sonia's relationship with Keith Nicholls. Sonia told them Nicholls was divorced when they had started seeing one another. He was a couple of years older than her, but after six months, she decided there was little hope the relationship would lead anywhere. She wanted marriage and children, so Sonia had told him it was over. Nicholls went ballistic, broke down her front door, and punched her several times. Sonia reported the assault, but no action was taken.

Sonia had given them the name of the WPC who accused Nicholls of rape two years later. When they tracked down Tammi Short, she confirmed she'd withdrawn her statement because other staff at Malmesbury had made her life unbearable. Lydia coaxed the details of the attack out of her, and they had left Tammi's home with another lead to follow.

Lorna King was their next home visit, and she told them about an initiation ceremony every new female had to suffer. On Friday afternoon, at the end of her first week, she was grabbed by two male officers and bent over a desk. Her skirt was raised, and her buttocks were stamped with the day's date with the office date stamp. When she complained to her sergeant, he told her it was a man's world; she should get used to it. The only way a woman would get three stripes on her sleeve in his station was by sleeping with the correct three superior officers.

Grace prayed more women would be encouraged to come forward once word got around.

Alex and Neil had uncovered hundreds of dusty note-books in Shrivenham that had enabled the team to create an almost unbroken timeline for the men Gus had termed the brotherhood from 1983 to 2008.

Blessing and Divya had analysed data held by the Hub, which added flesh to the bones of the timeline and filled some crucial blanks.

Grace was convinced that by Friday, they would have enough evidence to charge every name on their list. She hoped by then Geoff Mercer would have identified the men who threatened Suzie Ferris.

Wednesday, 23 January 2019

GEOFF MERCER ARRIVED in his office at London Road at nine. His phone rang five minutes later.

"Good morning, Gareth," he said. "What can you tell me?"

"We traced the van that drove to Urchfont on Monday evening, sir," said Gareth Francis. "The registered owner reported it stolen at four that afternoon. CCTV images from the Magic Roundabout were blurred, but when we enhanced the images, they convinced us the officers involved were Harry Anderson and Simon Rutty."

"That's DS Anderson," said Geoff, "And DS Rutty worked on the Clare Dyke murder investigation. So perhaps we can understand now why they made so little progress."

"We believe Anderson relayed the threat to DI Ferris, sir, and Rutty was the passenger."

"Thank you, Gareth. You know the score, we add your evidence to the growing list, and when we're ready to strike, it will be quick. They won't know it's coming."

"You can rely on me, sir," said Gareth. "I'm sat in my car in the car park to avoid anyone overhearing this conversation."

Geoff ended the call and immediately rang Gus Freeman to pass on the good news.

"I was always a big fan of Gareth Francis," said Gus, crossing his fingers.

"How's Suzie?" asked Geoff.

"Not stress-free, but we're getting there," said Gus. "Grace rang yesterday evening. She hopes to have everything ready by Friday. I want to go to the office if that's okay?"

"I can't see any objection if Suzie's happy. I've got

people keeping watch on the bungalow. What about our lady driver?" asked Geoff. "Has she got cold feet yet?"

"Far from it, she can't wait."

Friday, 25 January 2019

SUZIE HAD JUST GOT out of bed when Gus left the house for work. As he drove down Caen Hill, Gus couldn't help feeling the hours before a daring raid felt like the calm before the storm.

Grace and Blessing had arrived before him, so Gus grabbed an empty spot next to the Smart car. Gus rode the lift to the first floor.

"Morning, guv," said Blessing. "Good to have you back. Is Suzie feeling better?"

"No further bulletins will be issued, Blessing," said Gus. "When Suzie hears our suspects are under lock and key, I'm sure her recovery will be complete."

Grace gave Gus the latest situation report.

"Every box ticked, Gus," she said. "Even Harry Houdini couldn't escape from what we've gathered."

"If confirmation were needed you've spent too long with Neil Davis, that was it, Grace," said Gus. "One last run-through, then. Who's where on Sunday afternoon?"

"Mervyn Hill is due to tee off at La Manga golf course at eleven o'clock. The Guardia Civil will arrest him as he leaves the eighteenth green at around three in the afternoon. Mick Reynolds will be at Crystal Palace's ground for the FA Cup tie against Tottenham Hotspur. Keith Nicholls won't be working, so his home will be under surveillance from the end of his Saturday shift on the M6 until the order for the coordinated series of arrests is given. If he moves, Wednesbury police will fine-tune their strategy, but they've had eyes on Nicholls on other days off, and he rarely leaves the house before the evening."

"Only one principal brotherhood member to go," said Gus.

"Frank Pickering will arrive home in Exeter at two-forty-five after completing his 6-2 shift," said Grace. "Devon and Cornwall police will arrest him at three o'clock precisely. He might have time to enjoy a cup of tea. Officers from our Armed Response Unit will arrest Calderwood, Rutty, and Anderson at the same time."

"That leaves us with Gerry McLean and John Pearce," said Gus. "Sunday can't come quick enough.

Sunday, 27 January 2019

GUS AND SUZIE had enjoyed a meal at the Lamb with Brett and Clemency last night. Suzie contributed most of their side of the conversation. She knew Gus was fretting over today's events. There was no rush this morning, so they had a lie-in.

"Where will you watch things progress, darling?" she asked as they ate a late breakfast.

"Geoff proposed we went to one of the training rooms at the Hub," said Gus. "Divya and her technical staff moved various pieces of kit in yesterday. They played with it for twelve hours straight, checking all the links were in place. We must hope nothing crashes during the important bits later today. So what will you do with yourself while I'm away?"

"I thought I'd drive over to the farm," said Suzie. "Mum will be on her own for most of the day. Grace and Blessing will be with you at London Road, and Dad will be in some far-flung field, no doubt mending a fence."

Gus gave Suzie a hug.

"I'll get my stuff together and drive into town," he said. "Grace and the others will be there soon."

"What about your mystery woman?" asked Suzie.

"She's staying with her sister in Newbury," said Gus. "They've spent more time together in the past few weeks than they had for several years. Contact with our targets was made at the Northcroft Leisure Centre on the seventh. The sisters have attended casual swim sessions between eight-fifteen and nine on three evenings a week since. McLean and Pearce swam in nearby lanes, then stood at the poolside, and watched."

"Creepy," said Suzie. "Is Geoff positive they can keep her safe?"

"Timing is crucial," said Gus. "We took a leaf out of Divya's book and added a belt to the pair of braces."

Suzie followed Gus to the door just before noon.

"Good hunting," she said.

Gus drove into Devizes and parked in the visitors' car park at London Road. He walked to the Hub Building and went up to the training room. The rest of his team was already there. Geoff Mercer was in danger of wearing out the carpet as he paced from side to side in front of a wall of TV screens covering the width of the room.

"Any problems?" asked Gus.

"Everyone is where they should be," said Geoff. "Friend or foe."

"Don't panic, guv," said Neil Davis. "We used the six 'P' principle. Proper planning prevents poor performance."

"That's only five, Neil," said Blessing.

"There are ladies present," said Neil.

"Now we're in the final furlong, Gus," asked Geoff. "Will you tell us who we're going to see on these screens in a few hours?"

"I felt I couldn't use a serving officer," said Gus. "There was too much of a risk someone from Wiltshire Police connected to McLean and Pearce would suss what we planned. Look at what happened with Calderwood, Anderson, and Rutty. I didn't have either of them pegged as being involved, but it shows how deeply entrenched this cancer has become. We didn't know who we could trust, and then I thought of a lady I met in Bath last year. She was a WPC in Chippenham in 2005 who had an affair with her boss. He was over twenty years older and drank more than was good for him. The relationship soured; her boss became controlling and lashed out with his fists. The WPC threatened to report him if he didn't leave her alone. He laughed and said nobody would believe her. The complaint went nowhere, like several we've heard of in the past few weeks. Finally, senior officers at Chippenham station questioned her integrity, her card was marked, and she felt her only option was to quit."

"Annie Drew," said Alex. "The lady we spoke to at Wood Security Services, near Bath Abbey. Her elder sister, Penny, worked for Brentwood Borough Council, and Annie moved away from Wiltshire for twelve years or more to work with her."

"Well, now Penny has changed jobs and works in Newbury," said Gus. "Annie is thirty-eight, and with brown contact lenses, her appearance at the leisure centre made Gerry McLean look twice."

"It sounds like Annie Drew has an old score to settle,

Gus," said Geoff. "No wonder you were able to persuade her to fall in with your plans."

Divya Yadav entered the room at one o'clock with her team to carry out their final checks, and after they gave Geoff the thumbs up, they left. Divya stayed behind to watch the fun.

"All the screens will be live from ten minutes to two," she said. "Top left is from La Manga golf course where the first arrest is due. Murcia is one hour ahead of us, and the Guardia Civil reckon Hill will have shaken hands with his golfing companions by five past three local time."

"Thanks, Divya," said Geoff. "I can't wait for the main feature when we sit and watch the drama unfold on the other screens."

"We should have phoned Kassie Trotter, guv," said Neil. "She could have brought popcorn."

"We've confirmed Hill was on holiday in Benidorm when Joe Gorse's daughters were photographed, sir," said Grace. "That's another charge we can bring."

"The more, the merrier," said Geoff.

"Unless you're Ms Robbins," said Gus.

Mervyn Hill looked shocked to see four armed policemen waiting by the side of the green. His three companions were left to deal with his golf trolley as Hill was led away in handcuffs.

The Guardia Civil didn't hear the light applause from the Hub.

Annie Drew left her sister's Newbury home and drove her Ford Kia onto Western Avenue. She followed the A339 to the A34 Oxford Road, and only four miles later, she was engulfed by the complex Chieveley interchange. Annie checked her exact position, stayed in the inside lane, and carefully brought her car to a halt near a bridge. Highways

England had determined this was the safest place for Annie to break down, and it had no CCTV coverage for half a mile.

Geoff Mercer and the others watched from London Road as Annie's hidden onboard camera showed her climbing out of the passenger door. She climbed up the grass verge to a place of safety as the Kia was straddling the white line. The hard shoulder had ended two miles back.

"McLean and Pearce have received the call," said Geoff. "They won't be suspicious once they learn where the car has broken down. The driver isn't in immediate danger, but the vehicle must be removed immediately. So they've heard that a recovery vehicle has been summoned. It's timed to arrive five minutes after McLean and Pearce reach the driver."

Blessing Umeh found it hard to know which screen to watch as the clock approached three o'clock. Every screen buzzed with activity as cars fitted with dashcams closed on the brotherhood members in different parts of the country.

Gerry McLean sat beside his pal, John Pearce, in their Highways England Mitsubishi Shogun. They had been diverted from the London to Newbury section of the M4 and had left the motorway at Junction 13. A lone female driver in a Ford Kia required assistance. They were to take her to Chieveley Services, where she could call family or friends to collect her. Her car would be towed away within minutes of them leaving the scene.

"This should be a doddle," said McLean. "Probably ran out of petrol, silly mare."

"They'll be with Annie in two minutes," said Grace. "Screens 4 and 5 contain the GPS signals for the Shogun and the Kia."

Alex and Lydia watched as both screens suddenly

contained two pulsing signals. If there were a chance of something going drastically wrong, it would happen in the next sixty seconds.

"Well, would you look at that," said McLean. "It's that lady from the swimming pool. The lassie with her sister. It won't be a hardship to give *her* a lift. This could be fun."

McLean got out and walked up the grass verge to speak to Annie. John Pearce sat in the Shogun, wondering whether Gerry would let him play with this one for a while. He'd made it clear on Thursday night, when they last saw the two women, that the younger one reminded him of his mother, Jennie. When they'd grabbed the first woman, he'd had to stand by and watch as Gerry tormented and strangled her. John had been aroused, but it wasn't until the third time Gerry let him join in.

Pearce could see Gerry helping the woman down the ramp to the Shogun. A mile away, the recovery vehicle was closing on them at seventy miles an hour. Gerry opened the rear passenger door, pushed the woman inside, and jumped in behind her.

"Go," said McLean. "Right, sweetheart, there's been a change of plan."

Pearce looked for a gap in the traffic to pull out. Annie Drew struggled in the back seat with McLean as he tried to secure her wrists with zip ties. The next thing Pearce saw in his wing mirror was a car crossing from lane two, which stopped him from moving forward. A second car pulled up behind them, and a dark van drew alongside. The doors were wrenched open, and McLean and Pearce were face down on the grass verge in seconds.

Geoff Mercer glanced from screen to screen. They all showed a positive image.

"It worked like clockwork," he said. "Congratulations.

222

Now for the bit that sticks in my craw. I'll have to tell Kenneth and the others the good news."

Two hours later, the PCC gave a press conference. Stuart Midwinter stood on the steps outside the London Road HQ and announced that two men had been arrested in Berkshire. They had been charged with the murders of four women between 1998 and 2014. Additional charges may follow. Seven men had also been arrested in connection with historical offences of hate crime and sexual assault. The combined operation was led by ACC Sylvia Robbins and involved Highways England and several regional police forces.

Gus and Suzie watched the rerun of the announcement on regional TV later.

"Not even a mention of you and the team," said Suzie as she searched for an album to suit the occasion. 'Two Low For Zero' by Elton John caught her eye.

"Kenneth thanked us while the PCC and Ms Robbins were hogging the limelight," said Gus. "Annie Drew got her opportunity to embarrass the idiots who forced her out. As long as I can see everyone settled before the axe falls, I reckon I've deserved to put my feet up for a while. I've nothing left to prove."

Epilogue

Luke,

Many thanks for the card congratulating us on the birth of John Albert. He arrived a little earlier than planned on February the twenty-eighth, weighing five pounds, five ounces. All three of us are doing well; thanks for asking.

His first name was Suzie's choice, and I felt Bert Penman deserved to leave his mark on our firstborn. Bert passed away in his sleep in the third week of February at eighty-seven, and I've just finished my eulogy, 'The Countryman', which I'll be proud to deliver at his funeral service.

Kenneth Truelove will soon be off on his first cruise with Elizabeth. Geoff Mercer and Christine have moved into their Clench Common cottage. The new Chief Constable is searching for the right person to become an ACC. Suzie reckons her links to the Jurassic period might rule her out of contention, and with hopes of a daughter to complete our family, she's in no rush to return to work.

After the Lime Kiln cowboys saga, my concern was ensuring my team found new homes.

Maxine Devereux has returned from maternity leave to become a DI across the county border in Dorchester. She begged London Road for the services of Lydia Logan Barre, and I'm pleased to say they saw sense and agreed.

The fallout from my last case led to vacancies at Gablecross for two detectives. Alex and Neil will transfer there next month. Alex and Lydia won't work in the same office anymore, so I don't think we'll have long to wait before we hear wedding bells.

Blessing is well on her way to becoming a DS, and she'll move in with her fiancé, Jamie, when she transfers to Bourne Hill to work with DI Chris Stanton. At least one of us impressed the locals when we were there in December!

Grace Packenham leaves at the end of March to join the Met. She shone during the Extinction Rebellion protests, and it was only a matter of time before Grace moved closer to the centre of power. Her romance with Major Marcus Sanders is smouldering rather than ablaze, but Suzie has high hopes they'll find a way to stay in touch.

Well, that's pretty much all the loose ends tied up. Kenneth will need to leave a weekend free next year to walk Kassie Trotter down the aisle when she marries her rugby-playing junior doctor, Noah Edwards.

There's little point asking what you're up to, Luke. You could tell me, but then you'd have to kill me, I expect. Perhaps we'll get a chance to have a drink together one day?

Time to close the Freeman Files and our cold case reviews. It's been fun. I'm off to the allotment later with The Reverend and Brett. They're having trouble with their leeks and want me to find the note-book I put in a safe place in my shed packed with Bert's sage advice.

There was no return address on your card, Luke. So I'm relying on Annie Drew to see you get this letter, wherever Olympus sent you.

Gus Freeman – Urchfont – March 15th, 2019

More by Ted Tayler

vinci-books.com/phoenix-box-set-1

From the depths of despair, an assassin rises...

A ruthless assassin with a dark past finds redemption in the Olympus Project. Tasked with preventing a catastrophic terrorist attack, he must face his toughest mission yet. Can he save London before it's too late?

Turn the page for a free preview...

The Olympus Project: Chapter One

THE LATE EVENING sunshine bathed everything on the far bank of the river. The man in the water was barely breathing. He hooked his right arm over a lower branch of one of many overgrown bushes and trees scattered along the waterline.

A thinning group of people peered across the water, shading their eyes. The glare of the sunlight blinded them as it disappeared behind the rooftops of the nearby buildings. The group continued to gaze across to the opposite bank. They searched and searched for a glimpse of their quarry but saw nothing. He was too tired to move. The bushes and tethered barges strung along that stretch of water below the Pulteney Weir provided the perfect shelter.

The man rested. Safe, for now, his mind drifted back to the last few hours' events. His plans had gone out of the window when that stupid female copper recognised him and shouted. A bullet shut her up, but an old bag, no doubt her mother, chased after him and lashed out with her handbag. He remembered descending the steps to the towpath in a blind panic, trying to calm his nerves and gather his thoughts.

He thought he could make it back to the Land Rover. Get the hell out of this city. Then he spotted a uniformed policeman running towards him. He had no choice but to turn and sprint back towards the steps. The man remembered running alongside the Weir. He was only a few strides from the spiral steps leading to the street. At least there, he might see a chance of escaping among the city crowds.

He had heard a shout feet away. As he glanced over his shoulder, he spotted his nemesis. That meddling policeman had pursued him the length and breadth of the country. With a warning shout, the policeman was on his heels and launched himself towards him. They both fell headlong over the railings and into the river's murky waters. Both men surfaced, gasping for the air knocked from them by the force of the impact.

At first, the man struck out for the opposite bank, with confidence, despite his lack of experience. The policeman followed. The man soon realised his adversary was a much stronger swimmer and any thoughts of a quick escape were futile. The two men grappled, and while both concentrated on gaining the upper hand, they drew closer and closer to the Weir and its lethal foaming waters. The nature of the water altered around them as they fought, and both men realised the danger they faced. Finally, they disappeared under the surface and got tossed around under the Weir like socks in a washing machine.

The water clutched at the man's legs, dragging him further under the water. He cracked his knees and elbows on the concrete buttresses of the Weir. He punched and kicked at the policeman as they both tried to swim back towards the surface. When they did, the respite was brief. A second to take in an invaluable lungful of air, and then the water snatched them back under the churning waters. They resumed their battle at once, but their struggle took its toll. Their actions grew more and more laboured. Both men soon reached the end of their tethers. Neither man knew which way was up any longer. Battered and winded, each swallowed large quantities of water. The man sensed the policeman release his hold and watched as he drifted away.

The man didn't know if his nemesis had sunk to the riverbed or surfaced and reached safety. The man felt happy he no longer needed to fight and was prepared to resign himself to his fate. He sensed his lungs giving up the ghost as an excruciating pain built within his chest. The man broke through the surface and took a desperate breath. The pain increased. Successive breaths brought little relief, but he willed himself to press forward, away from the direction the policeman had gone.

As he surfaced again for a moment, he realised that he was near the far bank. He drifted in silence behind a barge. The man forced himself, against his instincts, to swim under the near side of the barge's hull, keeping the river wall at his fingertips. When he surfaced once more, he continued to breathe. Each breath was becoming more manageable, but it exhausted him.

With a supreme effort, he got his right arm over a branch and rested; he needed to stay focused because if he slipped under the water again, he understood there was no chance of saving himself.

From his place of sanctuary, he saw people running on the towpath. He heard sirens blaring somewhere nearby. He tried to check his condition. He had suffered cuts to his legs and shoulder, but he didn't appear to have any broken bones. He felt bitterly cold. He was suffering from shock.

There was no time to worry. A helicopter throbbed over-head. As night fell, a searchlight would soon probe the little nooks and crannies trying to find him. If only he could evade capture long enough for them to believe he drowned in the Weir. To assume his body had floated downstream. Maybe he could yet escape this mess.

An hour later, the towpath had emptied. The armed response men had withdrawn; the paramedics and onlookers had disappeared. He looked across to the oppo-site bank where a distinguished-looking, elderly gentleman stood in the shadows of a bridge talking on his mobile phone. The man looked right at him as if this man knew where he was hiding. Had the man near the bridge called the police? Was this how it ended?

The elderly gentleman smiled to himself. Then he spoke aloud as if talking to someone in a crowded room. Someone who struggled to hear what he said: -

"Hold on for a few minutes more, Mr Bailey. There's a good chap. Our people will be along in a tick to remove you. You'll be safe then and among friends."

Still hidden on the opposite bank, Colin Bailey had been afraid to breathe. He exhaled raggedly and allowed himself the briefest of smiles. Colin didn't know who the well-dressed man was, but he oozed class both in the cut of his suit and the way he spoke. Colin wasn't sure what lay ahead for him, but he convinced himself the police couldn't be involved and friends were always welcome.

Moments later, an inflatable dinghy appeared from downstream and inched its way closer to the bank. Two pairs of powerful arms hoisted Colin Bailey from the icy river. Without a word, the men stripped him of his wet things and helped him don multiple layers of dry, warm clothing. They even supplied a cosy ski hat and thick socks to help with the warming. He struggled to get these on while a man offered him a hot drink poured from a thermos flask.

The other man returned to the wheel and manoeuvred the craft along the river. The dinghy stuck to the far side, hiding from the odd dog walker on the towpath. It carried them further from the city centre. Finally, they moved clear of the dangerous Pulteney Weir, where Colin had escaped a watery grave.

They travelled for a minute, and then the driver deftly turned the wheel, and they darted across the river to the opposite bank. Under the weeping willow trees, only yards from the water's edge, an ambulance waited, its rear doors open, the engine idling.

His two companions grabbed one of Colin's arms and lifted him onto the towpath, where a man dressed in a paramedic's uniform waited. Colin's legs buckled under him as his feet touched dry land for the first time in several hours. The man dressed as a paramedic took a firm hold of him as he stumbled and, surprisingly, swept him up in his arms and carried him into the ambulance. He laid Colin on the stretcher, covered him with a heavy blanket, and closed the doors behind them. With that, the ambulance drove into the night.

In the Royal United Hospital, DCI, Phil Hounsell rested after his ordeal in the water. His wife Erica had visited him earlier. Now she lay tucked up at home with their children. DS Zara Wheeler was enjoying a drink with her two male colleagues in a crowded Bath hostelry. Her beverage was non-alcoholic, but the two young policemen were heading for a hangover.

Colin Bailey wasn't heading for a hangover or an NHS hospital; his ambulance soon drove out of the city towards a

Georgian manor house ten miles away. The only clue to his destination was the unmistakable sound of a cattle grid. He experienced the distinctive rattle when they drove between the stone pillars at the entrance to the property.

Satisfied to be in safe hands, Colin closed his eyes and fell sound asleep before the ambulance negotiated the long arc of the driveway to reach the main house.

COLIN SAT UP IN BED. He was suddenly wide awake.

"Where am I?" he wondered. Then yesterday's events came flooding back. He remembered the ride through the countryside in the ambulance and a gradual warmth returning to his body. He must have fallen asleep because he couldn't recall being taken from the ambulance, then into the building and finally reaching this magnificent bedroom.

The bright sun shone outside, and from its height in the sky, he deduced it to be late morning. He had slept for just short of twelve hours. His bedroom had two large sash windows, and the sunlight allowed him to view his surroundings with growing admiration.

The white-painted solid timber bedstead and woollen or flax-filled mattress had been ultra-comfortable. Colin brushed the clean white sheets with the palms of his hands. He gazed around the room and took an inventory, bedside cabinet, check, cheval mirror, check, and a double wardrobe with drawers at the bottom. The sage green walls, intricate ceiling swags, and moulded cornices complemented the idyllic scene perfectly.

"Someone is going to an awful lot of trouble," he thought, "considering they know exactly who and what I am. I wonder if I've missed breakfast."

Colin no longer wore the layers of clothing his rescuers

233

provided him for the short dinghy trip. So he got out of his far too comfortable bed. As he did so, he discovered he wore a nightshirt, which was not out of place in Georgian times.

Colin tiptoed to the window. Before he could look outside, the door opened behind him, and someone crossed the floor. The elderly gentleman from the towpath came to stand beside him.

"Good morning Mr Bailey. I trust you slept well?" he said.

"Yes, thank you. What is this place? Who are you? And what am I doing here?"

"Time enough for questions, old chap," the old man replied with a chuckle. "What's the rush? The en-suite is through the door to the left of the mirror. Once you've completed your ablutions, you'll find a choice of casual clothes in the wardrobe. Please don't insult me by asking if they'll fit. Instead, I invite you to join us for a light luncheon on the ground floor, and I'll give you the grand tour."

Sensing Colin would soon ask where the meeting was or who he meant by 'us', the elderly gentleman stopped at the bedroom door. With his hand on the door handle, he said, "I appreciate you have questions, Mr Bailey. Sometimes we need to shelve our curiosity and take things on trust. Follow your nose, and the excellent food will bring you to the right door. Of course, if you're wandering around the corridors in an hour, we'll have selected the wrong man to join our enterprise. But, if I were a betting man, I'd say you'll be tucking into a plateful of excellent English fare within twenty minutes."

The bedroom door closed. Colin stood at the window a while longer. Then he checked the second sash window and confirmed that both were locked. There were no signs of a method of releasing them. He should have been at ease in

these gracious surroundings as he gazed out at the mani-
cured garden and lawns. Yet he couldn't help thinking he
had little choice other than to join this 'enterprise', whatever it might be. To refuse might lead to an unpleasant
outcome, and Colin was intelligent enough to let things
move along at their own pace for now. Apart from that, he
was starving.

It didn't surprise Colin when he found the en-suite bathroom as well-appointed as the rest of his new accommodation. He lingered in the refreshing hot shower for a moment
or two longer than usual and speculated on what might lie
ahead for him. He imagined he'd discover what he had let
himself in for in due course. What he did with that knowledge involved serious thought and meticulous planning.

Colin Bailey had made a career out of doing just that.
He towelled himself dry and walked back to the bedroom.
He opened drawers and wardrobes to reveal a variety of
shirts, tops, and trousers. There were several pairs of shoes
and socks and assorted styles of underwear. Colin made his
choice, and everything was a perfect fit, as predicted by his
host. Minutes later, he stood in front of the cheval mirror
and nodded with satisfaction.

"Cool bastard," he exclaimed. Then with a hearty
laugh, he assumed the time-honoured position favoured by
the inimitable Commander James Bond and said, "the
name's Bailey, Colin Bailey."

The corridor and staircase he discovered outside his
door didn't disappoint. With each successive step, he
descended to the ground floor, admiring paintings of naval
battles and personnel. Finally, Colin strode along the pale
marble floor towards the nearest door on the lower level.
The delicate aromas that enticed him further only height-
ened his appetite. He entered the room to find the old

gentleman, whom he assumed to be his host, talking with three men and a striking-looking woman.

Four faces turned towards him. Finally, the elderly gentleman approached Colin and led Colin back to join the group, taking his arm.

"We can dispense with formal introductions for now. Your reputation precedes you, old chap, so we know who you are and how efficient a killer you have been. That's why you're here. There will be plenty of opportunities to discuss that side of things in due course. For now, you need to know that we share a common goal, and this estate is the centre of our operations. We selected you as the ideal candidate to join The Olympus Project. We will train you to bring a swift end to any direct action we decide is necessary in the cesspit that passes for a civilised world outside this estate."

While the older man talked, servers slipped into the room. They carried the contents of the dishes from the long side table to serve up a sumptuous luncheon for the six potential diners. Colin couldn't help noticing that the servers on duty were men in their late thirties to mid-forties, and each had a military bearing. They moved and conducted themselves in a manner that suggested there wasn't an ordinary seaman, airman, or plain squaddie among them. Colin was sure every one of them had been Marines or even ex-SAS before leaving the services.

Just what nature of outfit was this Olympus Project? An inflatable dinghy on-call at a moment's notice, a fake ambulance to use, and a protection squad that worked in the kitchens. This lot may have former guardsmen mowing the lawns and digging the vegetable patches. Heaven help any burglar who thought this Georgian mansion had a few trinkets worth stealing.

Everything was ready. Colin's dining companions took

their places, and he found his seat at the end of the table opposite his host. The formidable-looking lady sat at the older man's right-hand side, and her three male companions sat on Colin's right.

The remaining chairs that had stood at the elegant table for its eight place settings when Colin first entered the room now stood against the wall. No late arrivals were joining this happy band. The pecking order of this group was pre-ordained.

Colin casually tried to assess the people around him as the servers served their starter dish. By his estimation, the three men to his right could be in their mid to late fifties. The man to his host's left appeared to be a civil servant or a professional. The other two showed every sign of being ex-military. While the waiter attending to him poured a small glass of Cedar Creek Chardonnay, he looked across at the lady and felt his face redden. She gave him a look that, without uttering a word, told him she knew he was sizing up his companions and that she disapproved.

Colin switched his attention to his plate. He felt uncomfortable under the gaze of the lady he was convinced had to be the second-in-command of this outfit. His comfort didn't improve when he saw the warm squash veloute with soft poached egg and pink grapefruit jam. Colin hadn't eaten in ages, and his stomach ached for a full English breakfast. When he had been with his late wife, Sue Owens, in The Gambia, they ate well enough, although they generally preferred simple food. He wasn't a total stranger to fine dining. Heaven knows she and Colin could afford it with the money she'd made selling her home and business.

As soon as he tasted that first mouthful, Colin had to revise his opinion. It tasted fantastic. He forgot his fellow diners and his dream of a big fry-up for the time being and savoured every moment of this first lunch at the manor house. The main course of young Welsh lamb arrived with crushed broccoli, sheep's curd, Provencal figs, and toasted hazelnuts. It was even more delicious. A large glass of Cabernet Sauvignon was more than a welcome companion. Later, the wild honey ice cream proved the ideal dessert for warm summer days. As the stewards cleared away the last few dishes away and served coffee, Colin leaned back in his chair and relaxed. He looked up to find the eyes of his fellow diners, who had remained silent throughout the whole proceedings, turned towards him.

"That was excellent," he said, "I'm looking forward to the grand tour more than ever now. The exercise is essential."

"I shall take my coffee on the patio," said the lady, "I want to enjoy this sunshine while I have a few minutes to spare. There's work to do later. Good afternoon gentlemen. Mr Bailey." With that, she swept out of the room. A waiter placed a coffee pot on a silver tray and added other necessary items for her excursion. When he had finished, he trotted off in her wake. His destination was her sun-kissed and sheltered haven a few steps from the door to the rear of the main building.

"Reminds you of a galleon in full sail, doesn't it, old chap?" said his host with a conspiratorial grin. He looked at the three men on his left-hand side. "No doubt you have things to attend to this afternoon. Don't let us detain you. I propose we six reconvene at 1900 hours. There is much to get through this evening. Mr Bailey will have a better idea of The Olympus Project by then. He'll appreciate how his particular skill set fits into our organisation."

As the others left the room, the elderly gentleman beckoned Colin to bring his coffee to more comfortable seats in front of the large fireplace. "Right you are then," he said, "let's finish our coffees in peace, and then we'll be on our way."

Colin and his host sat silently, savouring their drink and that excellent three-course meal. Colin could sense his eyelids growing heavy. Indeed, the older man had his head on his chest and was dozing peacefully. The period French clock on the mantelpiece struck two o'clock. The elderly gentleman stood up stiffly.

"Time to go, Mr Bailey. Let me take you through the delights of my family home and show you what we've done to update the old place. I'm sure the changes will interest you."

The two men entered the hallway, and the grand tour began.

"LARCOMBE Manor is a Grade One Listed Manor House lying in a secluded spot eight miles outside Bath. It has been my family's home, without a break, since 1550. Queen Elizabeth the First stayed here for two nights in 1585. I've searched high and low for a written account of her thoughts on the place, but to no avail. So, I can't tell you whether she was enamoured enough to stay an extra day. Nor that she intended to descend upon the place for a week but skedaddled back to London in high dudgeon. The eleven bedrooms, the seven-bathroom house comes with three and a half acres of gardens. We have a formal garden you can see from your bedroom window and a walled kitchen garden to the side. That's where we grow our vegetables and flowers. The reception rooms are full of character and keep many original features from the major extension and overhaul my ancestors carried out in the middle of the nine-teenth century."

His host was warming to his task, and Colin strolled alongside him as they moved through the main building. The grandeur of the building was plain to see at every turn. They paused here and there as the older man commented upon the décor, the artwork or the period furniture. Colin had a question.

"If this is your family home, do you have them living with you and the members of The Olympus Project I've met so far?"

His host stopped and emitted a long sigh.

"My wife is in a nursing home nearby. She suffered a breakdown a few years back, old chap, and there's no one else here."

Colin didn't pursue that line of questioning any further. It had raised a painful memory for his host. The next few minutes of the grand tour continued in a far more sombre mood. The older man's mood brightened as they went outside into the gardens. Colin looked across to the patio, but any lingering signs of the ship had gone. She must have returned indoors to work, and the ever-efficient staff tidied up behind her.

The two men walked across the lawn. Colin could only wonder at the immaculate grounds, with trees planted with a precision that protected the house from nosy passers-by in the far-off adjoining fields. Yet, when he looked towards the main building, the magnificent edifice always remained visible as you walked towards the other estate buildings. His reverie was broken by his elderly companion speaking: -

"The orangery, of course, is over there to the right."

"Of course," said Colin under his breath.

"Just here in front of us, to our left, is where the old

stable block stood. When the idea for Olympus took shape, we converted that into staff accommodation. The building you can see one hundred yards further on is the ice-house. Let's wander over and take a look, eh?"

Colin had read about ice-houses. He knew they were in everyday use before the invention of the refrigerator. Most comprised hand-built underground chambers within yards of a water source, and the winter ice and snow were taken inside and packed with insulation. The wealthy owners of manor houses on estates such as this could store perishable foods, chill their drinks, or prepare ice-creams and sorbets. Oh, how the other half lived.

As they approached the door to the building, Colin prepared himself to see a grill covering a brick-lined forty-foot pit. Perhaps he would see the decaying signs of a drain to take away any water. Once they agreed that little remained worth seeing, they could move towards the remaining buildings. From his current vantage point, Colin thought those resembled a terrace of two-up, two-down cottages.

As soon as they stepped through the outer door of the ice-house, Colin gasped.

"That was a shaker Mr Bailey, wasn't it?" chuckled the old man.

After he pressed the call button, Colin heard the lift rise for a few seconds, and then the steel doors opened.

"Shall we?" asked his tour guide.

Colin followed his host into the lift and watched as the older man selected the button for the first of the three levels. A few seconds later, they stopped. When the doors opened, they walked into a room where a computer nerd would have believed Christmas had come early.

"This is our command centre. Operatives in this facility

monitor the movements of our identified criminal targets. They track every possible terrorist threat yet undefined and keep us abreast of any potential global catastrophe. That may be a tsunami, an earthquake, or a volcanic event, everything that has the potential to threaten our social equilibrium. The corridor leads to recreation rooms, a dentist's surgery, and a fully functional operating theatre from this room. We have a few sleep pods at the far end for operatives to use on those occasions when the criminal fraternity keeps us extra busy. Don't confuse this with the old-style Burlington bunker near your neck of the woods at Shaw Park; that's more of an enlarged foxhole. Did you enjoy your wine at lunch today?"

Colin nodded. His host continued -

"We have a constant relative inside temperature in this foxhole, and the insulated hull surrounding it makes this environment ideal for storing our wine. I think we've seen enough here for now. Let's drop to level two, shall we?"

On the next level, they met two armed personnel. The men wore no uniform, just a white t-shirt with Olympus on the left breast, black combat trousers, and boots. Each carried a gun in a holster at the hip. Both had a physique that looked like they used the recreation rooms to good effect. Again, Colin recognised his rescuers from last night. These two had manned the dinghy.

"Good afternoon, men. You've met Mr Bailey. I'm delighted to tell you he is joining our group."

Colin looked at the old gentleman. He couldn't recall getting asked if he wished to join whatever set-up this was, let alone tell anyone he had agreed. The locked windows in his bedroom and the distance between himself and fellow diners led Colin to believe his host was used to giving orders. To say 'No' was inadvisable.

The older man continued, patently aware of Colin's feelings over what he had said to the two guards. "I'm sure he will be in to visit you from time to time. Can I show him what we have available?"

The two men moved aside, and one entered an access code on a pad to the side of the main door. Once inside the room, Colin could see this was the armoury. There were racks of assault rifles, which his host informed him included several varieties of AK and a WASR3. In addition, they had a range of Heckler and Koch rifles that various police and even special forces preferred. The racks contained several items Colin had seen before, mostly in films. He spotted M4 Colt Carbines that had been everywhere in Iraq and Afghanistan when the US forces were in action. The ubiquitous Uzi was among several light machine guns, and the weaponry included far more than rifles. The armoury even stocked hand-held rocket launchers.

Below the racking lay drawers containing handguns and knives; H&K, Browning, Glock, and Sig Sauer models were abundant. The latter's P226 was no surprise since the SAS had favoured this model for years. The elderly gentleman moved from the racks to the drawers with evident pleasure. Now and then, he picked up a gun and spent a moment or two in contemplation. Colin wondered whether he was reliving an occasion when he had used it in action.

"I don't have the key for the other drawers, but they contain our supply of gas canisters, flash bombs, incendiary devices and, of course, hand grenades."

"Of course," replied Colin, allowing himself a brief smile. If you want to wage war on someone or protect your organisation against attack, you may as well have something of everything he thought.

"The rest of this level includes a shooting range, where I

expect you to improve your accuracy. You will reach the Olympic standard if possible, although, now you're one of us, you'll never represent your country in competition."

The two men walked along the corridor, which ran along the side of the range. No operatives were honing their skills this afternoon. The door at the end was locked. The older man turned on his heel and encouraged Colin to walk back with him towards the armoury.

"That's the ammunition store; there's something for everything. Once you've seen one magazine, you've seen the lot I find, old chap. Rather boring to stand around inspecting bullets. Much more fun firing them at the enemy, eh?"

With a nod to the two guards, his host led him from the armoury to the lift. A bony hand hovered over the button for the third level.

"Well, we've come this far, so you might as well see the rest," he sighed.

The final level was dark and eerily quiet. A long corridor stretched to the left, and low-wattage security lighting highlighted the pair as they moved past various rooms to their right. The older man pointed a finger. He informed Colin that they were passing the cells and the interrogation rooms. Colin was familiar with a windowless room at the far end of the quiet corridor where a slight odour lingered.

"To add to the information we gather in our command centre, it's necessary, on occasion, to invite people to stay with us for a while. They arrive using the same transport as you, without knowing where they are. We encourage them to answer our questions, and if they give useful data, they leave us unharmed and return to their loved ones."

His guide began the long walk back to the lift. As Colin

hurried to catch up, the older man shook his head and glanced back along the corridor towards the final room.

Wearily he added, "If they get to the far end, then it's not likely they'll see their families again. I'm afraid those visitors' final destination is a plot in the family pet cemetery we have in the woods on the outskirts of the estate."

"I wondered why someone had pinned a small card to the door with 'Hotel California' printed on it," Colin muttered.

Colin and his host rode back up to the surface in silence. The sun still shone when they emerged from the ice-house, and Colin automatically headed towards the final group of buildings, which were the terraced cottages.

"We can give that place a miss. Everything is not as it might appear. We converted the worker's cottages to incorporate a staff canteen, a cinema and a swimming pool."

As he walked back towards the main house, he added, "Of course."

He laughed at his little joke at Colin's expense. Colin drew level and saw that his host was smiling.

"I think you'll fit in well here, Mr Bailey. Let's find a place to rest our weary bones. I'll chase up a pot of tea, and then I'll tell you the history of the Olympus Project."

The woman followed their walk across the lawn to the house from an upstairs window. No doubt the old gentleman knew she was there, but he gave no sign. Finally, Colin spotted her and hung back as they climbed the steps onto the patio. He gave her a friendly wave and a smile. The woman stepped back from the window and disappeared from view.

The Olympus Project: Chapter Two

TWENTY MINUTES LATER, the two men sat in one of the elegant drawing-rooms. Their wing chairs faced the enormous windows that gave full access to the sweeping panorama of the Larcombe Manor estate. The sun continued to beat down on the grounds, but it was calm, peaceful, and serene here in this sanctuary. Colin had forgotten the chill he felt as the older man showed him the lengths this organisation would go to.

After they had returned indoors and taken a chance to freshen up, Colin sought and rejoined his host. Erebus summoned a steward. In no time, they had cups of tea, tiny triangular sandwiches and a tray of fancy cakes to refresh them after their long walk.

"I know you are eager to discover the nature of the work The Olympus Project carries out, Mr Bailey. I have tested your patience long enough. My entire career was in the Royal Navy, as I'm sure you deduced. I believe I served my country well. As each successive decade passed, each one quicker than the last, I stood by, unable to help, as my superiors lost their moral courage. I watched them abandon their comrades to political correctness. Governments of whatever colour have continued to shrink the fleet to an unacceptable level. The country is at the mercy of bands of brigands, let alone massive navies. My comrades in the army and air force have suffered the same humiliation. The quality of our armed forces is still among the highest anywhere in the world, Mr Bailey, I have no doubts on that score, but the numbers are far too low. We are vulnerable to attack as a nation in a way we haven't been for five hundred years. The armed services' effectiveness suffers in four corners of the globe. At home, the police and judiciary are falling into the hands of the same weak, hand-wringing milksops. They have stepped away from tackling crime with a big stick and meaningful sentencing. They are now reaping the wind as organised gangs, drug cartels, and people traffickers operate carte blanche the length and breadth of this once great country. I had my reasons for wanting to redress the balance. One man alone could achieve little. Even one with a large family fortune such as mine, I placed an advert in The Times personal column four years ago. It stated: - Help required. Anyone eager to prevent Britain from going to hell in a handcart. Write Box 1815, etcetera. I soon weeded out the time-wasters. I found a handful of people who thought the same and possessed the intelligence, will, and access to added funding to help bring my ideas to fruition. A few of our backers have remained silent partners and do not live here at Larcombe Manor. The four people you met at lunch today are the founder members of Olympus. What do you know of Greek mythology, Mr Bailey?"

"I've heard of the Gods, Zeus, Achilles and um…."

"No matter. There are just six names you need to

remember. While here at Larcombe, we use these names only when we speak of one another. Do you understand?"

Colin nodded.

"It's for our protection, old chap, in case you fall into the hands of a terrorist group or the bumbling fools that pose as our police force while on one of our direct actions. Then you can only reveal your identity, and hours of interrogation or torture are futile. You don't know the names of your masters. So, you have nothing to tell."

"Yet everyone here knows I'm Colin Bailey," Colin blurted out.

The elderly gentleman tapped his forehead. "Think deeper young man. Have you seen the papers or television today?"

Colin shook his head.

"As far as the police and the media are concerned, Colin Bailey and his many aliases perished in the deadly waters of the Pulteney Weir last evening. That body remains undiscovered yet, but no one is looking for you. No one believes you could have survived. Miraculously, you did. From this moment forward, you will be called Phoenix. We will keep you here at the Manor for a few months. You will train in new techniques and hone your existing skills. You will receive treatment in the medical unit to alter your features. It is nothing too drastic, though, as it doesn't take much to fool the authorities on these shores. We will continue to name targets for direct action, and dossiers will be available for you to study. The action planning gives you as much satisfaction as the endgame itself, so the future is bright for you. Don't you agree, Phoenix?"

"It appears so," Colin replied. He realised that this organisation had committed itself to tackling the malaise crippling his country by eliminating the worst criminals.

Instead, his pathetic Street Cleaner idea was elevated to a global scale. What he started years ago with Scott Hall, Leroy Ambrose, and their rotten gangs; then followed up this summer with the evil Neil Cartwright, who had murdered his sweet, innocent daughter Sharron, paled into insignificance.

They had paid the price for their crimes, as had Pete Howlett, the Manchester drug-running affair overlord, and four gang members. Colin had rid the world too of Usman Khan and Mustafa Jobe, just two of the men responsible for the systematic abuse and death of Khalima Darbo. A family friend trafficked the poor Gambian teenager to London for sex. That swine Hounsell had thwarted his progress. In his small way, any others he had identified for elimination continued to abuse children and peddle drugs on estates throughout the country. Heaven knows what else. Colin wished he could start these direct actions his host was so fond of describing.

The old man looked at Colin, "All in good time, dear boy. Be patient."

Colin paused for a second. How did he know what I was thinking? Did I say something out loud without realising it? He gathered his emotions in check and asked: -

"What are you called? What of the others too? What's your story?"

The old man replied, "I'll tell you my story. After dinner, the others will explain their code names and histories. Then you will understand where our motivation for Olympus originated. Finally, you will appreciate what drives us to right wrongs and make criminals pay for their crimes. Our ultimate aim is to remove any threat to the natural order of things."

Colin listened intently, and question after question sprang into his head.

"How do you keep what you're doing here a secret? Surely, people knew your colleagues before they came here. You must be on a naval pension, apart from your state pension. The DVLA, your bank or building society, the list of people who know you must be endless. How did you ever get planning permission for your underground foxhole on a Grade I listed property?"

"Steady on Phoenix. One thing at a time. I'm not getting any younger. I can't cope with this machine-gun questioning. Let me explain. Larcombe Manor lies in secluded spot three-quarters of a mile from a minor road. That minor road carries only a few vehicles. It's a 'No through road.' Just over a mile further on, the road ends in the farmyard of our neighbours, the Davis family, who have lived and worked on Larcombe Farm for three generations. The other families who have lived there have been tenants of this estate since the seventeenth century. We don't bother them as they carry on their dairy farming enterprise, and they don't bother us. As the occasional car or farm vehicle passes our gateway, they can see a sign on the left-hand stone pillar. A plaque signals The Olympus Project's home with a registered charity number. We, five founder members, are the trustees of that charity, and, as you point out, the authorities and many other organisations know *who* we are. We can carry on our business without hindrance. We supply the necessary papers in full to support the illusion that a charitable organisation operates on this site. As a result, we attract no unwanted intrusion, and we can take steps to protect the truth of *what* we are."

"What type of charity is it then?" asked Colin.

"As you are undoubtedly aware, Help for Heroes started

in 2007. They helped offer better facilities for British servicemen and women wounded or injured in the line of duty. This organisation took shape the same year after my advert in The Times. We set up our charity and announced that it would concentrate on service staff whose injuries were far from visible. Our mission statement shows we help service members suffering from Post-Traumatic Stress Disorder or combat stress if you will. This step proved more than useful in camouflaging what we do here. Charity commissioners visit us from time to time. They are not shocked to find men tending to the lawns and gardens or exercising in the swimming pool. They might see men learning new IT skills, playing computer games in the old stable block, or baking cakes in our kitchens. Each is a very therapeutic activity — just the ticket to help them get through the dark days. In time we hope they can return to a position where they can rejoin the hustle and bustle of the modern world beyond the walls of this estate. The general opinion of our efforts has been that we carry out highly commendable work."

The older man chuckled. "We keep them away from the ice-house, of course."

The two men chorused together, "Of course."

"The ambulance driver that brought you here and his companion, who played the role of a paramedic, is our transport section. They have a few vehicles at their disposal. We are in a remote location, and we arranged with the Post Office four years ago to collect the mail for everyone housed on the 'No through road'. After the daily trip into Bath, our driver drops any post into each property for supplies. He acts as a paperboy, too, even on Sundays. It's the least we can do. You arrived in the late evening. We keep the pretence of more PTSD sufferers coming by using the ambulance during daylight hours for our occasional trips into the city. The drivers have to be extra careful on those occasions. We don't want a member of the public hailing them for a real medical emergency. In the past four years, we have attracted no unwanted attention in that regard. The operatives you have encountered are service personnel who have joined us after their armed forces careers. Many left the forces before they wished to go. They were on the scrapheap through these abominable government cuts or court-martialled because they were considered old school by the numbskulls that pass for officers today. They are highly trained and motivated people who need a purpose in life. We gave them that purpose."

The older man rang for a member of staff to collect their tea things. He stood up, walked to the window and stretched, "I'm tired, Phoenix. Let's take a break for a while. I'll go to my room for a nap. I'll see you back here at 1800 hours. My story will be over well before we meet up with the others for dinner. We should have time for me to answer a few questions you may still have. I bid you good afternoon, Phoenix."

With that, the elderly gentleman left the drawing-room. Colin remained seated and reflected on everything he had learned so far. It hadn't even been twenty-four hours since his unscheduled dip in the River Avon, yet so much had changed. If he allowed himself to be dragged along by his host's enthusiasm for his pet project, his life would never be the same. But what options did he have? He had spotted the printed card on the door to the torture chamber. The much-used reference to the song's lyrics that 'you can check out but never leave' sprang to mind. The locked windows in his room and the shadowy presence of staff suggested that he was a virtual prisoner wherever he was on the estate. Colin wondered what the outcome might be if he ploughed his furrow and refused to join the Olympus Project. What if he got back on the road with another band and picked up where he left off with his street cleaning? Although the woods looked like a charming spot, he wasn't in a rush to end up there along with Fido and Smokey.

Colin realised the elderly gentleman was right. Nobody believed he could be alive and had stopped hunting for him. That should have been a relief. Yet Colin was only too aware; it emphasised he was alone once more.

As a child, he had suffered abuse and neglect in equal measure from his parents. As a young man, Scott, Leroy, and their thuggish companions had bullied him. So when he got Karen Smith pregnant and married her, they were little more than children. Although she loved him, he never experienced that same depth of feeling. Sharron, their daughter, had shown him how to love, to experience that feeling of belonging over and above everything else going on around him.

Neil Cartwright had snuffed out Sharron's young life. Then followed the committed relationship he developed in his affair with Sue Owens. She gave Colin the only other period in his life when he didn't feel alone in the world. Colin and Sue married in The Gambia, and he had loved and cared for her until her untimely death.

Everything had come full circle. While Colin was still grieving for Sue, he had resolved to return to the UK to tick a few more names off his list. He had been so busy planning and carrying out those plans that he hadn't found time to consider his loneliness. A few snatched hours with Therese Salter had given him a brief glimpse of a possible future. He might have forged a new life somewhere with her, but she'd be checking the news over the next few days looking for confirmation he had died. It had only been a glimpse of the future. Therese would move on and get on with her life, whether in mainland Europe or wherever she went.

Colin looked across the lawns towards the woods. He had little choice when he had gone over it in his mind. He was invisible once more.

Colin awoke to find the old gentleman standing over him. It was six o'clock; he had fallen asleep in the chair. The older man gave him a brief smile and said -

"It's time for my story Phoenix. Shall we begin?"

Commodore William Horatio Hunt OBE, Royal Navy Retired (code name Erebus)

EREBUS -the primaeval god of darkness and shadow. He was the consort of Nyx (Night), whose dark mists enveloped the world's edges and filled the deep hollows of the earth. Nyx drew these mists across the heavens to bring the night to the world while their daughter Hemera scattered the mists bringing the day.

The older man stood in front of the fireplace and began his story.

"I was born in 1940 here at Larcombe Manor. Male members of my family have served in the Royal Navy for centuries. I had it impressed upon me from a very early age that this was my chosen profession. At no time did I entertain doing anything else. My father took me on a visit to Portsmouth for Navy Day when I was five years old. My enthusiasm for the service and my ambition to do my duty never faltered. I left school and joined up in 1957. I passed out of Britannia Royal Naval College, Dartmouth, and graduated from Plymouth's Royal Naval Engineering College. My sea service included several County-class destroyers, and I sailed on the carrier HMS Eagle. Missions included helping to deter an Iraqi invasion of Kuwait in 1962 and blocking oil supplies to Rhodesia in 1965. We played silly buggers with Iceland and Spain over cod and Gibraltar. I then had the opportunity to move back to these shores. I transferred to Portland and joined the FOST (Flag Officer Sea Training) staff, which had opened there in 1958. FOST was a major success, and the harbour became the world's premier workup and training base. It was a world centre of excellence for basic naval and advanced operational training. Almost every ship in the Royal Navy has participated in training programmes, including simulated warfare exercises. Many ships of NATO countries trained and frequented Portland too. I enjoyed my time there immensely but still longed for another spell at sea. Part of the Falklands task force sailed from Portland in 1982, and I was fortunate enough to be a privileged member of that task force. Several ships and crew were lost. It was not a good time. I saw things in the South Atlantic that I'd have been happy to miss. On our return, I took shore leave. In addition to my rehabilitation, family matters needed attention. I will cover that later. Shortly afterwards, I received the OBE. They described a 'diverse and selfless career' and an 'outstanding commitment to my country'."

"You must have been very proud," said Colin.

"I did my duty Phoenix. No more, no less. They then consigned me to the scrapheap. I just hadn't received the letter from my superiors advising me my career was coming to a premature end. My forthright views on those superiors had harmed my cause. More than a few admirals in naval operations were only interested in promoting their careers. To stay on the right side of Her Majesty's Government was more important than protecting the integrity of the honourable traditions of the Royal Navy. Morale throughout the chain of command had plummeted. Good officers left the service based on hearsay and unsubstantiated evidence. Other senior officers stood by and allowed civilians to say a cultural problem in the Navy needed addressing. They didn't defend the way of life my whole career had helped to shape and to protect. It was diabolical. After generations of our family following the same career and upholding the highest values with pride and dedication, they palmed me off with a gong and a pension. I would not go quietly into the night, Phoenix. I resolved to do whatever I could to redress the balance. If the Navy went down the toilet and I couldn't stop that from happening, my good works must concentrate on other areas. God knows I had plenty from which to choose."

Colin watched as William Horatio Hunt, whom he would only ever know as Erebus, moved from the fireplace to one of the side tables. Erebus took items from a drawer. He came back and took his seat in a chair next to him.

"This is a photograph of my wife, Elizabeth. We were on holiday in this one, in Ibiza in the late Sixties."

"What a beautiful woman," said Colin as he took hold of the photograph. It showed a smiling, tanned couple relaxing on a beach.

"She still is to me, old chap," replied his host. "We had been married for a couple of years here. Elizabeth always stayed here at Larcombe Manor while I travelled overseas. My folks were still alive then, and they looked after my wife. I got home on leave as often as I could. Our daughter Helen was born soon after that holiday in the Balearics. Elizabeth struggled with being a mother and with me not being at home to share the burden. I didn't appreciate that at the time. We never had another child. We tried, but for whatever reason, it didn't happen. Elizabeth was adamant; we should keep ourselves to ourselves and not involve the doctors. I suppose she was already struggling with her demons, and I never stopped here at Larcombe often enough or long enough to see the signs. Helen was a smashing young woman. She took after her mother. Helen was twenty-one in this photo taken after graduating from Reading University."

Erebus handed Colin another photograph. The sheer beauty of the girl staring back at him left him breathless.

"I always wonder whether my daughter Sharron might have been clever enough to go to University," said Colin wistfully, "as she was so artistic."

"Helen got a first. She was passionate about ecology and wildlife conservation. We still kept horses here then, and Helen rode every day around the countryside. She would have made a difference in the world. Of that, I'm certain."

Colin looked at the picture he still held.

"What happened to her?"

"Helen worked at various jobs around the country. Footloose and fancy-free, with no deep ties to mention. She moved when the mood took her, working on different projects and building an impressive reputation. The time may well have been coming when she thought of getting married. Who knows? She worked for the local Wildlife Trust in Cheddar Gorge in her last post. She met a young chap called John Maunder, who taught at a school in Bath; they were a good match. I liked the young fellow, at least. One terrible November evening in 2004, Helen came home from work in a happy mood. She looked forward to John taking her into Bath to watch the rugby. Helen wasn't keen on the game, but he was an avid fan. I told her the sooner you leave, the sooner you'll be back. I never saw her alive again. It surprised me when he hadn't returned her by midnight, but I still didn't think anything untoward had happened. John talked to anyone, particularly about rugby, for hours. Then the police arrived at the door. Elizabeth had retired to bed early, so I was alone when they told me the devastating news that Helen and John were both dead. Elizabeth must have heard the doorbell. She had just reached the foot of the stairs when the police told me what had happened. I remember Elizabeth collapsing on the hall floor. Nothing would ever be the same again. When we found out what happened, it was devastating. Helen and John walked along the pavement towards a pub John and several friends used on match nights. A VW Golf hit them from behind, travelling sixty miles an hour in a thirty zone. The driver was a foreign chap, Adam Bosko. He tested three times over the drink-drive limit in a stolen car without a license or insurance. He'd been at odds with the authorities in his home country of Poland since the age of fifteen. Bosko had been in a UK court seven times before in the few years he lived here. He faced dozens of other offences on those occasions. He overstayed his work visa by eleven months and should never have been in the country. I felt sure his record ensured this Bosko received a long sentence. It appalled me when he got just seven years. That was all he got for taking the lives of two people, let alone the other charges of theft and drink driving. It was a shattering blow. We were still reeling from the death of our beloved daughter, and by the time of the sentencing, Elizabeth was depressed. I lost both of them that night. This Bosko's wife and family in Poland got ready to appeal to the European Court of Human Rights. They argued that he should return to serve his sentence as he was due to be deported back to Poland because of the visa situation. His family could visit him in prison more easily. The Home Office caved in, and I later learnt he served only four years before his release. That didn't reflect true justice in my eyes. I couldn't get my head around it then, and I still can't. Adam Bosko got a few years in prison, but Elizabeth and I had to serve a life sentence. Can you understand what motivates me now, Phoenix? Elizabeth's condition has never improved. To live here at Larcombe, with the memories of her only child, became intolerable for her. I got rid of the horses, and the stables stood empty for a while, but this didn't help. Her black moods made me imagine it was always nighttime in my beloved house. I longed for the days when my Helen breezed into the drawing-room with a piece of toast, eagerly relaying a shred of news on whatever project she was undertaking. I couldn't forget how she rode across the grounds on one of her horses or waved as I sat on the patio reading the morning newspaper. Helen had been my Hemera, scattering the dark clouds and bringing blessed sunlight into my life. I arranged for Elizabeth to go into a nursing home. At least she's well cared for there, and I visit her as often as I can, although she hardly knows me, dear boy. While I lived here at the Manor alone for a time, I formulated my plans for Olympus. In due course, I wrote to The Times, and my quest for a return of true justice to our courts began."

Colin looked at Helen's face again in the photograph. He stood up and collected the picture of William and Elizabeth that Erebus was still holding. The older man was somewhere far away. On the high seas, maybe with one of his destroyers or with Elizabeth and Helen in happier times, no doubt. Colin now understood his motivation.

Anyone who lost a wife and daughter cruelly had a right to lash out at those responsible. Sharron's murder proved the final straw for Colin. He lashed out at the thugs who strutted around his town, arrogant, believing they were untouchable and above the law. He showed them they were wrong.

Colin had waited patiently for her killer to leave prison. He was glad, odd though it may seem, that Neil Cartwright served only a decade behind bars. As Erebus remarked, no sentence for Adam Bosko equated to two lives taken with such callous disregard for the law and human life.

Colin returned the two photographs to the drawer in the side table and walked over to where Erebus still sat. Erebus looked at him, and Colin sensed tears were close. Erebus collected himself and stood up, back ramrod straight as ever and took his place in front of the period fireplace. He invited Colin to sit one more and continued -

"Right then, Phoenix, my story is complete. We've a few minutes before the others join us in the dining room for dinner. Do you have any questions?"

Grab your copy…
vinci-books.com/phoenix-box-set-1